Twice Shy

The Shelter Series, Book Three

Kate Sherwood

About The Book You have Purchased

This story is a work of fiction. Names, characters, places, and incidents are either the product of the author's imagination or are used fictitiously to further the plot in this story. Any resemblance to actual persons living or dead, business establishments, events, or locales are entirely coincidental.

Cover Art by: A.J. Corza

website: www.ajcorza.com

Cover content is for illustrative purposes only and any persons depicted on the cover are models.

Formatting by: All Indie Publishing Services

website: www.allindiepublishingservices.com

Twice Shy

The Shelter Series, Book Three

www.katesherwoodbooks.com

Twice Shy

Micah's a junkie who hit rock bottom and is trying to claw his way back into the world. Jake is a landscaper trying to look after his business and his family, with no time for distractions.

But when Jake's brother Austin runs into Micah at a Narcotics Anonymous meeting and impulsively offers him a landscaping job, Jake's life gets more complicated. Sure, there's a strong attraction, but an addict brother is more than enough; Jake just doesn't have room in his life for an addict boyfriend.

And Micah isn't looking for love either. He's working the program, trying to reconcile with his friends, and following all the rules, including the one about no new relationships right out of rehab.

Unfortunately, Austin's own recovery isn't going as well as Micah's. Working together to try to help him, Micah and Jake find their attraction growing into a relationship. But when tragedy strikes, they're driven apart, and it will take more strength than either thinks he has to pull them back together.

Word Count: 69,613

Genre: Gay Contemporary Romance

Warning: This book contains graphic language and sexually explicit content. Intended for adult audiences only. Not intended for anyone under the age of 18

Chapter One

"HELLO. MY NAME IS MICAH, and I'm an addict. Mostly heroin, but really any of the opiates—I'm not too picky. But I've been clean for ninety-two days."

"Let me guess," a grey-haired lady with a smoker's rasp said from two seats away. "You spent ninety of those days in rehab."

"And two in the hospital," Micah shot back at her. "This is my first meeting on my own. And I'm sure enjoying it so far."

"We're not here for your enjoyment," someone growled from behind him. Micah didn't even bother turning to see who was speaking.

Instead he addressed the man at the front of the room. "Isn't there usually a 'Hi, Micah,' chant right about now? Come on. I was really hoping for some chanting."

"Hi, Micah," the man said dryly. "We usually save the responses for when members share, not when they introduce themselves."

"Oh. How disappointing." Micah sat down. He was probably being an ass. Petulant, maybe. That's what Tristan would call him. Except Tristan wasn't talking to him, and for damn good reason. Reasons. Not that this memory inspired Micah to be any less petulant.

"If you'd like to stick around after the meeting, we can talk more," the man said. He seemed friendly, kind, maybe even gentle. Absolutely not the kind of person Micah wanted to be around, not when his head—his whole body—was buzzing like it was. Like he was composed entirely of bees, all of them angry and looking to sting.

But he managed to keep himself at least somewhat under control, and he nodded at the man like he was considering the offer. Then he slumped back down in his seat. And regretted it immediately, because he was way too restless to sit still. Way too restless to suffer through another sanctimonious damn meeting, another lecture about how it'll work if he works it, another empty argument trying to persuade him that he could still be something, still contribute.

He couldn't do it. He couldn't bore himself with another series of painfully earnest, totally humorless stories from his fellow inmates. Because he was still an inmate, out here, just as much as he'd been when he was in rehab. Stuck in a damn prison of addiction, facing a fucking life sentence.

Of course, that sentence might not be too long. Not if he kept drowning in his bottomless pool of self-pity, or if he was crushed under a mountain of his overworked metaphors.

That thought made him smile, just for a moment. It was the sort of thing Tristan would have come up with, back when their fighting was just play. And Shane would have been there, watching and listening, amused at first, then impatient. Trey and Becky, bored even from the start. Noah, so busy admiring Shane he'd barely even notice Tristan and Micah.

They were all still out there, somewhere. They hadn't visited him in rehab, hadn't even called or sent a care package, and the counsellor said it was because she'd told them not to. Maybe she actually had, or maybe the counsellor was kind enough to break her own rule about always telling the truth.

But even if they hadn't wanted to visit, even if they'd forgotten all about him, they were still out there, and that made it a bit easier for Micah to sit still. He might never earn his way back into their lives, but at least he could try. And the first step in that was going to these stupid meetings, one every single day for the first month. He wasn't sure he was going to get anything out of them—well, he was pretty damn sure he wasn't, considering how little attention he was paying to any of it—but at least it was one more hour out of the day, one more hour of sobriety to add to his total.

So he sat, trying to accept his new reality. His life wasn't going to glow anymore. He wasn't going to be buffered from reality. When he was in a boring place with boring people, he was going to be bored. That was just how things were when he wasn't high, and he wasn't going to get high any more. He *wasn't*.

About half way through the meeting he noticed the guy across the room, about his own age, looking vaguely familiar. That wasn't good. He was supposed to be starting fresh, leaving his old druggie friends behind, and that was all this guy could be. If he was something more, Micah would have recognized him with more certainty.

But then the guy grinned at him, threw in a conspiratorial eye-roll, and Micah smirked back before he knew what he was doing.

It couldn't hurt, could it? The whole point of these meetings was to find fellowship and support, after all. So if Micah made a friend, would that be so bad?

He tried to remember where he knew the guy from. Olive skin, high cheekbones—too far away to see his eyes, but Micah somehow knew they were green. Yeah, green eyes, dark lashes falling to cover them, then lifting back only halfway, too tired or too blissed out for full consciousness. If Micah had led a different sort of life, maybe he'd think the guy in his memory had just come, or was just about to, in a slow, languid sort of way. But in the life Micah had actually led, that look meant something else completely.

But that only made sense—who the hell was he going to meet in a Narcotics Anonymous meeting besides other addicts?

And this guy had quit, obviously, and was trying to stay clean. Nobody would come to one of these meetings just for fun.

When everyone who wanted to talk was done, the guy leading the session read a page or two from his little brown book, and everybody nodded like they believed it all, and Micah saw the other guy looking down at his hands. Being polite about his skepticism, Micah figured, and followed his example. When the prayer started, everyone chanting along, Micah kept his mouth shut. There were groups that tried to work the twelve steps without dragging religion into it and he was definitely planning to hit those meetings, but they mostly met once or twice a week; if he was going to achieve his meeting-every-day goal, he was going to be hearing more about God and prayer and all the rest of it than he really wanted.

Of course, compared to the pain of giving up smack a little God-talk was barely a mosquito bite.

The group hug was a bit much, though, so he dodged backward out of it and started for the door. He was half-way there when he sensed someone walking next to him and turned his head to see eyes just as green as he'd remembered.

"You made it, then," the guy said.

And that was all it took to jar the rest of Micah's scattered memory into place. They'd been together on New Year's Eve, the night of the overdose that had sent Micah to the hospital and then to the rehab facility.

"Always a bit hard to be sure," the guy continued. "When someone disappears like that—did they leave the scene, or the planet?" His smile was easy and relaxed as they jogged up the stairs from the church basement. "Glad you were the first, not the second."

"Yeah, thanks." They stopped at the top of the stairs. "Sorry, man, I forget your name—that night's a bit hazy. And I guess I wasn't paying attention when they did the introductions today."

"I'm Austin. We were at Moby's party." Austin shook his head. "What a shit-show. You just got out of rehab, right? Haven't really talked to anyone. Do you know there were six ODs that night? Moby just about killed the guy who was selling for him, 'cause he fucked up and made everything way too strong."

Micah shook his head. He didn't want to talk about this anymore. Didn't want to think about it, didn't want to remember the ecstasy, the pure, soaring freedom that had lifted him out of his body, left the vessel behind while the contents explored the universe. Didn't want to remember that it had almost killed him, and absolutely didn't want to remember that he could never do it again.

"I gotta go," he said, and started for the door, but Austin caught his arm, then released it quickly when Micah spun around.

"Take it easy," he said. "I just wanted to know if you've got a job, yet. My brother's got a landscaping business and it's about to kick into gear for all the spring clean-up stuff. So he's hiring, and he's—you know, he's a bit less of a prick than most bosses would be. He'll give you a chance, if you want one."

"I, uh—that's supposed to be one of my 'tasks' this month. Go to a meeting every day, go to counselling twice a week, and try to get a job."

"Be kind of nice to get one of those things out of the way right off the bat, right?" Austin's grin was encouraging. "He's picking me up, if you want to meet him."

Tristan had always said Micah was born with horseshoes up his ass. He'd said Micah got high because life was too damn easy for him and he needed to find ways to make it more challenging. Not exactly how Micah would have characterized things, but it was hard to argue with the general point. He had no employment history, no skills, and he'd been out of rehab for less than twelve hours. But someone wanted to give him a job, or at least a chance at one?

"Okay," he said. "Sure, I guess."

Why the hell not? Talking to this guy would at least be a couple minutes taken up, a couple less minutes to be thinking about finding a fix.

JAKE DESANTIS WATCHED AS HIS BROTHER bounced out of the church. Not alone.

Jesus Christ. Jake wasn't sure if it was a blessing or a curse, but Austin could find a friend anywhere he went. He seemed to *need* to find a friend, seemed unable to ever just be alone.

But on the list of things to worry about in regards to Austin, "excess sociability" was somewhere near the bottom.

Of course, "compulsive need to adopt kicked puppies" was a little higher, especially when, as seemed to be happening right then, the actual adopter ended up being Jake instead of Austin. Austin had met this guy at a meeting, so the guy was an addict. Not exactly what Jake needed more of in his life. But Jake kept a calm expression on his face as Austin led the other guy around the hood of the pickup and waited expectantly outside the driver's window.

For a moment, Jake thought about ignoring them. He could lean over, turn up the stereo, get distracted by his phone—just generally behave like a brother sometimes should, gently tormenting his younger brother. But he and Austin weren't playful like that anymore. They hadn't been like that for years.

So he hit the button to lower the window and waited patiently.

"Hey, man," Austin said with a too-bright smile. "This is Michael. Old friend of mine from way back. I just ran into him, and he's looking for work. I said you might be able to hook him up."

Of course Austin had said that. Jake looked at Michael, took in the dark, serious eyes, wondered if he caught a glimpse of something impish, something that suggested a sense of humor, then completed the inspection with a quick look down his body. Seemed fit enough. "It's pretty hard work. If Austin told you it was easy, he was lying, and if he keeps goofing off like he has been, he's gonna get his ass fired, brother or no brother. So if your plan is to get paid for sitting around like he thinks he's going to do, then you should find somewhere else to work."

"Hard work is fine," Michael said.

"You got any experience?"

"Landscaping? Not really. Used to mow my parents' lawn. My mom gardened, so I picked up a bit from her. But nothing professional."

Jake appreciated the honesty, he supposed. "Where you living?"

"Halfway house down in Ranier Valley."

"Damn, you're getting the deluxe treatment, huh?" Austin interrupted. "Ninety day rehab, counselling, a halfway house— who's paying for all that?"

"My parents," Michael said. He didn't sound too thrilled about it. "I guess they figured I wasn't really going to need my college fund, the way things were going."

Well, that would shut Austin up, at least. He and Jake really didn't discuss their parents. "You have a car?" Jake asked into the silence.

"No."

"So I'll give you somewhere to be, a bus stop or a Link station or whatever, somewhere that's on *my* way to the job site, not yours, and you'll be there *on time* for me to pick you up. You aren't there on time? I keep driving and you're fired. Is that clear? I'm running a real business here, not a co-op or an internship or whatever. It's not designed to be a damn learning opportunity for your social enrichment."

Michael nodded his understanding, so Jake shrugged. If the guy didn't work out, he didn't work out. He dug out his phone and took down Michael's number. "What's your last name?"

"Porter. And the first name's actually Micah." He glanced over at Austin, and Jake could tell from the look that the two weren't old friends, or at least not *good* old friends. Still, Micah tried to cover. "Sometimes people call me Michael. Like a nickname."

"Yeah," Jake said with a frown toward his brother. "Of course they do."

Austin knew he was busted and clearly didn't care. Because Austin was Austin, sure he could cruise through life on charm and enthusiasm, and Jake was Jake, the one left to pick up the pieces after Austin's disasters. And Micah, this new addition to their happy little circle? Likely going to be one more disaster. Still, Jake tapped the contact information into his phone and said, "We start early. I'll text you tonight and tell you where to meet us. One chance. Clear?"

Micah nodded.

Probably about fifty-fifty odds of the bastard showing up the next morning, and way worse chances of him making it through a whole week of work. That was the way with junkies. But Jake could never forget that junkies had brothers, people who loved them and dreamed of their recovery. People who sat bolt upright at night, yanked out of a nightmare of the junkie *not* getting better, dying instead, lying in some damn flophouse with a needle and an expression of gentle surprise—

"Get in," Jake growled at his brother. *Get in the truck, stay beside me so I know you're safe, let this be the time when the program actually works for you. Please. God, please.*

But none of that came out in words. "Tomorrow," Jake said to Micah as Austin climbed in. And then they drove away, Jake leaving someone else's nightmare behind while he tried to get some kind of control over his own.

Chapter Two

JAKE HADN'T BEEN KIDDING WHEN he said they started early, but the 6:15 pickup time was actually a gift for Micah. Having to get up early meant he could go to sleep early, and that meant fewer hours of consciousness at night, less time to torture himself with memories of all the chemicals floating around out there in the dark, dreamy streets, all the different ways he could alter his reality. All the different reasons to *want* his reality altered.

So Micah went to bed early and woke up early and was at the designated corner, waiting, when Jake deSantis pulled up in his pickup. Did the guy look a little surprised to see Micah there? Maybe, and just that possibility was enough to give Micah the first tiny burst of pride he'd felt in far, far too long. He wasn't quite as flakey as this guy had thought he was. Not much of a victory, but Micah would take it anyway.

He climbed into the cab of the truck and looked at the narrow bench seat in the back. It was empty.

"Austin's meeting us at the site," Jake explained. "He couldn't get his ass in gear this morning, and after my big lecture yesterday about you not being late, I didn't want to be a hypocrite and show up late myself. So I left without him."

"I'd understand if you were late," Micah said. It wasn't exactly true; he totally would have thought Jake was being a hypocrite. But he wasn't *supposed* to think that way. "You're the boss, and I'm the one mooching a ride."

Jake shrugged. "It's good for Austin, too. I think. Wouldn't kill him to learn a little discipline."

Micah didn't think he wanted to start a conversation about Austin's character flaws, not when so many of them were likely to line up with his own. So he kept his mouth shut and his gaze focused out the side window.

Jake's thought process must have been fairly similar, because after a couple blocks he asked, "You going to meetings every day? You got one lined up for today?"

It was a gift, Micah realized, to have a boss who already knew about all that. It would have been a lot harder to make things work if he'd had to be sneaking around, wanting to leave the job at certain times for reasons he couldn't really explain. Damn, Austin really had done him a huge favor. Or at least hooked him up with someone who was doing him a huge favor. "I've got a few listed— I'll pick one based on where we are and what time work ends."

"The meetings come first," Jake said. He sounded like he was ready to fight about it. "You tell me what time you need to be off work to make it to your meeting, and that'll be the time you're off work."

"Wow. You're a true believer in the program, huh? It really helps Austin?" And then Micah wanted to kick himself, because Austin had been at Moby's party ninety-three days earlier, and nobody would be at one of Moby's parties if they weren't partaking. So even if Austin had been clean ever since, it was pretty early to say anything was *working*.

"I'm a true believer in trying," Jake said. He didn't sound pissed off, exactly. Maybe frustrated? "If NA is what you're doing, then you need to *do it*. Austin needs to do it. I'm not going to let 'I had to work for Jake' be anyone's excuse for not doing what they're supposed to be doing to stay clean. That's all."

Micah turned his head, just a little. Not enough to be obvious, not enough to make it look like he was trying to establish eye contact or anything. Just enough to get a bit of a glimpse of the guy.

Micah was pretty sure that he hadn't always been a self-absorbed asshole. He could remember, vaguely, a time when he'd paid attention to other people, a time when he'd cared about the impression he was making and the feelings he might be creating. But heroin was such a solitary drug. Sure, he might have taken it with others, but that was for convenience, not sociability. When he was high, he was on his own, living in his own protected bubble, floating away on his own adventures. He hadn't needed anyone else, hadn't valued anyone else.

Well, there had been his friends. Tristan's band of misfits, hiding from the world together. Micah had cared about them, in his own way. It was just too damn bad he'd cared about drugs more.

Now, sitting in this pickup truck, sneaking glances at Jake deSantis, brother of an addict, Micah felt like something long forgotten was stirring back to life inside himself. The rising sun was casting a strange light on the angles of Jake's face, the same green eyes and olive skin as his brother, and Micah could feel the warmth on his own cheeks. They were together. In this cab, on this street, in this city, country, continent, and world. Two human beings, and that connected them somehow.

It was empathy, Micah supposed. It had been kind of nice to go through life for a while with his empathy turned off, kind of nice to let himself be a sociopath, someone who didn't really care about others. Everything was easier when you only thought about yourself, and easier when you were willing to take whatever chemicals you could find to keep from remembering anyone else. Easier, but not better. He had to believe that, or there was no damn point in going through all this rehab bullshit. If he wasn't firmly committed to the idea that his life would be better without drugs, he might as well go find a needle right then.

And if being off drugs was making things better, then this feeling, this understanding and connection, must be a good thing, as scary as it was. Someone was helping Micah out, and Micah was feeling grateful because of it. Unfamiliar, but good.

"Yeah," he said. "Okay. Thanks." He took a breath, then said, "I'm doing NA, so I might need to leave work sometimes to get to a meeting. But not too often, hopefully—there's a lot of different times and places for the meetings, so I can make things work out."

"Just let me know," Jake replied. "And—" He stopped as if rethinking whatever he was about to say, then sighed and went ahead anyway. "If you can take Austin along with you, I'd appreciate it." He glanced over, frowned, then turned his attention back to the road. "If you guys can support each other, that's great. But if you can't? If it seems like you being around is making it more likely that Austin will fuck up again? Then you're gone. And if I see *any* sign of you actively making it worse for him? If I hear about you using around him, or taking him places where people are using? You're not only fired, but I'll also beat the shit out of you. That clear?"

"Clear." It might not be strictly professional for a boss to be threatening his new employee with bodily harm, but it also wasn't too professional to hire a known addict just to be a good guy, so Micah wasn't going to worry too much about professionalism. "I appreciate you giving me a chance."

Jake's grunt might have been acknowledgement or it might have been a sign of regret. Micah figured he'd better keep his mouth shut and not push things. So they drove in silence for another five or ten minutes, then pulled up in front of a small office park. Jake had explained on the phone that most of his clients wanted their landscapers to be invisible—hence the early hour. The team was supposed to get their jobs done and be gone before the office employees arrived. Then the crew would head off to the residential customers, since they'd mostly be at work or school by then.

It reminded Micah of that story about the shoemaker and his elves. Like the people they were working for wanted to pretend the jobs were being done by magic, not by actual human beings. They wanted to look at mowed grass and trimmed hedges, but didn't want to have to actually see any laborers. *The best proletariat is an invisible proletariat.* He wished Tristan was around so they could be aggravated together.

Then he thought of Austin's words of the day before. Micah was getting the deluxe rehab treatment, and it was coming at his parents' expense. Because his parents could *afford* the expense, which a lot of other families couldn't. Maybe Micah should keep his mouth shut about the treatment of the underclasses.

He should probably keep his mouth shut about pretty much everything. This was a good chance, and he couldn't afford to blow it.

So he nodded politely as he was introduced to Alex and Eduardo, the two workers who'd driven their own truck to the site, complete with a trailer full of Jake's equipment, and been waiting for the day to begin. "Alex is an old pro," Jake told Micah. "If I'm not around, he's in charge. You don't use any of the chemicals until you get trained and certified, you don't prune a shrub or a tree until you know what you're doing, you don't pull out a weed until he or I confirm it actually is a weed. You and Eduardo are mostly going to be mowing lawns until you learn to do more. Landscaping isn't brain surgery, but there's stuff to learn, and I'm trying to grow this business—word-of-mouth is the best advertiser. So you're always dressed tidily, you're polite to anyone you see but you keep your head down and try not to be seen most of the time, you keep your shirt on even if you want to work on your tan, you don't play loud music, you don't swear so anyone can hear you—you get the general idea?"

"Yeah," Micah said. "I got it." *Invisible proletariat.*

Jake squinted at him so intently that for a moment Micah thought maybe he'd spoken his thoughts out loud, but then the conversation shifted to unloading tools and getting to work. Micah did as he was told, and the day progressed.

Austin got off a bus just as the crew was packing up. He had a big smile and a cardboard tray with five cups of take-out coffee, cream and sugar in his pockets. "I almost got mugged for these," he told the others as he distributed his gifts. "It is *not* safe to take public transit in Seattle with what seems like extra coffees. Could have been ugly."

"You wouldn't have to take public transit if you got your ass in gear," Jake bitched at him, but he took a coffee.

"But I found you a good worker," Austin protested, gesturing toward Micah. No evidence of what sort of worker

Micah was, really, but apparently Austin was ready to believe the best. "I'm more of a people-person, I'd say. A recruiter, a manager, a problem-solver. Not so much with the manual labor."

"Great." Jake sipped his coffee. "You should start looking for a job that matches your skills. I'll lie in order to give you a good reference. But until you've got that job? You need to get better at doing *this* job."

Micah glanced at Alex and Eduardo, but neither seemed too concerned about the family spat they were witnessing, and Austin didn't seem upset either. He just smiled at his brother, sipped his own coffee, and said, "Where's the next job? I can drive."

"I should make you take the bus over there, too," Jake groused. "And there's no damn way you're driving. You don't even deserve shotgun."

But being relegated to the backseat did nothing to quell Austin's good mood, and he chatted happily away as they drove to the next job. By the time they'd arrived, Jake had stopped scolding and Micah had relaxed. Still, when they got out of the truck he wasn't sorry to see Austin getting right to work, helping Alex unload the equipment and then starting with the weed wacker.

"Come here," Jake ordered Micah, and he complied. "This bed needs weeding and then mulching. You don't know all the weeds, so you're going to be our grass specialist. You know what grass looks like, right?"

"Like—like lawn grass?"

Jake squinted at him. "We're not pulling marijuana out of our customers' flower beds. Yes, lawn grass."

"Okay, sorry, yeah. I know what grass looks like."

"If there's a big clump of it, don't pull it. Might be ornamental or something. But all these stupid little bits sneaking in from the edges?" Jake crouched and pointed at something in the flower bed.

And there was something about the way he moved, the way his shoulders bunched and shifted under his work shirt—something that sent Micah's thoughts in all the wrong directions. He was at work, and he needed this job, which meant he shouldn't be wondering what his boss's shoulders would look like without the fabric. And he absolutely shouldn't let his thoughts wander any further along the path they seemed to be exploring.

"I'll pull out the stupid little bits," Micah said, just a little too fast and too loud. "Everything else stays, stupid little bits go."

Jake squinted at him, probably trying to figure out if he was being sarcastic or something.

"I'm on it." Micah had been trying to sound reassuring, but he had a bad feeling that he'd come off sounding way too enthusiastic. "Because I want to do a good job, not because I have any personal anti-grass sentiments."

Jake grinned, and damn it, Micah hadn't needed to see that. He hadn't needed to know how the guy's square, almost plain face turned into something totally different when he smiled. Something a bit lopsided and totally appealing.

"Okay." Jake stood up, one smooth movement that Micah tried desperately to ignore. "Good. Don't let it get personal, but do your job. The grass needs to respect its boundaries and stay the hell out of the flower beds. If you pull it gently enough you can get a lot of the root and you won't have to do the same damn thing next week."

Next week. So Jake hadn't already decided to fire him. That was something.

Micah just needed to make sure he kept it that way.

When he'd been using, he'd lost pretty much all interest in sex. About the second week in rehab his desire had come back, but there hadn't really been anyone to mess around with. Sex was discouraged at the facility—they were all supposed to be focusing on themselves, on their issues. And even if it had been allowed, he'd been at a small facility; nobody else seemed to be gay, and while Micah was open to bisexuality, he had a very specific type when it came to women. Short hair, lean bodies—yeah, bisexuality wasn't really the right label for Micah's desires. He liked guys, or women who reminded him of guys. Gay but willing to compromise? Was that how he'd advertise himself?

Didn't matter. The point was that he'd gotten his sex drive back but hadn't been able to use it for anything, and that was leading him to have inappropriate thoughts about his boss, who'd shown no sign of being gay and was statistically likely to be straight. Perving on your straight boss was not a recipe for emotional stability, and stability was what Micah was supposed to be focusing on. Easier to stay clean if he avoided drama.

"Got it, boss," he said, and crouched down to start weeding. No more perving. Just recovery. Lots of soul-searching and whatever. Ninety-three days clean. He needed to make sure he made it to ninety-four, and anything else was just a distraction.

Chapter Three

AUSTIN WAS LATE FOR DINNER, and Jake was trying not to go crazy.

Austin was late for every damn thing, he reminded himself. He'd been *born* late, the doctors about to induce labor just before the little brat finally got off his ass and started working his way out. It didn't mean anything that he was late now.

Except—damn it. Hiring another addict to work alongside Austin? That had just been stupid. Sure, they'd said they were going to a meeting together, and Austin had said he didn't need to be picked up because the meeting wasn't far from the apartment and the walk would do him good. But the bastard should have been home more than an hour ago, and he *wasn't*, and it was too damn easy to think of the other places he could be. Micah had seemed like a good guy, seemed like he was taking things seriously, but Jake had never met an addict who wasn't pretty damn good at lying. Jake should have known better.

Now the two of them were out there, somewhere, getting into god only knew what kind of trouble, and it could have been avoided if Jake had been smarter. He shouldn't have trusted Micah, and he shouldn't have trusted Austin.

Jake started for the apartment door. He'd go for a drive, check out the street between home and the meeting, then try some of Austin's old hang-outs, the spots he was supposed to be avoiding, the places where he'd met stupid Micah in the first place.

The doorknob twisted just as Jake was reaching for it, and he had to jump back to avoid the door as it swung toward him. "Hey, man," Austin said as he strode inside. His eyes were bright, but not too bright. Nothing suspicious. "You heading out? Did you already eat? Check this out—I got free asparagus at the market! Remember? We can do the pee test afterward, if you're up for some nostalgia."

"The market?" Jake said, trying to catch up and let his body figure out what to do with all the adrenaline it apparently didn't need.

"Yeah. Just a little one, a couple blocks down? I don't know, maybe it's just a store—I don't really know what the difference is between a store and a market, in a technical sense. They have all those vegetables out on the sidewalk? One of the women from the meeting owns the place and the guy who usually works for her is out sick, so she had some heavy stuff she needed lifted." Austin stopped talking long enough to flex his biceps in a manly fashion, then grinned. "Micah did most of it, to be honest. She gave him a whole bag full of stuff. Me? She gave me the funky-pee vegetable. But, whatever. It's free. Have you already eaten?"

If Austin's drug of choice had been a stimulant, Jake never would have been able to tell when his brother was high. As it was, though, if Austin was talking and bouncing around like this? He was just being Austin.

"I haven't eaten. I was waiting for you."

"Cool. We can have asparagus, and—I don't know, what goes with asparagus?"

"There's chicken in the oven. It's going to be a little dry by now, though."

"Marta—that's the market lady—told me how to make a sauce for the asparagus. I could make more of it and put some on the chicken, too." Austin smiled happily. He'd solved the problem, he had a free vegetable, and his pee was about to smell funny—all was right in his world.

And he was home, safe and sober, so all should be right in Jake's world, too. But he was still wired, still jumpy, still pissed off that he'd been worried. That Austin had made him worry. "Is your phone broken?" he asked as he trailed after Austin toward the kitchen. He sounded like a jealous housewife, but realizing that did nothing to make him less angry about the situation.

And Austin's big-eyed innocent look, now that he was finally picking up on his brother's mood, wasn't calming, either. The son-of-a-bitch was anything but innocent, and they'd had this same fight enough damn times that neither one of them should be surprised by it.

And that realization was what finally took the edge off Jake's anger. This was their pattern, their relationship, and he played just as much of a role in it as Austin did. Austin was just pretending to be surprised, but wasn't Jake kind of pretending, too? "You never asked me to make dinner," he said slowly. "Just because I took something on myself doesn't mean you have a responsibility to go along with my plans."

Austin frowned, caught on to what Jake was doing, and shrugged. "But I know you worry, and it wouldn't have killed me to give you a call. I've given you lots of reasons to worry about where I am or what I'm doing, and you're helping me out in a lot of ways, and I need to pull my head out of my ass and work on giving back sometimes instead of just taking. A one-minute phone call could have saved you a lot of stress."

"I can't keep you locked up all the time. I have to start trusting you, or—" And that was the hard part. "I have to start trusting you, or stop caring what you do."

Austin's smile was gentle and almost sad. "But you're my brother, and we're the only family we have left. I can't expect you not to care, and I don't *want* you not to care."

Jake snorted. Their fights might be a little less volatile when they reversed roles like this and presented the other's arguments as their own, but they didn't really get any closer to a solution. Austin was an addict who'd quit and started again more times than could be easily counted; Jake was his brother, who loved him but couldn't change him. That was the truth of the situation, and no amount of discussion or argument was going to make it anything different. "Okay," he said. "Is the sauce hard to make?"

Austin gave him a cautious look, obviously expecting some sort of trap, then shook his head. "Didn't sound that way. I'm not saying I won't find a way to mess it up, but the way she described it seemed pretty clear."

"You'll do fine. You want help?"

"Probably best," Austin agreed.

The incompetent act was mostly put on, Jake knew. Austin had long ago discovered learned helplessness as an excellent way to get out of work. But some of the insecurity was genuine. Austin did think of himself as a screw up, which only made sense, considering how many times he'd screwed up. But, still, Jake didn't want his baby brother seeing himself that way, so when he had time and energy he tried to work with the kid and build his confidence. "I'll mostly watch; you're the one who got the instructions."

"Okay," Austin agreed. "Where's the butter?"

"No," Jake said.

Austin frowned at him. "What? We're not using butter?"

"Give me a break, Austin. You know where the butter is. You use it every day. Don't try to con me on this; I'm not going to fetch and carry while you give me orders."

Austin scowled at him. "I'm sorry—when you offered to help, I thought you meant you'd help. You can see how I'm confused, I guess."

"No one in this apartment is confused about anything, including the location of the damn butter. Get it yourself, you lazy-ass piece of shit."

Austin grinned. He always liked it when Jake swore at him, for reasons that weren't completely clear. "You're a terrible sous-chef," he announced, and headed toward the fridge. Toward the butter.

Jake pulled a stool up to the breakfast bar and watched his brother puttering around, making his sauce. It was boring, really, but so much better to be bored than terrified. If it could always be like this? If Austin could always be right in front of Jake, safe and healthy? Jake would damn well accept the boredom, just for the peace of mind.

"Micah did a good job today, huh?" Austin said, cutting his eyes slyly in Jake's direction.

Damn, the kid was up to something. "Yeah, I guess," Jake agreed carefully. "He doesn't know shit about landscape maintenance, but he worked hard."

"He's not hard to look at either, right?"

"What?"

Austin pulled the butter out of the fridge with a triumphant gesture, as if it had been hidden but he'd persevered. "He's good looking. You like guys with thick, dark hair and dark eyes, right?"

"What are you talking about? Jesus Christ, Austin, this had better not be some matchmaking bullshit you're working on right now! Did you want me to hire him because of *this*?"

"No." Austin was completely calm as he found a saucepan and squinted down at the butter, clearly trying to find a way to guess how much he needed. "I wanted you to hire him because he seems like a good guy and he needed work and I thought he'd be fun. Turns out he's pretty much *zero* fun, because he's too busy trying to kiss your ass and be a good little employee. But that could translate into fun for *you*, right? A hot, young guy kissing your ass? Is that, like, a gay fantasy or something?"

"Jesus, Austin." Jake was too tired for this. "He's not a party favor. You can't give him to me just because you think I'd enjoy him."

"No, I can't give him to you. But I can give you the opportunity." Austin smiled happily. "That's my gift. From me, to you: a chance to score with a hot, young guy."

"Why are you emphasizing the *young* part? I'm young too, you know. I'm only four years older than you are!"

"I just don't see how that can be accurate. I think you've prematurely aged yourself with all your responsibility and whatever. So now I'm giving you the chance to reverse the process a little. Hang out with someone who's acting his own age, get your ass kissed, get laid—seriously, man, when's the last time you got any action?"

It would be too easy to fire back with something hurtful. The last guy Jake had dated had dumped him because he said Jake was already too wrapped up in his business and his brother and there was no room left for anyone else. Jake hadn't really been able to argue with him. But Austin didn't need to be loaded down with more guilt. Not that it wouldn't be well-placed, but it sure wouldn't be constructive. So instead, Jake asked, "Is he even gay? I mean, not that I'm interested. I'm just wondering whether you're deluding yourself a lot, or just a little."

"I don't know for sure, but I've seen him making out with guys, at least sometimes. Under certain circumstances."

It was the vagueness that put the image into Jake's mind. Micah, lying back after shooting up, relaxed and languid and content, trading slow, easy kisses, no rush, no finish line, just kissing, just gentleness and lazy affection. It was such a beautiful picture, such a seductive one, as long as Jake could ignore the chemical assistance required to achieve it. But he couldn't ignore that, not at all.

So he said, "No, thanks. I don't need the complication. If I want to hook up, I'll find someone else. Someone who isn't my brother's friend."

Yeah, those were the words he used. But he knew Austin heard the real reason, just as clearly as Jake knew it. *Someone who isn't a junkie.*

Well, damn it, it was true. That was the main problem with getting involved with Micah. Sure, there were others, like the fact that he might not even be gay. But even if he were totally into guys, totally into *Jake*, he'd still be a junkie, and that meant he'd be a terrible idea.

"Is there more to the sauce than butter?" Jake asked, looking pointedly at the stove. "Because if there is, you'd better get to it. And are you steaming the asparagus, or what?"

Austin looked startled. "Shit. The asparagus. I don't know—I'm really more of a sauce specialist. How do you cook asparagus?"

"I know what you're doing," Jake said, but he stood up anyway. He was hungry and wanted his dinner. "You're not manipulating me, you're just pissing me off."

"But you're going to take care of the asparagus for me, right?" Austin said.

"On one condition." Jake waited for his brother's attention. "No more matchmaking. I'll make the asparagus and you can do your weird pee-smelling-thing, which, honestly, you should have outgrown when you were seven. But no more matchmaking. Deal?"

Austin raised an eyebrow. "I bet I could find you a guy who's totally into pee smelling. Like, as a kink. If I find that guy, can I match-make you two?"

"If you find that guy, you've found a guy who you should never, ever match-make me with."

"So white-bread," Austin sighed. Then he nodded. "But, yes. Deal. Make my asparagus, kitchen-bitch. And I will stop trying to make you happy. It's been very frustrating for me anyway."

"Sorry about that," Jake said, and he headed for the bag of asparagus lying on the counter. He had his brother, safe. He had dinner, even if it was going to be of questionable quality. He had a business and a place to live and a TV in his bedroom for porn. That was all he needed, surely.

He just wished Austin hadn't mentioned Micah's dark, deep eyes. He wished he hadn't had that image of the slow kisses, the anonymous male hand running up over Micah's torso, under his shirt....

Damn it. Life would be a hell of a lot easier if Austin would stop messing with Jake's peace of mind. Or if Jake had more peace of mind to begin with.

~*~*~*~

THE PEOPLE AT REHAB HAD WARNED Micah about returning to his old hang-outs. They'd also told him to stay away from his old friends, if he could manage it. He needed new habits and a new habitat—he needed a new life. He hadn't liked the idea, but he hadn't resisted it, either. After all, his old friends had made it clear they were done with him; there was no point fighting for the right to see people who didn't want to see him.

But now, only two days out of rehab, he was already back in the old neighborhood, just down the street from Tristan's apartment, trying to build up his nerve or beat down his shame or otherwise find some way to—to what? To beg for forgiveness?

That likely wasn't necessary. Tristan would forgive him. Micah had done horrible things before, and Tristan had gotten past it. Their relationship had never been quite the same after Micah stole from him, but it had still been good. Tristan had a big heart, and there was room for a lot of messed-up friends in it.

This time, though? Tristan had told Micah to choose, and Micah had chosen. He'd stood there right in front of Tristan, he'd seen the hurt of his most recent betrayal in Tristan's eyes, and when Tristan had told him it was the drugs or his friends, Micah had popped a pill. He'd made his damn choice. So, sure, Tristan would forgive him for the betrayal that had led to the standoff, but Tristan wouldn't forget the choice Micah had made.

If it had been something less important, it would have been easier to do to the right thing. That was what Tristan would never understand. If Tristan *hadn't* been so hurt, if Micah *hadn't* cared so much, then it wouldn't have been so damned important to run away from it all. But the hurt and caring were real, and Micah wasn't strong enough to deal with anything like that. He hadn't needed to be, as long as he could wrap himself in oxy or heroin or whatever other chemical insulation he could find.

But now he was raw and exposed. He walked half a block down until he could see the windows of Tristan's apartment, rectangles of yellow light shining out into the misty darkness. Micah wondered who was in there. Just Tristan? Unlikely—the apartment was like a club house. Maybe Tristan's new boyfriend, Simon, was up there. They'd barely been getting started when Micah had gone to rehab, and three months was a long time for a new relationship to last. But Micah bet Simon was still in the picture. There'd been something about the way he looked at Tristan, a warmth and steadiness that seemed as if it would take a lot to shake. Micah wrapped his hand around a light post and let his eyes almost close, picturing the scene.

Tristan and Simon would be on the couch, half-lying, half-sitting, totally entwined with each other. Noah in the big armchair by the window, Shane leaning over behind him. Trey, glowering somewhere in the shadows, looking for a fight. Becky and Amanda would be there, maybe, Amanda soft and Becky so damn hard, both of them quiet and watchful.

They were Micah's family. His parents had kicked him out when he'd started acting like a junkie, and his new family had taken him in. His parents had paid for his rehab, but his new family had been the reason he'd agreed to go, the reason he'd put so much effort in while he was there. The reason he was still putting so much effort in.

And they were the reason he turned around and headed back down the street toward the bus stop. He'd let them down. He'd rejected them. They were better off without him.

But it still made him feel good to know they were around, and hopefully still all together.

Chapter Four

WHEN JAKE PULLED UP AT the bus stop where he and Austin were supposed to meet Micah the next morning, there was nobody there. Jake felt the expected irritation, but also a strange stab of disappointment. Just another irresponsible addict, he told himself. Nothing to be surprised about, and definitely not something to care about. But then he saw Micah jogging across the street, coming from a stop on the other side.

"Sorry," he said through Jake's rolled-down window. "I thought you meant over there."

Jake had just given the intersection—he hadn't even realized there were two different bus stops. "No problem." He tried to sound casual about it; he wasn't going to admit to the assumption he'd made, that was for sure.

Austin, of course, wasn't quite so discrete. "We thought you'd bailed," he said as Micah climbed into the back seat. "Got a better offer, or decided to just sleep in and find an easier job somewhere else. Maybe somewhere that *doesn't* make you wake up in the middle of the damn night."

"No," Micah said. "I couldn't. I'd miss you too much."

Austin nodded with exaggerated sympathy. "That's a common problem, I'm afraid. Everybody wants a piece of me, but there's only so much Austin to go around."

Jake let himself fall out of the conversation, but he felt his whole body relaxing as he listened to the inane chatter that swirled around him. There was no tragedy in the cab of his truck. No junkies, no lost parents, no struggle or pain. Just two easy-going young men, killing time and enjoying each other's company. Two easy-going young men and one uptight, slightly older man trying to believe in the illusion.

"You guys are on your own for the start of today," he announced as they pulled up to the job site. "Well, with Alex and Eduardo. So, remember, Alex is in charge." He turned to give Austin a pointed look. "None of your bullshit about being the boss's brother. Clear?"

"Well, technically, I *am* the boss's brother," Austin replied. "And I'm a little hurt that you want to deny our relationship. I will not live in the closet, Jake! Not for you, not for anyone!"

"Please shut up," Jake said. "You know what I mean." And then, mostly as a way to move the conversation the hell away from any talk of coming out of the closet, he said, "In fact, I'm instituting a merit-based hierarchy for this team, starting right now. So Alex is in charge, then comes Eduardo, then comes Micah, because he may not know much but at least he puts in a solid day's work, and then, my *brother*, comes you."

Micah leaned forward. "So, if I tell Austin to do something, he has to do it?"

"That's the theory," Jake agreed, not bothering to point out that he'd never had much luck exercising his own theoretical authority over his brother. "Austin, you clear on that? You're number four in the pecking order."

"But number one in your heart." Austin pushed his door open with a jaunty energy that would certainly disappear as soon as there was any real work to be done. "At least, I'm number one until you find the right guy, right? And then I'll have to fight him for the spot."

And there it was. Austin couldn't let anything rest, couldn't stop poking at things that were better left alone. At least the bastard wasn't sending any pointed looks in Micah's direction. Yet. "Get out of the truck, Austin. I'll be back in a couple hours. Alex knows what to do."

"Don't worry," Micah said, opening his own door. "I'll keep him in line."

"God help us all," Jake said, mostly to himself. He waited until the doors were shut and Austin and Micah were on their way over to Alex's truck, then pulled back out into traffic.

Austin had just outed him to a possibly-gay, definitely-attractive junkie. And the junkie hadn't seem too worried about it. Hadn't seemed at all interested, really.

So that was good, Jake tried to tell himself. No need to be secretive, but also no need to worry about temptation. Austin was an asshole and needed to get better at minding his own business, but really, this was the best possible outcome from an awkward situation.

Yes, good to just put the whole thing in the past and move on. Work was important; Austin was important. Getting laid? Not important, not right then. And getting mixed up with a junkie? Last thing Jake needed.

Still. Might have been kind of nice if Micah had at least paid a little attention to Austin's announcement. Might have been nice to be something other than a sexual non-entity in the eyes of an attractive potential partner.

"You're an idiot," Jake said to himself as he drove. And there was no one in the car to disagree with him.

~*~*~*~

IT DIDN'T MATTER THAT JAKE DESANTIS was gay. Didn't matter at all. The rehab people had been totally clear about the stupidity of starting a new relationship until everything had settled down, and that was one of their rules that actually made sense to Micah.

No relationships, of course, didn't mean no sex, but Jake was Micah's *boss*. Not a good candidate for the position of fuck buddy or, even worse, one-night stand. Whatever Austin was up to—and it was pretty damn clear that he was up to something—was a terrible idea. So Micah would just ignore him, focus on getting his work done, and keep plugging away at rebuilding his life.

Easier said than done, of course, once Jake returned from his meeting and they all piled into the trucks to go to the next site. Austin continued his campaign of insanity by insisting he wanted to ride with Alex and Eduardo, and there was just no graceful way for Micah to avoid climbing into the passenger seat beside Jake.

They'd been alone in the same truck together the day before, Micah reminded himself. There was nothing to feel self-conscious about. No reason to be hyper aware of the way Jake's hand rested on the gear shift, the loose grip that tightened a little whenever something happened on the road in front of them. No reason to imagine the same fingers wrapped around something else, tightening and loosening....

"You guys from Seattle originally?" he asked, hoping he didn't sound as desperate for a distraction as he felt. "You have family in the area?" Small talk—boring, stupid small talk. That was what he needed.

Then he realized that Jake was pausing a bit too long before answering, and wondered if the talk was something other than small. "You and Austin don't really know each other that well," Jake said finally. "He hasn't had time to lay all his stories on you." He glanced over, saw Micah's confusion, and added, "Or maybe it's because you're a ju—an addict—yourself. Maybe he doesn't think he needs to explain himself to you."

"I'm a bit lost," Micah said. "And, sorry, if this is a bad subject or something. If it's none of my business, you can just tell me."

"Shit. No, I'm sorry. I don't know—I didn't think I was still so touchy about it. But, seriously, the more time you spend around me and Austin, the more landmines you're going to stumble over. Not your fault at all, just a lot of history."

"We could talk about sports," Micah suggested. "I mean, I don't really follow sports, but—what do you think about the Mariners this year?"

"I don't follow sports either," Jake admitted. "And if you're okay hearing it, it might not be a bad idea for you to have a bit of background. Mostly just to know when Austin's bullshitting you." He glanced over, then back to the road. "I admit it, I'm kind of hoping you'll help keep him in line. I mean, I know it has to be his choice, his responsibility, all that. But I'm giving him all the support I can, and it's likely not enough. It never has been before."

Micah didn't think he was ready for this. Hell, he *knew* he wasn't ready for it. "I've been out of rehab for three days. I'm barely holding myself together. I'm in no kind of position to—it's not that I don't *want* to help. I just don't think I'm someone that anyone should be counting on."

"No," Jake agreed slowly. "Not counting on. I get that. But at least not—not enabling? I don't know if that's realistic or not. I talked to one counsellor who said it could actually be *good* for junkies—addicts, sorry—to hang out with other addicts because they're the only people who know all the games and can call each other on their shit. That's why they do group therapy, right?"

"I think they do group therapy because it's cheaper." Micah shifted in his seat so he was twisted a little toward Jake. "And it's okay to call me a junkie—I know what I am, so there's no point sugar-coating it."

Jake paused, then nodded his understanding before moving on. "So hanging out with Austin—you don't think that's good for you? I mean, I don't know what I'm doing with any of this. If you think it's a bad idea for you and Austin to be hanging out, let me know. I've got a couple friends who have businesses like mine and I can trade you with one of them if you want the job with a different set of people—"

"No," Micah said quickly, and a little too loudly. He was surprised by the strength of his reaction. "I mean, thank you. Sincerely, I appreciate you even thinking about that, instead of just firing me. But I actually do think it's kind of good for me and Austin to be hanging out. I don't know if I can say why—I guess because it's someone I don't have to explain things to? I mean, even talking to you is easier than it would be with another boss, right? You know the meetings are important, I don't have to hide anything—it's great, for me. And I don't think I'm hurting Austin. So if it's okay with you, I'd like to stay."

"You just don't want to be responsible for him."

Jake didn't sound angry, just resigned. It was a tone that seemed to invite honesty, so Micah decided to give it a try. "I don't

43

want to be responsible for a house plant. That's the order they suggested at rehab—plant, pet, person. I think that's kind of bullshit, because pets are totally dependent on people and they shouldn't be used as training aids or test cases or whatever. At least people would be able to walk away if things got bad and pets can't really do that. But the point is, I've been out of rehab for *three days*. I'm just not a good bet, not for anything."

Jake was quiet for long enough that Micah started to think about ways to make it clear that he was a good bet for employment, at least, and shouldn't be let go because he was so likely to be irresponsible. But when Jake finally spoke, it was clear he'd been thinking about something else. "We don't have any family in the area—me and Austin. We have aunts and cousins and whatever, but they're back East and we're not a close family. Our parents—" He exhaled through his nose, a little too strong to be normal but not strong enough to be a snort, then said, "Austin tries to get people to believe he's a junkie because of our parents. They died in a car crash a few years ago, and it was pretty tough for him. But he was a junkie before they ever died. The crash they were in? He'd been missing for almost a week—he was only sixteen, still living at home—off shooting up and having fun or whatever, and they had signs up all over the place, had a private detective trying to track him down, the whole works. And they got a call from someone who'd spotted him, so they took off. Rainy night, driving too fast—"

Jake stopped, shook his head, then said, "They slid off the road, hit a tree. So nobody else got hurt, at least. It could have been worse."

Nobody else got hurt. Nobody but Jake, who lost his parents and gained responsibility for a junkie brother. "I'm sorry," Micah said. As was so often the case, the words felt inadequate, almost insulting. As if Micah's sorrow could change anything, or matter to anyone.

But Jake smiled gently in response. "Kinda more than you were asking about, right? So, yeah, we're from Seattle. But, no, no family in the area. And if Austin tries to use the accident as an excuse for him being a fuck-up, don't let him get away with it, okay? He was a fuck-up long before it happened."

Micah nodded, but he wasn't sure he was really agreeing to anything. He wasn't Austin's keeper, and he sure as hell wasn't in any position to start deciding what lies other people had to tell themselves in order to get through their dark times. He had his own lies, after all. But he sure as hell wasn't going to share them with his boss, who just happened to be his own kind of hot and apparently gay. So he said, "It's a lot on you, though. Taking care of him."

Jake shrugged. "He's my brother."

And it was that simple, apparently. Maybe Micah should have had siblings instead of being an only child. Or maybe he should have been at least a little less awful toward his parents and he could have gotten this kind of support from them. But there had already been enough soul-baring for one day, so he said, "I learned about bindweed this morning. Alex says it's one of the few times you might use a chemical herbicide."

"It's a bitch," Jake agreed, sounding as if he was just as happy to be back on solid ground as Micah was. "If the customers are willing to be patient, we can usually starve it out, but if they want it gone fast? Chemicals."

"The cause of and solution to all of life's problems," Micah mused.

"Not quite all of them." But Jake didn't offer an explanation, and Micah didn't push for one. Instead, he let himself slide a little further around to the side so he could see more of Jake without getting caught staring. The guy was nice to look at. Strong body, almost stocky—he seemed solid, physically and every other way. For just a moment, Micah let his sex-starved imagination run, and, damn, what it came up with! Micah, the same height but without the bulk, pressed up against the wall, with Jake's hard body pressing into him, rubbing against him. Jake's cock would be as thick as he was, and it would strain against his jeans, pushing forward as Micah ran a hand down between their bellies. Straining toward him as Micah sank to his knees....

The truck stopped moving, and Micah blinked hard. "You should see the view they have here," Jake said, clearly and thankfully oblivious to Micah's perving. "The whole back of the house is glass, for good reason. I don't know why they even bother having gardens, to be honest, because I can't imagine anyone paying attention to anything but the view, but I'm not complaining."

"So this would *not* be a good place for me to start yelling obscenities and randomly cutting down plants with the weed-trimmer?"

"I don't think there are any good places for that," Jake replied calmly. "But a place of complete natural beauty, enhanced with tasteful architecture and a shit-ton of money? Yeah, it's one of the even less-good places."

"Noted," Micah said.

He and Jake walked together over to Alex's truck, and it felt good, natural, as if he'd known Jake for longer than he had and as if their friendship were deeper than it was. A stupid, dangerous feeling, he reminded himself. He couldn't afford that sort of illusion, and he definitely couldn't let himself be distracted by a whole new temptation, not when he was already using all of his willpower to avoid something else.

Chapter Five

TWO MORE LONG DAYS THAT WEEK, and Jake was still getting calls from new customers, still having trouble keeping up with all the work. So that Friday afternoon, he asked the guys if any of them were free to work the next day. He'd known it was a long shot—both Alex and Eduardo had other jobs where they would already have been scheduled, and Austin? Well, Austin had been pretty clear about his plans to stay in bed until afternoon both days of the weekend and then to spend the rest of the day not lifting anything heavier than various snack foods. He saw no reason to change that agenda now.

But Micah had agreed quickly, seeming almost—relieved? Jake knew enough about addiction to know that free time was the enemy of at least some addicts. They were fine as long as they didn't have time to think, imagine, and stray. He'd never been able to persuade Austin to keep himself busy but it wasn't surprising that Micah might be more disciplined in that area. The part that surprised Jake was that he'd almost completely forgotten that Micah even *was* an addict. Less than a week of good behavior and reliability and already Jake was forgetting that the guy had a serious issue he was dealing with. Austin had shared a bit more about Micah's past, and Jake knew about the party, the OD—he knew that Micah had been more than a dabbler in the scene, had almost died from it, and was still early in his recovery from it. He *knew* that. But he'd let it slip from the front of his mind to the back, and that had been a mistake.

Still, when he picked Micah up early that Saturday morning, he couldn't make himself sorry it was just the two of them in the car. If Austin had been there he would have dominated the conversation, and maybe Micah liked that, maybe Micah would rather talk to someone vivacious and funny and entertaining, but too bad. Austin was home asleep, and that meant Jake had Micah all to himself. He'd brought an extra coffee and Micah made an appreciative grunting sound when Jake passed it over, and all was right in Jake's world. Damn it. He was so stupid.

"This is good for you, huh?" Micah asked, and Jake's mind froze in guilt. Then Micah continued, "The extra work? This is because you have more business than you can handle, right? Not because we screwed up or something?"

"No, it's a good thing," Jake said once he kicked his brain back into gear. "A bit awkward, though." And maybe it wasn't completely professional, but Micah wasn't just an employee, he was—Austin's friend? Was that how Jake was going to categorize him? Well, he was someone who had at least some idea of what things were like at the deSantis house, especially if Austin bitched as much at the NA meetings as he did at home. So maybe it wouldn't be too bad to share a little from Jake's perspective. "I'd like to hire some more workers and start a new crew, to be honest. It'd just be seasonal, but that'd be okay. I've got enough money saved to buy another trailer, another set of mowers and everything, and I could get some students on board for the summer, at least. But I'd need supervisors. Alex is great, but if I had two crews, I'd have to be doing even more of the other work—meeting customers, bidding on jobs, doing the management side of things—so I'd want a supervisor for the second crew, too. And—" He shrugged. The problem was clear, surely.

"Austin?" Micah sounded confused. "He wouldn't expect to be promoted, would he? He knows he's not doing a great job. Hell, he takes *pride* in not doing a great job."

"Yeah, he does. So how am I supposed to ask someone else to be in charge of his bullshit? I mean, I should fire him—if he weren't my brother, I'd fire him. Hell, if he were my brother and he wasn't—you know—if he didn't need the stability so much, I'd still probably fire him. But he *is* my brother, and he *does* need the stability whether he likes it or not. So I'm stuck with him, but I can't expect anyone else to put up with him. So if I'm not on the site as much, if I'm off doing the other side of things, what the hell do I do with Austin?"

Micah sipped his coffee thoughtfully. "There isn't enough work for two, doing what you're doing? I mean, he's a charmer— you know that. I bet he'd be really good at the sales side of things.

He might make some promises no sane business could ever follow through on, so you might need to keep an eye on him, but other than that, he'd be good, I think. And could he help with the paperwork? He's not totally lazy, I don't think—he's okay with using his brain. It's his body he likes to keep still."

"Huh," Jake said. "I hadn't thought of it like that. It wouldn't be perfect, but—it might not be terrible. It's not like he's that much use on site anyway, so I wouldn't be making things harder for you guys, would I?"

Micah tried to hide his grin behind his travel mug, but Jake saw it anyway. "No, I don't think it would be a problem for us," Micah said carefully.

Jake groaned. "He's that much of a nuisance?"

"He's a good guy. Friendly, and funny and everything. He's totally entertaining, and I like hanging out with him." Micah seemed to be thinking about the next part. "But I need this job, you know? Alex and Eduardo? They need their jobs. I'm only here because of Austin, so it's easier for me to overlook it, but for them? Seeing him goof off while they work their asses off, and then hearing him laugh about it? I think—well, I think it wouldn't break their hearts to get a bit of a break."

"I would really like it if my brother didn't put me out of business," Jake mused, mostly to himself but not worrying about Micah hearing him. "And if either of those guys, but especially Alex, got so fed up they wanted to look for another job? They wouldn't have much troubling finding one, not at this time of year."

"I don't think it's that bad. They really like working for *you*. And they say that even when Austin isn't around, so they're not just saying nice things in front of the boss's brother."

Well, that was something. "You're not only here because of Austin," Jake said. He should have corrected the statement earlier, but he'd gotten distracted. Still, better late than never. "I hired you because of Austin, but you're still here because you're working hard and doing a good job."

Micah didn't answer right away, but finally said, "I'm kind of surprised by how much I liked hearing that. I mean, I shouldn't care, right? You're not The Man, really, but you're working hard to get there. Building your profits on the backs of your workers, alienating us from the products of our own efforts in order to feed into the capitalist machine—and don't even get me started on the customers, with their ostentatious displays of wealth and power."

"Okay. I won't get you started."

"Too late!" Micah sounded gleeful. "Because I have to examine my own reaction to what you said. I was *proud* when you said I was doing a good job—it's like Stockholm Syndrome! I'm hungry for positive attention from my captor!"

Jake glanced over and saw Micah grinning, his eyes dancing with good humor. "Do you really believe all that stuff? And if you do—how come you're not pissed off about it?"

"I don't know." Micah still sounded happy. "I guess I'm like Walt Whitman right? 'I am large; I contain multitudes.' I can believe one thing and feel something else, all at the same time."

"And it doesn't bother you?"

"It used to." Micah twisted around in his seat to look at Jake more directly, and Jake realized how often Micah did this, and how nice it was that he did. He wanted to have a *conversation*. He wanted to exchange ideas, wanted to see Jake's reaction to things and truly engage in whatever they were talking about. Micah might be a budding communist, but he sure as hell wasn't close-minded about things. And his enthusiasm was contagious, so Jake was listening closely as Micah said, "It was this deep schism in myself that led me to narcotics in the first place. I was torn asunder, and needed something to heal—no, not heal, just mask— my emotional pain."

Jake looked over with a frown, and Micah grinned back at him. "Bullshit," Jake said.

"Absolutely," Micah agreed. "I've always liked having different ideas—try one out for a day, try something else the next day. No schism whatsoever."

"I don't really know what schism is."

"But you're thinking of another word that sounds kind of the same, right?"

"Well, I am now." But this was dangerous ground. Jake couldn't talk about *jism* with an employee! Well, no, that wasn't quite true—it wasn't like he ran a totally 'proper' business, with no crude jokes or language allowed. As long as the customers didn't hear, Jake didn't give a shit what his guys talked about. But Jake couldn't talk about jism with Micah. It was possibly the least sexy word in the universe, but the association was clear enough to send Jake's mind all the places it wasn't supposed to go. An image popped into his imagination, completely unbidden—Micah, naked, on his back, eyes rolled back in pleasure, thick white drops shooting onto his stomach, his chest—Jesus, no, not the right time! "So how *did* you get started?" His voice was a little strained, maybe, but he sounded a hell of a lot calmer than he felt. "With drugs, I mean. It wasn't the big pain from your ideas not matching up, so what was it?"

Micah sighed, but he didn't turn away. "Just young and dumb and thinking I could handle it, really. I know there are lots of people who drink and smoke pot and that's it, but for me? They really were gateways. I started hanging out with people who smoked up a lot, and then someone offered me a pill and I figured, sure, why not, it's just a pill, and it *was*, really—I think it was oxy, but I took just one and it felt good and it wasn't like I turned into a raving lunatic or anything, so I guess I thought I was immune to addiction or something. I don't know. Something stupid like that."

"But you weren't immune."

"Doesn't seem like it," Micah agreed.

"But you're—I don't know, you're better? Rehab helped?"

"Rehab helped while I was there, for sure. Once I got past the physical side of things—the withdrawal bullshit, which I really,

really don't ever want to do again—I was fine. There were people there who were trying to smuggle shit in or sneak out to get a fix or whatever, but for me? The therapy stuff was annoying, because—" He stopped, and Jake glanced over to see him looking sheepish. "Well, you might not know it from listening to me right now, but generally I'm not huge on sharing and caring, you know? So sitting around in a circle with a bunch of people I barely knew, being expected to spill my guts, and expected to be supportive of them when they spilled their guts? Not a good time, not at all. But I didn't hate the individual therapy sessions, and there was a pretty good gym and lots of activities and stuff. Some of them were stupid, but some were okay. I made a stained glass window for my mom—she paid thirty grand for rehab and got a cheap chunk of glass out of it, so not a great deal for her."

"She got her son back," Jake corrected. "I'm sure she thinks it was a bargain, even without the stained glass." Micah didn't say anything, and Jake looked over again. The light was gone from Micah's face, replaced with an unpleasant tension that made Jake's stomach tighten in sympathy. "She didn't get her son back?" he guessed.

"I don't know." Micah turned away, squirming around to look out the front windshield. "They live in Portland now. Moved down a couple years ago. They—they came to see me in rehab. Every week, as often as they were allowed to. But we didn't really talk about anything. Just small talk, you know? But I still kind of thought I'd go stay with them when I got out. Stupid of me to assume that, I know."

"They said you couldn't?"

"Not my mom. My dad—he said he'd prefer I didn't. For my mom's sake. He said it would be better if I could prove I was over it, you know? He said if I could stay clean for a couple months on the outside, away from all the supports and everything at rehab, then maybe they'd be able to start trusting me again."

Jake wasn't sure what to say, and Micah didn't seem to need a response. He just kept his gaze locked on the traffic ahead of them and said, "It's totally fair. I was an asshole when I lived with them—typical junkie shit, stealing and everything. They'd be stupid to let me back in. And they paid for rehab, so it's not like they've abandoned me or anything. They're just protecting themselves. It's hard to—" He stopped, then said, "Well, you know. It's hard to love a junkie."

Yeah, it was. Not hard to feel the love, just hard to live with it. So Jake didn't think he could judge Micah's parents for their decision. Still, "The problem is we love junkies anyway. I mean, whether you're here or in Portland—whether Austin is with me or not—the love doesn't go away."

"That's the *problem*?" From the corner of his eye, Jake could see Micah's slow nod as he thought it through. "Yeah. I guess for you, it'd be a problem. A hell of a lot easier if you could just take a pill and stop caring."

"That's kind of what *you* did, wasn't it? Was it easier?"

"Short term? Hell, yeah."

"But long term?"

"I ODed at New Year's. It wasn't the first time. Dying is kind of a shitty side-effect of the 'not caring' thing."

"But if you could be more careful? If you could get the effects of the drugs, *without* the risk? Would you want to keep taking them?"

Another long pause before Micah said, "No." He turned in his seat again, suddenly animated. "Shit, that's what's different this time! I've quit before, done rehab before. But those times, I always would have said 'yes'. If I could have had the drugs safely, without worrying about getting into bad shit or OD'ing or getting busted or whatever, I always would have wanted to keep shooting up. But this time? No. Even if it was safe I wouldn't do it, because— because I don't want to stop caring, I guess."

"And what made you feel that way?" Jake asked. He wanted to pull the truck over so he could turn in his seat just like Micah was, so they could really *talk* and figure this out. But he kept driving; he didn't want to make this too intense, didn't want to scare Micah away from telling the truth. Because the truth was important, here. If Jake could figure out what had made Micah determined to quit, maybe he could figure out the same thing for Austin.

"Rock bottom, I guess," Micah said. He sounded serious. "When I fucked up with my parents, I found some friends—good friends—who turned into a sort of family. And they put up with a lot of shit from me, but I eventually managed to screw that up, too. The OD—the shit was stronger than I was expecting, sure. But also, I was being careless. Too chicken shit to actually kill myself, and too chicken shit to actually care about living. I woke up in the hospital and my friends weren't there. Nobody was there. And I just figured I had to either do a better job of killing myself, or a better job of staying alive."

"And you chose the second," Jake said, the words just something to fill the space in the conversation while he thought it all through. "It's a hell of a gamble," he finally said.

"For Austin, you mean? Yeah, it's—I wouldn't recommend it, really. Like, I wouldn't recommend forcing the issue, trying to *make* him hit rock bottom. My parents, and my friends, they didn't ditch me for *me*, they did it for themselves. To protect themselves. And if you and Austin get to that point, where it feels like instead of you pulling him up, he's pulling you down? Then I'd say you have to cut him loose. But from what I'm seeing, you're not at that point. You're still pulling him up, don't you think?"

"I—I think so, yeah."

Micah nodded. "So—so, shit, this whole conversation has been completely pointless, huh? I'm not helping you at all."

"No, it wasn't pointless. It was—it gave me hope, you know? You *are* helping me, and helping Austin." And even with the distracting, completely inadvisable moments of lust that had been plaguing him, Jake meant it when he said, "I'm glad you two ran into each other. I'm glad you're working with us. I think you're a good thing for Team deSantis."

"It's been a long time since I've been a good thing for anybody," Micah replied quietly. "I hope I don't let you down."

"I hope we don't let *you* down," Jake replied. "We're doing a lot of taking, me and Austin. Any chance we could do a little giving? You want to hold off on your parents for a bit longer, but what about your friends? They're in Seattle, right? You want—" It was dangerous ground, he realized, but he pushed on anyway. "You want some company going to see them? I can be a character witness or something, tell them how good you're doing."

"I've been out of rehab for less than a week," Micah replied. He sounded—wistful? Was that the word? Kind of sad and hopeful at the same time. "Might be a bit early to be making reports."

"Preliminary reports," Jake said. "Letting them know you're doing well and working hard. No guarantees." And he was probably pushing too far into something that was really none of his business, but he kept going anyway. They'd been ignoring boundaries for the whole conversation, so why stop now? "It'd be good for you to have some friends, wouldn't it? Something to look forward to, or a reward or something? I mean, you're doing great with just the self-discipline thing, but—I don't know. At what stage do you get to start thinking about enjoying your life again?"

"They don't even want us to get *laid* for the first year. I don't think they're too worried about overall life enjoyment, really."

"They don't want—for a whole year?"

"It's bullshit, because if you were married or dating someone when you went into rehab, even though that person is part of your old patterns and clearly wasn't keeping you from abusing before you went in, you still get to go fuck them all you want. But if you were single when you went in? They think you should stay single. Every other damn thing is about changing patterns and doing things differently, but on this one thing they're all prudish. It might be tied in with the religious side of it all. Their 'higher power' is a fucking cock-block."

Well, boundaries were looking sort of good all of a sudden. Not because Jake didn't want to keep going with this line of conversation; his carnal side could imagine five different ways to turn things around so he'd be doing poor, horny Micah a damn *favor* by taking advantage of his desperation. But the responsible side wouldn't let him get away with that sort of behavior, which meant this conversation could go nowhere good. "There was no one from before? None of your friends, or anything? You couldn't kind of manipulate things so it seemed like you were just going back to an old relationship?"

"You sound like me all the other times I tried to get clean," Micah said with a grin. "But the thing is, there's no one else to fool. I mean, if I think the rules are bullshit, I can just ignore the rules. You know? I'm already pretty much doing that with all their God stuff. There's no—okay, the jury's out on whether there's a higher power, like, cosmically, but there's definitely no higher earthly authority. I'm not on probation or anything, not reporting to anyone. They don't even have a sponsor for me yet, and I kind of like it like that. The last two times I had sponsors the bastards brought me down, struggling with their own shit and making my life harder than it had to be. But the point is—if I decide the 'no sex' rule is bullshit, I should just break it. And if I think it's a good rule, I should follow it. I don't need to play games and twist shit around; I think it's kind of important that I *not* play games and twist shit around."

That totally made sense. God, had Jake just been trying to persuade an addict to sabotage his own recovery? Had he been trying to do it because somewhere, in the back of his mind, he was thinking that maybe *he* could be the one who was an exception to the rule? Had his next line been destined to be something about friends-with-benefits? Was he that fucking pathetic?

Luckily, they were at the first job site and he didn't have to answer those questions. Instead, he said, "Yeah, sorry. That makes sense," and then "You're on lawns. Trim, then mow. You know the drill."

"No problem," Micah said easily, pushing his door open and swinging down out of the cab.

Jake made himself stay still for a moment longer, collecting his thoughts and his self-discipline. His need to take care of himself was fading, being replaced by a need to take care of Micah. It wasn't a bad idea for him to get involved with an addict, it was a bad idea for Micah to get involved with anyone until— well, shit, until a whole *year* had passed? Well, until Micah thought it was time, probably. Until he figured he was stable enough to start ignoring that rule.

But he clearly didn't think it was time for that yet. And realizing this made it a lot easier for Jake to behave himself. *It's not what Micah wants,* he told himself as he climbed out of the truck and retrieved his gear from the back. *Not what Micah needs.*

The corollary was obvious, of course. Not what Micah wants, not what Micah needs; not what Jake should be thinking about. So he steeled his will and tried to think about overgrown rhododendrons instead.

Chapter Six

IT WAS ALL JAKE'S FAULT, REALLY.

Well, no. That wasn't fair. Micah had come back to the neighborhood on his own, after all, before Jake had even mentioned it. And nothing he did was anyone else's fault. That was one of the lines from therapy that had been kind of hard to swallow, at first, but now that he had it down, he liked it. Micah was in charge of Micah. So if Micah worked all day Saturday and then went home, got cleaned up, and went to stand outside Tristan's apartment, looking up at the lighted windows by himself? That was *Micah's* weird-ass decision, and Jake couldn't be blamed for it.

Even if he *had* been the one to put the idea in Micah's head this time around.

It was tempting to think about calling him. Just something casual, maybe. Just a simple, "Hey, I was wondering if you were serious when you said you'd vouch for me to my old friends? No, it doesn't have to be now, of course not. But—well, as it happens, I *am* in their neighborhood right now, and, well, are you busy tonight? Saturday night? A young, good-looking guy with his own business and shoulders begging to be scratched with desperate fingernails? You wouldn't have plans tonight, of course."

Yeah, that was a phone call Micah was never going to make. He might not have a lot of pride left, but he had that much.

So he stood, alone, and looked up at the apartment windows. They'd likely go out at some point; it was Saturday night, after all. But they might not. The group was so self-contained, so complete in and of itself, that they often didn't bother finding any other people to socialize with. They were all they needed; they'd been all Micah had needed, except—

"You can go in if you want," a neutral, vaguely familiar voice said from far too close behind Micah. He spun to see Simon, Tristan's boyfriend, standing calmly a couple feet away. "I called up and checked, and Tristan says you can go in as long as you're clean. And you're clean, right?"

Micah didn't want to answer. It was a personal question, and who the hell was Simon Yeung to ask it? Tristan's boyfriend, maybe, but big deal!

But—he was Tristan's protector, too. He'd been something else before, but by the time Micah had gone away Simon had been doing his best to stand between Tristan and danger. Danger like Micah.

"I'm clean," Micah said, looking down at the pavement. "But I shouldn't go up, I don't think."

"He wants you to." Simon was quiet for a moment, then added, "That wasn't his message. We got a call that someone was out here, staring at the apartment—I have people keeping an eye on things, in case trouble comes—and I came down to check it out. When I saw you, I called Tristan and he said you could come up if you wanted, as long as you were clean. He didn't say he wanted you to. But—he wants you to."

It was a lot of information, especially coming from Simon, who Micah barely knew. But it wasn't enough. "What about the rest of them?" Micah asked. He felt pathetic, grovelling for any tidbit, but he needed to know. The idea of walking into that apartment, the place that used to be his refuge, and being met with hostility? He deserved it, but that didn't mean he was strong enough to take it.

But apparently Simon had reached the end of his interest in offering reassurance. His voice was bland and uninterested as he said, "It's Tristan's apartment, so I asked Tristan. I have no idea what anyone else wants."

"I'm clean," Micah repeated. Was he trying to convince Simon, or himself? "Ninety-seven days."

Simon stood and waited, his expression calm.

"I just—I mean—I don't know. I just wanted to say 'hi', I guess." But, no, he wanted so much more than that. Just saying 'hi' and then leaving? It would be—it would be too final. It would be admitting that the friendships were over, rather than just suspended. "And I need to make amends." He hadn't planned that part, but maybe it made sense. "You know, for the twelve steps. I'm supposed to make amends to the people I hurt. It's kind of a vague step, to be honest—I mean, am I just supposed to apologize, or should I actually try to make reparations of some sort, and if I try to make reparations, what would that even look like? But I know I hurt people here, so I thought—well, obviously I wasn't done thinking about it, or I would have done something, right? I'm still working it all through."

Finally, Simon nodded. "So, when you've got it worked through, if you want to see Tristan, he'd like to see you." He stepped back. "Until then—good luck."

Micah watched as Simon turned and crossed the street. He was going back to his place by Tristan's side, and Micah was still out in the dark, alone.

Because he'd chosen to be, he reminded himself. Cowardice or wisdom, he wasn't sure, but his choice. He looked up at the lighted window and saw a dark shape looking down at him. He raised his hand cautiously, and the shape raised its own arm and returned the wave.

It wasn't much, but it was enough. Enough to let him turn around and go back to the half-way house, enough to let him relax and fall asleep without too much trouble. He wanted more, of course, but he'd take what he could have.

~*~*~*~

"NINETY-NINTH DAY CLEAN," JAKE SAID as Micah climbed into the cab of the truck Monday morning. He made it sound like a statement, but really it was a question, and he was relieved to see Micah nod in confirmation.

"I hit two meetings yesterday and spent three hours working out," Micah said. "And without the guys at the half-way house to distract me, I—I don't know. I *think* I still would have made it? But I'm glad they were there, for sure."

"So it's the free time that's hard for you?" Jake asked as he pulled out into traffic. He was strangely pleased to see Micah reach for the extra travel mug of coffee as if he took it for granted that it was his.

"Seems like, yeah. My brain's kind of my enemy sometimes, you know? If I have time to start thinking about stuff, I can come up with all kinds of excuses and stupidity. Like, there *are* people who use opiates recreationally. Why couldn't I be one of those people? Get fucked up on Sunday, then lead a normal life for the rest of the week."

"But it wouldn't work for you."

"Nope. And I mostly know that, except for when I have too much time for thinking." Micah twisted around and looked in the backseat as if noticing the emptiness for the first time. "No Austin?"

"He's got the morning off. I talked to him about your idea, having him do more of the business side of things, and he's really excited about it. Wants to take some classes in bookkeeping and whatever. All the stuff I hate, to be honest, so if this works out, I'll totally owe you. Anyway, he's got the morning to check out courses and see what he can find. I'm going to pick him up at lunch." Jake glanced over. "Or, actually—do you have your license?"

"My driver's license? Yeah…"

"So maybe you could pick him up. We're going to be at Robertson's by mid-morning, and they've got a lot of beds, not that much lawn. So your expertise would be—"

"Non-existent," Micah said easily. "I bought a book, though. *Weeds of the Pacific Northwest,* or something like that. I'm working through it."

Jake tried to imagine Austin taking that kind of initiative, then caught himself. Austin *was* showing initiative, now that Jake was giving him a bit more freedom to do the kind of work he actually liked. "So, you'll be up to speed in no time. But for today, maybe the driving?"

"You realize you're talking about lending your truck to an addict you've known for less than a week, right? Does that really seem like a good idea?"

"In the abstract, not at all. But with the specific addict in this case, I feel like I'm pretty safe. Besides, the truck's insured, and there's something weird going on with the transmission. You'd probably be doing me a favor if you stole it and wrecked it so I could get the insurance money instead of paying for the repairs."

He paused. "Not that I actually want you to steal and wreck my truck. For the record."

"Got it," Micah said. "So, sure, now that the instructions are more clear, no problem. I can go pick Austin up if that works for you."

"You also shouldn't let Austin steal the truck."

"Valuable clarification. Thank you."

It felt good, talking to Micah. Easy. It reminded Jake of how long it had been since he'd hung out with anybody but Austin. Nothing fancy, nothing planned, just sitting around, shooting the shit. Maybe watching TV. Would Micah want to do that? Come over after work, or after a meeting, have dinner and just watch TV or something?

Jake honestly wasn't sure if he was thinking about making a friend or getting laid. Either way, though—maybe it would be okay? He was trusting Micah with his truck; couldn't he trust him with a little more? Micah had his no-relationship rule, of course, but he'd already sounded like it wasn't one of the more important ones for him to follow. It could be good for him, surely, to spend time with someone who could support his recovery. And didn't people say that doing heroin was kind of like the longest lasting orgasm in the world? Maybe Micah wouldn't miss the chemical kind so much if he were having more of the physical kind. Jake could help him with that, he was pretty sure.

If the bastard was even gay. Sure, Austin had mentioned him making out with guys, but junkies did all kinds of crazy shit when they were messed up. It was a bit different when someone was—well, if they were "straight" in the no-drug sense, maybe they'd be "straight" in the sex sense, too. And even if he was gay, there was still the problem of figuring out if he was even a little bit interested in Jake, sexually, when he'd never shown any sign of it.

And if Jake was the kind of selfish bastard who let himself make decisions based on his own desires instead of what was best for someone else. Damn it.

So he didn't let himself look over at Micah, didn't give in to the temptation to make any sort of invitation.

But when Micah said, "I talked to one of my old friends on Saturday," Jake was genuinely interested and genuinely wanted to be supportive. Micah added, "Well, I talked to my friend's boyfriend, not my friend himself." And Jake barely noticed the pronouns, barely wondered if they could be a hint about Micah's own orientation. Mostly he paid attention to the content of the words.

"But it went well? You think there's room there? Like, you could maybe be friends again?"

"I don't know. Maybe. But I feel like—" Micah stopped suddenly. "You must be really, really tired of hearing about all my shit, right? Twice-weekly therapy sessions for the past three and half months have got me used to talking about myself all the time. But you don't need to hear all my whining."

"I haven't heard much whining," Jake replied. "You're working through some stuff, for sure, but that's fine. I like listening." He glanced over and saw Micah still looking unsure. "Some of it's been really useful, in terms of me figuring things out with Austin. And even the stuff that hasn't been has been interesting, you know? You're an interesting person." Another glance made it clear Micah wasn't convinced, so Jake shrugged and said, "What else are we going to talk about? We've already established a shared lack of interest in sports."

"We could talk about you, maybe? Like, outside of Austin, what are you interested in? What did you do yesterday? Anything fun?"

Well, Micah had been honest, so maybe it was Jake's turn. "I cleaned the apartment in the morning, and then when Austin woke up we talked about changing things around at work, and I helped him figure out where he should go to look into courses, and then I went for a run and then got groceries, made dinner, and went over the business paperwork with Austin. That's my exciting life, right there."

"What about Saturday night?" Micah asked. "I actually thought about calling you to see if—I don't know, something to do with being my character reference with my friends, but mostly just—I don't know. Just to hang out or something. But I figured you'd be doing something better."

"I was watching TV." Jake felt as if his breathing wasn't quite right when he added, "You should have called."

"Maybe next time I will."

And there it was. Jake didn't even need to look over to see it because he could feel it, the sudden buzz in the air of the cab. A gentle hum of flirtation, of attraction acknowledged, of a possible future *something*. Nothing concrete, but that didn't make it any less real. Or any less exciting.

Jake had missed this, he realized. He'd known he missed sex, but he'd somehow forgotten about everything else. He felt alive, excited about his life and its potential. He looked over at Micah with a grin, and Micah grinned back, and Jake knew they were both feeling it. Life was fun; Micah had reminded him of that.

Chapter Seven

FOR THE FIRST WEEK, WORK had been Micah's salvation; it had been what kept him busy so he didn't have time to get into trouble. The second week, though, after that conversation with Jake? The second week, work was fun.

Well, not the work itself, really. Mowing lawns and pulling weeds out of flowerbeds was alternately loud and backbreaking. But the Jake part was fun. The morning rides to the job site, even when Austin was with them, started every day off right. Austin seemed to have picked up on the new vibe between them and, being Austin, fed off the energy like it was his own. It wasn't always clear whether he was trying to be his brother's wingman or trying to flirt with Micah himself, but it didn't really matter. It was fun either way, and Jake seemed fine with it, too.

Then there were all the extra opportunities during the day, chances for a quick exchange of looks, little jokes or exchanges, even a few 'accidental' touches that lingered as a tool was handed over or something heavy was lifted. Stupid high school crap, really, but Micah kind of liked that. It was like he was being given the chance to go back into the past to do things over, and maybe get shit right this time.

The rides home at night were perfect, too. Everyone tired after a long day's work, relaxed, but still with that extra energy cracking between Micah and Jake. Micah knew just what it would be like if he and Jake hooked up at that time of day—they'd both be slow and languid, their bodies already sticky with dried sweat, and there'd be no need to feel shy or self-conscious. Smelly armpits? Yeah, maybe, but for both of them, and earned with hard work. There'd be something sexy about it, something primitive, even animalistic. But still slow, not frenzied. Yeah, Micah had definitely spent some time thinking about that.

But every day he had a meeting to go to after work. And since Austin only seemed to hit meetings every other day, if that, Jake had his brother to deal with. Micah could have called Jake after his meeting, he supposed, but he never really had the nerve. What was he going to say? Were they at the "do you want to go to a movie" stage or the "get over here and fuck me senseless" stage?

Which brought up the "over here" issue, of course, because they weren't supposed to have overnight guests at the half-way house and somehow the idea of getting together with Jake while Austin was watching TV in the next room wasn't too sexy. Back to the high school stuff, but not quite as much fun in this instance.

Friday was pay day, and that should have been a golden opportunity. Austin was working at home that afternoon, doing the books or whatever, and Alex and Eduardo had been full of jokes as they collected their pay envelopes, full of crazy ideas of how to spend their money. It should have been easy for Micah to say something then, or just after, as he and Jake climbed into the truck together and pulled away. They had money, they had time—a cheap motel would fit into the ragged, primitive sex model pretty well, wouldn't it? They could shower together afterward, or maybe take turns, considering how wide Jake's shoulders were and how small the bathtubs were in most cheap motels. But the point was, with the sweat of the day gone, they'd be able to explore a whole new kind of sex, the clean kind, maybe the faster kind that ended up getting them sweaty all over again. There were a lot of opportunities, there.

But Micah had to go to a meeting.

It wasn't so much that he was getting a lot out of the meetings, he didn't think. They were pretty boring, really, and the religious stuff was just as annoying as it always was. But missing a meeting seemed like one small step off the path, one weakness that was too likely to lead to others. He had a follow-up appointment scheduled with his rehab therapist the next week and he was absolutely planning to bring up the idea of easing back on the meeting frequency. But until an actual decision had been made, he wasn't going to mess with what seemed to be working. Not even if his self-discipline cost him a chance to get Jake deSantis naked.

So he went home and got cleaned up and went to his meeting, where his internal eye-rolls were just a little more intense than they usually were, and then he went home. Alone.

But when his phone rang at about nine o'clock and he saw the name on the call display, a very interesting twisting happened in his lower belly, and he felt just a little breathless as he answered the call. "Jake?"

"Hey, Micah. Sorry to bug you, but Austin isn't picking up. Is he still with you?"

It took a moment for Micah to re-arrange his thoughts. "Austin? No—I haven't seen him since this morning at work."

A silence, as if Jake was having to do a little re-arranging of his own thoughts, and then, "This morning. He didn't go to the meeting with you?"

Shit. "No. I didn't see him there." But maybe it wasn't a big deal. Maybe it was just a misunderstanding. "I went to the one on Bronson Street. Was that where he said he was going?"

"Yeah."

Shit, shit. "Maybe he went to a different one instead. They're really uptight about people coming late to that one— maybe he realized he was going to be late and didn't want the hassle."

"He's not answering his phone, Micah. Not calls or texts."

Shit, shit, shit. "I'm going to call him, okay? Maybe he's just—I don't know, maybe he just doesn't want to talk to you for some reason? Let me give it a try. I'll call you right back."

"Yeah," Jake agreed, but there was a tone in his voice that broke Micah's heart a little. A tone that made Micah realize, again, how many people he'd hurt when he'd been using. At the time, he'd been full of bravado—they were stupid enough to care about a loser like him so they'd get what they deserved and maybe they'd learn a lesson—that sort of juvenile self-pitying bullshit. Seeing things from the other side made him want to travel back in time and beat the shit out of himself.

Kind of like he wanted to beat the shit out of Austin right then. But he wasn't going to get far if he called up and started screaming at the guy, so he took a few deep breaths, then dialed the number.

Austin changed his ring tone just about daily, but that morning it had been a Neil Diamond song—possibly a genuine favorite, possibly a choice based on irony, possibly a mix of the two. But as Micah sat there, listening to the buzzing of an unanswered call, he could picture himself standing there beside Austin, "Sweet Caroline" ringing out of his pocket while Austin ignored it, Micah punching Austin's stupid face one time for every "Bah" in the chorus.

When he got the chance to record a message, Micah tried to sound more relaxed than he felt. "Austin. It's Micah. Call me as soon as you get this, okay? Whatever time."

Then he hung up and sent a text. *Where r u? Contact me asap, k?*

And that was all he could do. He felt so completely helpless. Austin was—well, okay, maybe Austin was fine. Maybe he was at the damn movies or something, maybe he'd lost his phone, maybe he'd hooked up with someone and was too busy with that to even notice his phone was ringing. All totally possible.

But Jake obviously thought it was something else, and Micah did too. If it hadn't been payday, he might have been a bit less suspicious, but cash and addiction were a dangerous mix.

He waited a minute or two for Austin to respond, then called Jake back. "I left messages. Maybe he's fine."

"Yeah," Jake said. "There have been false alarms before. I need to remember that. It's just—there have been a lot of times when I was right to be worried, too. You know? And what am I supposed to do, just sit here, going crazy, waiting for the little bastard to call me?"

"We could go look for him."

Jake snorted. "I've tried that. Nobody will talk to me, nobody will open the damn doors to let me look inside. I end up just driving up and down the street, and honestly, if he's on the street I'm not all that worried about him, you know?"

Well, there were things that could happen on the street that Jake absolutely should be worried about, but probably Micah didn't need to point that out right then. Instead he said, "You misheard me. I didn't say *you* could go look for him. I said *we* could. People will talk to me. They'll open doors for me."

Jake was quiet for a moment, and Micah felt a pang of regret. He got the feeling sometimes that Jake didn't think of him as a recovering junkie, and he *liked* that feeling. But this was a reminder that it wasn't based on reality. Micah could get in places

Jake couldn't because Micah *belonged* in those places. And Jake wasn't going to be able to forget it, not after he saw it in person.

But Micah couldn't be selfish about this, couldn't try to maintain his illusion while Jake was suffering. So when Jake said, "If you have time—" Micah had only one answer.

"No problem. Are you at home? The places I'm thinking of—I mean, there are loads of spots he could be, all over the city. But the places I know, and where I know he used to hang out, are just south of downtown. They're all walkable from the neighborhood I used to live in. You want to meet there?"

Jake agreed, and Micah gave the address of the intersection closest to Tristan's place. He grabbed his coat and left his room, and was almost to the front door when he heard a familiar voice say, "Micah? It's almost curfew. Where are you going?"

Shit. Micah turned to find Andrew, who'd always seemed like one of the more reasonable house counsellors, standing in the kitchen doorway. "A friend's in trouble," Micah said, hoping honesty would be the best policy. "I need to go help him out."

Andrew drew closer. "In trouble with an abuse issue?" he asked softly. He clearly got all the response he needed from Micah's silence. "You know that's dangerous. You're doing really well with your own recovery, Micah, but you're not—you're not *better*. You know that. Getting involved with someone else who may be lapsing is an understandable impulse, but it's not a good idea. It's putting your own recovery at risk."

81

Yeah, Micah knew that. But he knew other things, too. "I think the biggest risk to my recovery is going to come if I start hating myself again. If I start thinking of myself as weak and useless, what the hell is going to stop me from acting like I'm weak and useless?" The words felt right as he spoke them. Of course, he'd fooled himself before. Still, he pressed on. "I'm going. I've got a friend who's meeting me—he's totally clean. So there's a risk, but, seriously, man—if the only way to stay clean is to let my friends down, then there's no reason for me to stay clean in the first place."

Andrew didn't look completely convinced, but at least he didn't get in Micah's way. "You've got the number here—call me if you need me. And expect to do some extra cleaning or something to make up for missing curfew."

"Least of my fucking worries," Micah said, but in a friendly tone, and Andrew nodded in response.

One of the best things about the half-way house was its easy access to the C line, so Micah was back to the old neighborhood—back to his old life—inside twenty minutes. He actually had to wait a while for Jake to show up, and outside of one quick glance to see if the lights were on, he studiously didn't look in the direction of Tristan's apartment. He didn't need Simon's spies ratting him out again.

So he checked his phone, sent a couple more texts in Austin's direction, then bit the bullet and sent one more in a different direction.

Within a minute of texting *anything going on tonight* to Moby, his old dealer, he got back a diatribe of cheerful obscenities and orders to present himself for inspection immediately. Moby was always pretty damn welcoming to his best customers. Especially the ones who'd done a good job sucking his dick when they didn't have enough to pay for what they needed.

I'm off the shit, he texted back. *But I want to see some people. Just to say hello.*

He knew how Moby would react to that—Micah was *counting* on that reaction. If he'd said he was trying to rescue a customer from Moby's evil clutches, he would have been shut down. But offering himself up, even cloaked in a denial of interest? An enthusiastic entrepreneur wouldn't just accept that he'd lost a customer, he'd look for ways to get the customer back. And, lucky for Moby, Micah had always been pretty happy with returning to the fold in the past. Welcome him back, make the product available—no harm giving a freebie the first time or two when you knew how many sales you'd soon be making—and let nature take its course.

For the first time, Micah felt real apprehension. He *had* always fallen into this trap before. Moby texted back an address with a smiley face and Micah stared down at his phone. Sure, he was on day 103 of clean living, but he'd been institutionalized for 92 of them! He was still a rookie, still a toddler, just learning to walk, and now he was heading into a swamp full of quicksand where one false step, one little toddler-stagger, could send him into a deadly—

A familiar pickup pulled into a parking spot down the street, and Micah's heart rate slowed. Jake was here. Jake was strong. Micah couldn't lean on him too much, not generally, because Jake already had enough to worry about. But just this one time, when it was for Jake's sake that Micah was taking the risk— no, wait. Not for Jake's sake, for Austin's sake. It wasn't fair to forget that and act as if Micah was doing *Jake* a favor by trying to keep Austin out of trouble. This was for Austin. Micah was risking himself for Austin.

But, fuck it, that wouldn't work, because Micah really wasn't sure he'd do this for Austin. The guy was a friend, sure, but was this actually going to do him any good? Or was it just a case of trying to make Jake feel better?

Micah took a few steps down the sidewalk then waited for Jake to join him. "I've got an address," he said. "Good place to start. But, Jake—what's the plan? I mean, we charge in there and haul him out, and then—what? I mean, assuming he's there. But if he's there, he's using. Right? He's back on the shit, and if you pull him out, you can't put him in jail—hell, even in jail, he could get stuff if he needed it bad enough. It's—I don't know. You've thought about all this, I guess. You've been through it before. This is just—it's my first time. From this side of things."

Jake didn't look exactly shocked. Just tired, far more tired than he'd been a few hours earlier. "What if we *don't* do it?" he asked quietly. "And what if this is the time he actually goes too far? A guy died at New Year's, you know. Same shit you got into—I don't know how Austin missed it, to be honest. But he did, that time. But what if this is the time it gets him? And I'm sitting at home, waiting for him to learn his lesson or hit rock bottom or whatever, while he's out here fucking *dying*. How would I deal with that, Micah?" He seemed to be genuinely asking. "How the fuck would I carry on, knowing that I left my only family to die?"

Micah had no idea. He thought briefly about giving his parents' number to Jake so he could get some advice on the subject, but that wasn't fair. Instead, he jerked his head down the street. "It's a couple blocks over, if you want to check it out."

Jake fell into step beside him and they walked quietly for a while. Then Jake said, "Why this place? You said there were lots of places he might be, so why is this one the most likely?"

"Austin's pretty social, right? He wouldn't want to just score and shoot up alone—even if he's totally fucked up, I figured he'd want to be around other fucked-up people. So one of Moby's parties would sound good to him. So I contacted Moby and said I wanted to see people. He gave me this address."

"You wanted to 'see people'? Is that some kind of code?"

Micah snorted. "Not officially. But I figured Moby would read it that way."

"He thinks you're coming back?"

"I'm not too worried about what he thinks."

Jake was quiet for a bit too long before he said, "Shit. This is really not a good thing for you. Right? You're doing it to help me out, but it's hurting you. It's taking you back to places you shouldn't be going back to."

Micah shrugged. "Life is compromise." He nodded down the street. "That's the place. I've been here before. Look, they'll let you in because you're with me, but keep your mouth shut, okay? Follow my lead? Honestly, it'd probably be best for me to go in alone, but if Austin's there and he's fucked up I might need some help to carry him out." *And if he's not there but Moby is, I might need you to drag me away from whatever he offers.*

"Just muscle," Jake agreed. "You're in charge. Got it."

In different circumstances it might have been fun to play with the idea of being in charge, but it definitely wasn't the right time. So Micah just nodded, led the way to the battered metal door, and banged on it a couple times before testing the door knob. Locked. He banged again and then the door opened, just a slit, with a chain clearly keeping it from going any further.

"Who the fuck are you?" a male voice demanded from the interior shadows.

"Who the fuck are *you*?" Micah responded. Maybe later he'd be amused by how insulted he was feeling to not be immediately recognized. Had 102 days been enough to erase him from the scene? "Moby told me to come by."

"Did Moby tell you to be a stupid bitch and not give your fucking name?"

"Fuck you, man. Is Moby here? Why don't *you* be the stupid bitch and go find your master?"

There was a mumbling sound, and Micah realized the doorkeeper was talking into a phone or a radio or something. Moby seemed to have gotten a bit more sophisticated in the last few months. Finally the voice got louder as the man returned to the slit in the door and demanded, "Who the fuck you got with you?"

"Friend," Micah said. He thought about it for a second, thought about how they'd look from the doorman's perspective. Jake was too damn clean cut, too bursting with health and vitality to be a junkie. Micah reached back, found Jake's unresisting hand, and dragged it up over his shoulder. "Boyfriend," he clarified.

It should have been fun and flirty, Micah thought as the door finally swung open and the two of them were allowed inside and pointed up a staircase. Fake relationship? Total rom-com fodder, great opportunity for flirting and innuendo and forbidden touches with meaningful eye contact. But there was nothing fun about the current situation, and the grip Micah kept on Jake's hand was related more to fear than passion.

Because he could smell it. He'd thought he was past the physical side of the addiction, but he could feel the fumes entering his body, travelling to his lungs, then out to every cell of his body, not enough to satiate them, just enough to wake them up and make them scream for more, more, more! Maybe he was imagining all that, but when they got to the top of the stairs and looked around at the occupants of the room, maybe a dozen people total, all reclining on battered couches or sprawled on a couple mattresses, there was no way he imagined the way his heart sped up, the way his senses sang in response to every part of the scene. It was smelly, dirty, debauched in practically every way, and he wanted to flop down on the floor and offer his arm up to the first person with a needle.

Then he felt Jake's fingers tighten around his and turned to follow his gaze.

Austin was sitting by the window, looking out at the street. He'd likely seen Jake and Micah approach; he certainly didn't seem shocked to see them now. Then again, he didn't seem to be in a state that would easily allow shock to be felt.

"Hey," he sighed at them as they approached. "You my car service, come to take me home?"

Jake released Micah's hand and turned away. The light wasn't good, but Micah was close enough to see Jake's fists clenching, and couldn't blame him. "You need to shut up," Micah told Austin. "And, yeah, we're here to take you home."

That was when Micah became aware of someone moving behind him, walking with more focus and energy than a typical junkie. He turned to be greeted with Moby in full charm-mode, smiling and stretching his hand out to shake Micah's. "My boy. Good to see you." He tugged on their still-joined hands, and Micah knew from experience that if he gave in he'd be pulled into Moby's body, into a kiss designed to dominate rather than excite, and then into god knew what else. Micah braced his feet, and when his other hand reached for Jake's, it was there.

"Hey, Moby," Micah said. "How've you been?"

"I'm all right, but I've missed you." He glanced over at Jake, then back. "You're busy tonight, I see. But you should come back when you're free. We could catch up on old times."

Jake's hand loosened its grip and Micah knew it was because Jake was trying to get free in order to go after Moby. It wasn't a good idea, and Micah squeezed tighter, hoping Jake would get the message. Moby wasn't someone who would ever really be an ally; he was far too dedicated to the cause of making money. But he was better as a neutral party than an enemy, especially while Austin was under his power. It was a lot of information to get across in a simple hand squeeze, so maybe Jake eased off just because he was remembering his promise to let Micah be the boss. Either way, he settled.

Micah nodded toward Austin. "He's done for the night, right? S'alright if I take him home?"

Again he felt Jake tensing; the disgrace of asking permission from a drug dealer, probably. But Moby inclined his head magnanimously and Micah didn't take time to worry about pride. He was there to get Austin out, and that was all. Jake let go of Micah's hand in order to heave his brother upright, and Austin smiled sadly in Micah's direction. "I missed the meeting," he mumbled. "Sorry."

"Shhh," Micah replied. He wasn't sure what Jake was feeling or how close he was to doing something stupid, but Austin wasn't likely going to say anything that was going to help calm his brother down.

And, sure enough, when Austin said, "He called me, and I just thought—"

"He fucking *called you*?" Jake demanded. He let Austin fall back into his chair and turned to face Moby. "Who called him? You did?"

"I was checking in with an old friend," Moby replied. He was good at seeming amused, good at keeping his voice light, but there was an undertone to it that Jake needed to be paying attention to. Moby tended to be armed, and he always had staff in situations like this, staff who wouldn't shy away from inflicting whatever damage Moby decided was appropriate. "Austin's always so lovely to be around, isn't he? So—lively. So it seemed only natural to invite him to my little gathering tonight."

He was gloating, baiting, and Jake was clearly about to take the hook. For a moment it seemed like an old painting—the dimness around the edges, the glow coming from the window to light up Jake's face as he stood protectively over his brother, and Moby, further into the shadows, taunting. An angel and a devil, fighting for a lost soul. But this was the devil's playground, and he had more tricks than Jake could even begin to guess. It wasn't a fair fight, and it wasn't going to happen, not while Micah was there. No, if someone was going to fight the devil, it wasn't going to be Jake.

Chapter Eight

"JAKE, GET AUSTIN OUT OF HERE," Micah said, and Jake tried to focus on the instructions. That was what they'd come for, after all. Just get Austin and go home.

But the bastard had *called* Austin. All the hard work, all *Jake's* hard work on top of Austin's, the glimmer of hope Jake had been starting to see for a future, and it was all blown because this fucker hadn't wanted to lose a customer and had made a goddamn phone call. *And because Austin wasn't strong enough to hang up*, a voice tried to remind him, but it didn't seem fair. Everyone knew Austin wasn't strong enough to hang up. It wasn't fair to take advantage of someone's weakness like that.

And damn it, Jake was done with tolerating unfairness, done with turning the other cheek. He took a half step forward and was met with Micah's strong hand on his chest, pushing him back. Then Micah leaned in and said, "It's not going to help anything. If we get the shit kicked out of us, it's not going to help Austin. Get him out of here now and we'll talk. I'm in charge, remember?"

It was the "us" that did it. Jake could risk his own skin—he *wanted* to risk it, wanted to take a few hits so he could be even more satisfied by those he gave in return—but he had no right to drag Micah into it. So he reached down and dragged Austin back to his feet. Austin wouldn't meet his gaze, but that didn't mean much—the son-of-a-bitch could go from abjectly guilty to sunny and carefree in about five seconds.

Jake had sort of expected Micah to take Austin's other side to help support him. Not because Jake couldn't do it himself, but just—for symbolic reasons, maybe? Instead, though, Micah had set himself between Moby and Jake, facing the dealer, clearly ready for something.

"Get him out of here," Micah said over his shoulder. He sounded calm enough, and he was in charge, so even though it felt completely wrong, Jake started toward the stairs. Micah would follow them, of course, and the stairs were too narrow for three people anyway.

He could hear the voices behind him, too low to make out words—but there was Moby, with that false, poisonous levity that had set Jake off, and Micah, sounding conciliatory, even fawning, and damn it, that made Jake angry too. Micah shouldn't have to kiss up to that fucker, shouldn't be asked to breath the same goddamn air as him.

"Hurry up," Austin muttered, trying to tug Jake down the stairs faster.

"You going to puke?"

"Not yet. But hurry."

So Jake sped up a little and he was all the way to the bottom when he heard the raised voice back at the top. Heard—

"Jake, let's go," Austin urged him. "He'll catch up." And now instead of Jake gripping Austin it was Austin gripping Jake, wrestling him toward the door or at least keeping him from climbing back up the stairs.

Jake had himself almost free when he saw Micah stumbling down the stairs after them, moving so fast he was almost falling. "Go," he ordered, and Jake let himself be pulled by Austin, pushed by Micah, tumbled out of the building and into the fresh, cool air of the street.

"Truck," Micah said. "Keep moving."

"They coming?" Austin asked. His words were still a bit slurred but apparently his brain was working better than Jake's.

"Don't think so," Micah said, hurrying along right in front of them. There was something a little strange about the way he was moving, and Jake wanted to stop and sort it all out, but then Micah added, "I don't want to give them time to change their minds," and Jake kept moving.

They got to the truck and settled Austin in the passenger seat, buckled him in and shut the door, and finally Jake could turn his attention to Micah. They stood on the sidewalk beside the truck, and the glow from a streetlight showed Jake what he'd been afraid he might see.

His hands tensed into fists and he had to make himself relax one before he reached for the reddened swelling on Micah's face. "He hit you?" he demanded.

Micah shrugged and wouldn't make eye contact. "It's no big deal. Could have been way, way worse. You want my help with Austin?"

"I—" God, Jake wanted to lock Austin in a cell somewhere, put him in a goddamn box so Jake could pay attention to something else for just a little while. "Did he hit you anywhere else? You were moving funny—where else are you hurt?"

Another shrug, this one with a bit of a grimace. "I'm pretty sure I'm fine. He kicked me in the ribs pretty hard, but I've had broken ribs before and I don't think this is the same."

"Shit. You want to go to the doctor? The emergency room?"

And there, in the middle of it all, Micah looked at Jake and grinned bright and easy. "Hey, you think they might give me some morphine?"

Jake stared at him for a moment, and then, despite himself, something loosened in his chest. The sound that came out of his mouth wasn't quite a laugh, maybe, but it was close enough, and the hand that had been ghosting over Micah's bruise shifted so easily, so naturally to Micah's neck, pulling him closer. Their mouths met in a kiss more friendly than passionate, Micah's lips still curved into a grin, Jake still almost laughing.

Then Micah leaned in a little more, his hands gently gripping the fabric of Jake's shirt, and there was no more laughing. Micah's mouth was hungry, his tongue demanding, and the adrenaline that had been circulating through Jake's body with no avenue of escape suddenly had a purpose. He held on tighter, spun them both back, hopefully out of Austin's blurry line of sight, and pinned Micah against the side of the truck. Micah, Micah. This skin, this body, these eyes, dark and so deep Jake felt like his whole soul could be drawn into them. No more flirting, no more indecision. He leaned in hard, lining their bodies up together, and his blood roared in his ears as Micah pushed back into him, need matching need.

But a door slammed somewhere and Micah's whole body jerked in alarm. Jake made himself pull away, at least a bit.

"We should get out of here," Micah said. His eyes were wide, his lips wet, and Jake's body responded to the sight even as his brain accepted the words.

Jake ran his hands down from Micah's shoulders as if saying goodbye to his body and Micah winced. Shit. Selfish, stupid, careless—"You're hurt. Can you—" Jake fought for a solution. "Yeah, can you come help me with Austin? Or if you need to go to the hospital—maybe without the morphine idea—?"

"I'm fine," Micah said. He tugged his shirt down a little, then nodded decisively. "Yeah, I'll come with you, make sure Austin's okay. We should talk about Moby, too. He's—I guess I should have handled that better, somehow. I didn't know he was going to be such an asshole."

"You didn't know I was going to take his bait," Jake added.

"Yeah, that too." Micah pulled open the back door of the truck. "So, let's get Austin home, and then sort shit out."

It all went fairly smoothly, really. After the shit-storm at Moby's, Jake was braced for everything else to go wrong, but Austin was compliant, apologetic, and generally pathetic, letting Micah and Jake pull off his jeans and shoes and tuck him into bed like an over-tired toddler. They propped him in the recovery position on his side, but neither of them was really too worried about him, not in an immediate sense.

Longer term, though?

Jake went to the fridge and found a bottle of Gatorade—his drink of choice since he'd decided he wasn't going to have alcohol in the apartment—and held it up as an offer to Micah.

"Sure," Micah agreed, and took the bottle, then sank down onto one of the stools at the breakfast bar. His face was turning purple along one cheekbone with a bit of swelling around his eye, but he didn't seem too concerned about it. Still, best to make sure Micah was okay before moving on to Austin.

"He kicked you, too?" Jake asked. "Just once? Your face and your ribs? That's all?"

"Got me in the thigh," Micah said. "Aiming for somewhere more delicate. Which is a problem, because, seriously, if he was pissed enough to aim for my balls, he was pretty pissed. I can ask around and see if he's been weird lately, but if it isn't a general thing? If this is specific, just to us in this situation? It could be a problem."

"A drug dealer beat you up tonight. I'd say that's more than a *could be* problem."

"*Could be*, like, future tense. Everything tonight is over with—no worries. But if he's still that mad? There could be more."

"What's he pissed about? Was what we did—did we violate some sort of code or something?"

"Not that I can think of, not just going to pick Austin up. I mean—" Micah stopped, frowned down at his bottle of Gatorade, then looked back up, decision clearly made. "From some of the stuff he said tonight, I think maybe this was a bit about me. He used to—if I didn't have enough money for junk, sometimes I'd—" He stopped again, looked at his bottle and said, "I'd do what he wanted. Blowjobs, usually. I thought—I don't know, I thought he liked chicks, to be honest, and he was just sort of fucking around. But he really didn't seem to like me showing up with you. Didn't like me having—I mean, I called you my boyfriend to explain why you were there, that's all. But I guess maybe he took it seriously. It's not like he ever cared about me at all—that's for certain. But maybe he thought he owned me or something."

It was another of those reminders Jake seemed to keep needing. Micah used to be—Micah *was*—a junkie. He'd sucked cock for drugs. Not that long ago, either. Jake wasn't a prude, and he'd had his own share of unemotional, impersonal sex. But—

99

"So, the point is," Micah said, charging on after Jake had failed to respond, "Moby might be carrying a bit of a grudge. He's not a total psycho; he's not going to send goons after anyone, not if we stay out of his way. But—yeah. He might call Austin again. I mean, he might do more than call. He might—" He frowned, as if realizing something for the first time, then slowly reached behind himself. Reaching into the back pocket of his jeans?

Micah froze, and Jake did too, staring at him, trying to figure out what had just happened. Then Micah brought his hand back around, under the counter where Jake couldn't see it, and stared down at what he'd pulled out of his pocket.

Jake made himself stay still. He wanted to lunge across the counter and grab Micah's hand, seize whatever he was holding, but he made himself wait, even when he saw the tremor run through Micah's body. And his patience was rewarded when Micah lifted his shaking hand and stretched it across the counter toward Jake. The baggie wasn't big, just a chunk of plastic that looked like it was cut off a shopping bag, wrapped around something and tied shut with an elastic band. Not big, but clearly far too powerful.

Jake still moved slowly, carefully, as reached out and took the baggie from Micah. He waited a moment, anticipating some sort of reaction, but there wasn't one, so he stood up and moved over to the kitchen sink. Water on first, then he twisted the plastic open and dumped the brown globs down the drain. He didn't look over at Micah until he'd carefully rinsed the plastic and then shoved it in his own pocket. A check of the sink to be sure everything was gone, then he turned the water off and stepped back toward Micah.

Who stood up as if he thought he was being attacked. "I didn't know!" he said. "I felt him touching me there but I thought he was just grabbing my ass, you know? I didn't ask for that shit! I didn't want it!"

"I know," Jake said. "I understand. I'm sorry it happened. I'm sorry I asked you to go there—I should have figured things out for myself."

"No," Micah said quickly. "That was fine. It's fine. I just— I should go."

"Wait," Jake said, and Micah froze. He stayed in place while Jake covered the space between them, and let himself be turned so he was looking Jake in the eyes. "*Should* you go?" Jake asked. "Tonight was—it was a lot of temptation, right? And you're obviously pretty shaken up. Can you stay here?" He held up his hands in the *I'm innocent* gesture. "No hanky-panky. Just sleep. Unless you have somewhere else to go. Is there someone at the half-way house?"

"There's a counsellor," Micah said slowly. "But—he'll be asleep, and there's all these rules I'm supposed to be following. Fuck. I—I hate asking you to babysit me. But—"

"It's not babysitting," Jake scoffed. "I'm the one who got you into this shit tonight; the least I can do is help you make sure you're going to be okay with it. And hanky-panky promises aside, I'd like to take a look at your ribs, and maybe your leg. Not that

I'm a doctor, but I'll feel better if—I don't know. If I can see the damage instead of just imagining it." It occurred to Jake just then that the worst of the damage wouldn't be visible even if Micah was completely naked; getting beat up wouldn't likely have an impact on his recovery, but going back to a drug den, having the shit actually in his hands? What effect was that going to have?

Micah seemed to have calmed down, though. He half lifted his shirt on one side, showing a red and purple blotch along his ribs, then said, "That's not bad, right? And the leg is even less. He mostly missed me on that one."

"Okay," Jake said. He still felt bad about the whole situation, but Micah was right about the bruises, at least—he'd be sore, but it didn't look bad enough to need medical attention. "Are you tired? Kind of a long day, huh?"

Micah nodded politely. "Yeah, I guess. Don't suppose you have a spare toothbrush or anything, do you?"

"There's new ones under the sink in the bathroom. Help yourself to whatever else you need—soap, or whatever. Do you want ice for your face? Or aspirin or anything?"

"Nah, I'm fine."

"Okay. I'm going to sleep out here, on the couch. You can have my bed."

Micah blinked hard, then said, "I'm not going to kick you out of your bed, Jake! The couch is fine for me."

"No, it's—I always sleep out here, when Austin's having a bad time. I don't get as comfortable so I sleep lighter and I'll hear

102

him if he needs me. And I'm between him and the door, so I'll wake up if he tries to leave." Jake saw Micah's doubtful expression. "I know, I'm an enabler or whatever. It is what it is." He smiled, not sure if it looked convincing or not, and nodded toward the bedroom. "All yours. I can get you fresh sheets, if you—"

"Jesus, Jake." Micah's voice sounded strained. "No. Thank you. Sleep well. Or don't, I guess, since that's your plan. I'll probably sneak out pretty early so you and Austin can talk or whatever without me hanging around in the way, so—"

"Don't sneak," Jake said a little too strongly, and moderated his voice to add a more polite, "please. Like I said, I won't be fast asleep, so—say goodbye if you leave, okay? Just so I know what's going on."

Micah nodded dutifully, and Jake went to find a blanket and pillow for the couch. He lay there, listening to the soft sounds of Micah settling in for the night, and dreamed about a different life, a different world, one where he could go into the bedroom and lose himself in Micah. So many things would have to be different, of course. If Austin didn't need watching out for; if Micah hadn't had a tough night or if Jake wasn't quite so responsible about not taking advantage of someone when he might be feeling extra vulnerable; if Jake were in any sort of position to actually have a relationship, to give as much of himself to Micah as Micah might be interested in taking. If, if, if.

But there was only this life, only this world, so Jake consoled himself with the memory of Micah against the car. Their bodies had fit together so perfectly, their desire had been so balanced and mutual.

But it had just been a moment, and a stupid risk to have taken, considering where they had been and what had just happened.

Just a moment. A stupid risk. True enough. But still a memory sweet enough to send Jake off to sleep with at least something positive to think about.

Chapter Nine

JAKE'S BED WAS BIG. KING size, Micah was pretty sure. Big enough for two, easily, but he supposed the problem was that there would have been so many more than two people in that bed. Austin never left Jake's thoughts, of course. And when Micah had told Jake about Moby, about how he used to trade sex for drugs, it had been pretty clear that Jake would have taken Moby to bed with them, too. Or maybe that was too easy, because it wasn't really Moby who was the problem. It was Micah. Old Micah, the guy he'd been, who'd made a hell of a lot of mistakes that someone like Jake wasn't likely to just forget about.

And Micah supposed he couldn't let himself forget about them, either. Because it would be far too easy to let New Micah turn into Old Micah. Just a few mistakes, and it would all be back. God, what would have happened if Jake hadn't been there when Micah had found the baggie in his pocket? Would he have used it?

You don't have any gear, he told himself. So that was something. A practical barrier, if not a long-term one. *Tinfoil and a lighter, asshole. You could have made it work.*

He could have. He'd thought, for one brutal, wrenching moment, about shoving the baggie back into his pocket. Not to take it, just to—to have it. To be able to think about it and decide. *To be able to talk yourself into it.*

But Jake had been there, so Micah had been saved.

But what the hell kind of a life was that for Jake? Lying out there on the couch, guarding not one but two junkies, making sure neither one of them went chasing after destruction that night.

That was what Micah could offer. A filthy past and a tedious present with no real promise of a bright future. That's all he had, all he was. And Jake was smart enough to realize it.

Micah thought about leaving. He was pretty damn sure he wasn't going to sleep, not with his body and mind buzzing like they were. But if he left, where would he go? He wanted to walk, to move, but if he was out on the streets right then he was pretty sure his feet would carry him back in old directions, taking him places he shouldn't be.

He'd taken a couple yoga classes at rehab, but not enough to really know any of the moves. Still, he could do something. He rolled out of bed onto the floor and did sit ups until his abs burned, savoring the extra pain from his sore side. Then pushups, again with a little extra stab as his skin stretched over his ribs. All the modified forms of exercises he could think of, working his body until the sweat dripped off his nose onto the carpet and he finally collapsed with a groan.

He stayed down there on the floor and tried to exhaust his mind just as he'd done with his body, but it refused to cooperate. Doing mental math, trying to recall song lyrics, even counting damn sheep, but the buzzing was always there in the background, the memories of sweet, dreamy numbness calling to him in a voice he couldn't ignore.

When the first hint of dawn showed through the bedroom window, he gave up on sleep and dug around for his phone. It was damn near inexcusable to call anyone at this hour, but compared to the other shit he'd done, it was nothing.

Tristan answered on the third ring, voice blurry and confused. "Micah?"

"Hey. Yeah, it's me. Look, man, I got paid yesterday—can I buy you breakfast?"

"It's five in the morning, Micah." And Tristan didn't sound so confused anymore. He sounded tired, disappointed, making the logical assumption about an addict making phone calls at inappropriate hours.

"I'm clean, man. I swear. I just—I don't know." *I had a rough night. I need to see you. I need you to see me, and tell me there's something in me worth saving.* "I want to beat the crowds."

Then Micah just had to wait while Tristan thought it through and finally said, "Yeah, okay. JoJo's?"

"If that's okay with you. It'll take me a while to get there—I don't know if the buses run yet, but I'll get a cab. Okay? Don't leave if I'm late."

"I'm going to shower first—I won't even be there for at least half an hour."

"Okay, good." God, Micah couldn't remember ever having been this nervous. Maybe when he'd come out to his parents? No, not even then. "Okay, I'll be there soon. Thanks, man. I—yeah, thanks."

"It's good to hear from you," Tristan said. Then he hung up.

Micah's stomach was churning so hard he thought he might actually puke. He'd done it. He'd called Tristan. He was going to *see* Tristan. He—oh, shit. He had a big bruise on his face and he was covered in dried sweat, wearing yesterday's clothes. He looked like a fucking junkie, and *this* was how he was going to present himself?

He heard the gentle knock on the bedroom door and whirled as it was cautiously opened. Jake peered in, softly saying, "You okay? I heard you talking."

"On the phone. Sorry to wake you. Yeah, I'm okay, I think. Shit, Jake, how bad do I look right now?"

"You got a job interview?"

"Friend interview. I called Tristan—he's going to meet me for breakfast. But I look like shit, right?"

"You look a bit rough. But you don't look fucked up. And if you want, I can still come with you and be your character reference. Seriously, man, all that shit last night? That was a test, and I'm not saying it wasn't hard, but you passed it. You know? You should tell him about that, or I can if you want."

That was a more positive spin than Micah had been expecting. "I might not have passed it if you hadn't been here."

"You might not have had to deal with it if I hadn't called you. I say it's a wash." Jake's smile was warm and seemed genuine. "So, what do you say? Should I come with you? Tell your friend how great you're doing?"

As nice as that was to imagine, Micah forced himself to stay in reality. "You've still got your other junkie to babysit."

"Enough with the 'babysitting', okay? And I can haul Austin out of bed and bring him with us. Him fucking up doesn't qualify him for extra special consideration or anything."

Again, surprisingly sweet. But Micah shook his head anyway. "I'm fine. Thank you, but—I'm fine."

"I guess it might not create the best impression," Jake admitted. "You showing up with a guy still oozing dope out of his pores—might not make your friend think you'd left it all behind, exactly."

"He'll either believe me or he won't," Micah said. "I just need to get it over with. But I'm gonna brush my teeth at least, okay?"

"It's your toothbrush now, man. You can leave it here or take it with you. Use it at will. You want me to call you a cab?"

Micah nodded absently. Damn, he wanted to leave the toothbrush behind. He wanted to stake just that tiny claim to belonging, that minuscule hold on Jake's life. And thinking about that made him way less nervous about meeting Tristan, so that was a plus.

He got cleaned up as well as he could in a few minutes, then went out to the living room to find Jake sitting on the couch, blanket wrapped around his shoulders. "Good luck," Jake said. "Call me when you're done." He held up a hand in front of himself. "And don't even start on the 'babysitting' bullshit. Call me because I'm nosy and want the gossip, okay? I'm not asking you to report in. I just want to know how it went."

"Okay," Micah agreed, and he made himself leave. He was going to see Tristan. Scary, but good. Something to look forward to. Something to make up for the empty feeling he was getting from leaving Jake behind.

His nerves kept growing as he travelled through the city toward JoJo's, a twenty-four-hour place down the street from Tristan's. They'd used to spend a lot of time there, when someone had enough money to pay for food. Usually Tristan.

And Tristan had earned that money whoring, Micah reminded himself. He wasn't going to meet with a fucking Sunday School teacher. Tristan wasn't going to judge for his sins against himself or against the rules of society. He would only be considering the sins against his friends.

Of course, there were more than enough of those to give Tristan good reason to shove Micah away for good.

So he was still nervous as he paid the cabbie and climbed out of the car, still nervous as he stood on the sidewalk and peered into JoJo's to see if Tristan was there already. And he was, sitting at the same booth they always tried to get, and when he saw Micah he stood up and smiled at him.

"What happened to your face?" he asked as Micah got closer.

"Kind of a long story. Short version, though? I had a test— and I passed."

Tristan nodded slowly. "Okay. Good. Congratulations. You're going to give me some more details though, right? I mean—you look really good, man, aside from the stubble and bruises. I want to hear about it."

Of course he did, because he was Tristan. Generous, forgiving Tristan, who was strong enough to let himself be hurt.

"Okay. Let me get some coffee. It's really fucking early, you know."

~*~*~*~

JAKE MADE LISTS. WHEN THE WORLD seemed to be getting out of control, he sat down with a pen and paper and started writing. Things he could control, things he couldn't. Things he needed to do, things he needed to not do. Things he should pick up at the grocery store, if it came to that. It wasn't the content so much as the ritual.

By the time Austin finally staggered out of his bedroom just before noon, Jake had the coffee table covered with his attempts to restore sanity.

Austin looked at them. "Are those for me?"

"Some of them."

"Let me piss first."

Jake busied himself pouring two cups of coffee and adding the insane amount of sugar Austin liked in his, then sat back down on the couch. Austin came, found his mug, took a sip, and said, "I think I want to go to rehab. An intense one, like Micah did. It worked for him, right? But he'd tried a couple times before, the four-week kind and they didn't do it, just like they didn't do it for me. But three months? And me really working it? Like, really doing the therapy, not just fucking around like I have before. I think it could work."

"I—" Jake looked down at his lists. "I was going to say you needed to change your phone number. You're obviously thinking a bit bigger than I am."

"Rehab's expensive," Austin said. "I know that. I don't know if I could get a loan from somebody—I kind of doubt it. But do you think you could? Like, co-sign or whatever? You could totally control the money—don't let me touch a cent of it. This isn't a scam, I promise. I really think it's time for a change. I think I can do it. But I need help."

It sounded so good, but it had sounded good before. Austin was a man of excellent intentions, but he didn't always do so well on the follow through. "You need to really think about it, really be absolutely sure you mean it. I expect I can get the money together, but just once. Like, if I pay for it this time and it doesn't work, and then six months from now you're ready to try again? I won't have the money. It'll be gone. So you need to be sure you're absolutely, completely committed to making it work *this time*. You know?"

"I do," Austin said. "I'm—I'm so fucking sorry about last night. And Micah—is he okay?"

"He's a bit beat up," Jake said. "And Moby slipped a baggie into his pocket and he was shook up when he found it. But he didn't use, so—he wins, right?"

"You and him are getting pretty tight, huh?"

"Me and him are none of your business." Jake looked at his lists. "Okay, I'm going to add 'research rehab facilities' to one of my lists. But you still need to do yours. Change your phone number—and leave the phone with me until you do. And all the freedom and trust you'd been earning? It's gone. We're back to the tightest rules. You don't go anywhere alone. You hit a meeting every damn day—you can either go with Micah, and I mean *go with* him, not arrange to meet him there and then not show up—or I'll drop you off and pick you up. Every fucking day, Austin. I don't care if they're boring and I don't care if they're bullshit. You do them until you come up with something better."

"Yeah, okay," Austin agreed. He was always so tractable right after a fuck-up. It was such a cycle, such a pointless, frustrating, soul-killing cycle. He'd be apologetic until they had a

113

plan, then gleeful and relaxed and optimistic right up until the plan kept him from doing something he wanted to do. Then he'd be a petulant, sulky pain-in-the-ass for at least a couple days before he levelled off to his usual slacking.

But he'd never been the one to suggest rehab before, and he'd never been to one of the ninety-day versions. Maybe—maybe. Jake sighed and looked down at his list. He wished, surprisingly, that Micah was there. Not to help with Austin, really, just—to be there. To be something positive in Jake's life, something to be excited about, someone to lean into to feel some warmth.

But Micah had his own shit going on and didn't need to get weighed down with any extra, so Jake was on his own. He sighed and looked down at the lists. "Get comfortable," he said. "There's more."

"Okay," Austin agreed, and sank into the armchair.

Jake rubbed a hand roughly over his face, trying to wake up. This was his life. He needed to suck it up and get on with it.

Chapter Ten

MICAH WASN'T SURE THE GOOD mood would last—well, of course it wouldn't, not forever. But at least temporarily, he felt as if anything was possible. He'd thrown drugs away the night before, Tristan had forgiven him, the rest of the old gang was apparently ready to welcome him back, and Jake. That was all, just—Jake. He existed, and that was enough.

Well, not quite enough, Micah thought as he stood outside the apartment building, phone to his ear. Jake answered and Micah said, "I'm downstairs. Can I come up?" and the door buzzed open.

Two flights of stairs and then Jake was waiting in the doorway, wary but welcoming.

"I'm a good person," Micah told him. Tristan had said so, and Tristan didn't lie to his friends. "I fuck up, but I keep trying. I'm redeemable; I'm forgivable. I'm not worthless. I deserve to have good things in my life."

"Yeah," Jake agreed, still cautious. "That sounds right...."

Micah stepped closer. He wanted to do this before he lost his nerve. "You're a good thing, Jake. I mean, a good person. Not a thing, of course. But in the context of my previous statement—do you get what I'm saying?" Shit, this wasn't going well. "Or, alternatively, were you completely grossed out by what I told you, about me and Moby? I mean, I understand if you are. I'd be disappointed and everything, but—"

"Micah." Jake was starting to look a little more relaxed. "Are you—is this your version of coming on to me? Is that what's happening?"

"Not if you don't want it to be. I can just—we can just talk, if you want. Things went well with Tristan. Obviously. So I was feeling all optimistic and stupid, I guess."

"And what if I *do* want it to be?" Jake reached out just as he had the night before, his hand finding the exact same perfect spot on Micah's neck just where it turned into his shoulder, the spot he wanted to be kissed and bitten and fucking devoured. He tugged gently and Micah let himself lean forward. "It's probably not smart," Jake warned him. "We both have a lot of other stuff going on."

Micah nodded, and their faces were so close their noses brushed as Micah moved. "I'm being smart about everything else," he said. He was pretty sure he meant it. He was doing well. "I think I can afford one little bit of not smart."

Jake kissed him then, just a gloss of contact before pulling half-a-breath away. "I can't make promises," he whispered. "I'm kind of worn out—I don't have that much more left to give anybody."

"So maybe it's time for you to do a little taking," Micah said, and he stretched his hands out to the sides, making an offering. "See anything you like?"

The heat in Jake's gaze seemed obvious, but for some reason the guy turned away, leaning back into the apartment. Then he yelled, "Austin? Turn the TV up and avert your eyes!"

Jake found Micah's hand and pulled him through the door into the apartment, pinned him against the wall of the short hallway, and growled, "I see a lot that I like. And I want it all."

Fuck, yeah. Micah let his body sag against the wall, threw his head back to expose his throat to Jake's lips, his teeth. Jake's leg slid between his and they pressed together, hardening cocks against strong thighs.

"Bedroom," Jake gasped. "Ignore Austin."

Easier said than done, with Austin lying on the couch grinning at them as they stumbled past, kicking his feet in glee and shouting, "I fucking *knew it*!"

"Volume *up*, you fucking pervert," Jake ordered. "I want it so loud the neighbors complain."

"Planning on makin' some noise," Austin said with obvious satisfaction. "Oooh, yeah." But at least he reached for the remote control and turned up the volume.

"I am so sorry," Jake said as soon as the bedroom door was closed. "This is not the most romantic situation."

Micah was trying to think of something reassuring to say when the noise from the next room changed from generic TV dialogue to an over-loud version of Marvin Gaye singing "Let's Get It On".

"Oh my god," Jake started, and turned toward the door.

Micah caught his hand and turned him around, laughing. "Ignore him," he suggested. "At least he's in a good mood."

"Got another couple hours of that before the self-pity starts." Jake sighed, still half-turned toward the door.

Micah let go of his hand. "Yeah," he said. "Okay. Yeah. You've got shit to do today, right? Things to take care of. This isn't a good time."

Jake frowned at him. "It's not a good time," he agreed, and looked back toward the door. "I've got shit to do and things to take care of." Then he turned to face Micah. "But I've always got shit to do. And I can't—I can't put my life on hold *forever*, waiting for a good time that might never come." He stepped closer. "I like you, Micah. I want you. I'm sorry this is such a fucked up—" He stopped, waved his hand around the room, then lifted his whole arm to indicate something much larger. "Such a fucked up life. But it's the one I've got. And I'd like you in it." He paused, then added, "Naked. I want you in my life, naked."

Well, finally something was simple. Micah pulled his shirt up over his head in one easy move, dropped it on the floor, and started on his fly. Jake caught his hands, slowing him down, distracting him with a kiss. One of Jake's hands slid up to explore Micah's chest while the other eased its way past his half-open fly, under the waist band of his underwear, and wrapped around his cock. Micah gasped in appreciation. It had been a long time since anyone but himself had paid any attention to that part of his body, and he'd almost forgotten how good it felt.

They both had their shirts off by the time "Pony" started blasting through the walls. "He's such a little fucker," Jake growled, but Micah grabbed his ass and pulled him closer and there were no more complaints.

They were horizontal on the bed, jeans undone but not yet off when "Sexual Healing" started. It seemed strangely appropriate. All the therapy in the world, all the rehab and 12-steps and all the goddamn effort to make himself okay without drugs, when what he'd really needed was just this. A warm mouth kissing his, strong hands exploring his body, and the solid weight of a partner who wanted to make him feel good. He arched up, moved his body with the song, felt the rumble of laughter in Jake's chest, and laughed a little himself, but didn't lose the rhythm.

They lost their jeans and underwear to "Sexy Thing", and Micah felt like he'd won something when Jake sang a few key lines to him. Won not for himself, but for Jake. Micah was no angel and he was a long way from a miracle, but he was making Jake laugh, making Jake hard, and those were both things to be proud of.

Micah found himself obsessing about Jake's shoulders, his chest. So wide, so strong, so solid. This was the body of a man who worked hard, and the angles of the bones, the curves of the muscles, the textures of the skin were all perfect. Jake hissed when

Micah dragged his fingernails across the hair on his chest, groaned as he shifted lower, bringing his mouth in line with Jake's cock, as thick and strong as the rest of him.

"You're going to fuck me, right?" Micah asked.

Jake nodded without sitting up. "If you want, yeah. I mean—I want to, but I don't have to."

"I want you to." Micah wanted a lot of things, really, but being fucked was definitely one of them. He made his tongue flat and wide and ran it from Jake's balls to the tip of his cock. "Just a taste, then," he decided, and engulfed as much of the feast before him as he was able to.

Jake threw his head back into the mattress with a muffled shout. "Jesus, Micah, that's so good. It's perfect."

And for at least that moment, Micah could believe it was true.

Even the drag of fingers through his hair, the gentle tug that got a lot sharper when Micah ignored it, was part of the perfection. He was driving Jake crazy, and as much as he wanted to get fucked, as much as he wanted the stretch and the fullness and the satisfaction, maybe this was even better. This was pure giving, and Jake seemed like he needed a little of that.

But then the tug on his hair became impossible to ignore and Micah let himself be dragged up Jake's body until their mouths met. "I don't want to come yet," Jake whispered, and that was fairly hard to argue with.

A new song started blaring and they frowned at each other, trying to figure it out. Then Jake snorted and said, "The little bastard better not think he's giving me tips."

Micah grinned at him. "Have you got a 'Slow Hand'?"

"The neighbors *are* going to kill us," Jake said, but he really didn't seem too upset, and Saturday mid-day wasn't a terrible time for loud music. Micah was worried for a second when Jake shifted to the side of the bed, but he just reached for the drawer of his nightstand and Micah relaxed.

"I got tested at rehab," he said. "I mean, we should still be careful and everything, but—I should be good. They tested me at the start and the end, so that's a good incubation period. We're pretty safe."

Jake nodded. "You're not the only one here, though." He caught Micah's look. "No, I don't mean anything specific, and I'm always careful. Just—who knows, right?" His smile was a little rueful as he added, "Besides, less sensation might not be a bad thing if I want to last much longer."

Good, back to the relaxed, playful mood. "Think the next song is going to be 'Mama Told me not to Come'?"

"It had damn well better not be," Jake said, shifting around and handing the condom and lube to Micah. "Besides, that's not what that song's about. But if he plays 'Relax' I'm going to go out there and kick his ass."

"After," Micah said, and savored Jake's quick inhalation as Micah added an extra squeeze to the condom-application process. "Kick his ass *after*."

The Pointer Sisters faded out and both Jake and Micah stilled, waiting for the next contribution from the living room. The first notes were confusing, kind of muddled, sounding digitized even through the wall, and was that—was it a laughing baby?

Jake's face contorted into a strange mix of amusement and frustrated anger as he recognized the tune. "There's something seriously wrong with that boy's brain."

A voice-over started, and Micah jerked his hand away from Jake as if he'd been burned. "Oh my god, it's the Teletubbies! We can't—I mean, to the Teletubbies? With the image of that fucking creepy baby watching us?"

"I know," Jake groaned.

"Jesus Christ. Can we wait it out, or is he going to come up with something even more twisted once this is done?"

"What could be worse than this?"

"I'm afraid to find out." But there was a sort of macabre fascination to the idea. "Hymns? Death metal?"

"Or something really new-age mystic-y," Jake speculated. He was lying on his back, looking up at the ceiling; his body was still obviously ready for action, but it seemed like his mind was disengaging.

"I wouldn't trust it if it were perfect," Micah said. The idea had just come to him, but it felt true as he spoke it. "If nothing was getting in the way? If it was all rose petals and candlelight? It wouldn't feel real."

"Oh, this is real all right," Jake said ruefully.

"Yeah." Micah tried to ignore the sounds from the other room—the Teletubbies seemed to have reached the introductions stage—and focus on the man in front of him. "And real is what I want. I spent too long running away from reality."

"Even if reality is an idiot brother blasting the fucking Teletubbies from the next room when you're trying to get it on?"

Micah thought about it for only a moment before nodding. "Yeah. Even if." He shifted over so he was straddling Jake's legs, their cocks lined up together. He looked down at the beautiful sight. Yeah, this was fine. This was good. He reached for the condom and savored the way Jake's eyes widened in anticipation.

"Even with the creepy baby watching?" Jake whispered.

"We're going to blow his creepy little mind."

There weren't many words after that. A few obscenities when the song after the Teletubbies was "YMCA" and they both found themselves unwillingly lifting their arms into the letter shapes. But then Micah let himself slide down and engulf Jake's cock and the swearing phased into something more appreciative.

Words were pretty much out of the question by the time "I Want Your Sex" came on. There was only warmth and pressure and friction and Jake's wide green eyes staring up at Micah as they moved in perfect rhythm with each other. And, yes, damn it, perfect rhythm with the song as well.

They came together, Micah gasping and Jake moaning and both sounds lost in the music. Micah managed to flop off to the side before he collapsed, and Jake fumbled around a little before stretching out alongside him. Their kiss was slow and easy and only heated up a little when Adam Lambert's "Fever" started blasting through the walls.

"The songs got gayer," Micah reflected when he mouth was temporarily free. "They started off as just regular sexy, then got weird, then gayer toward the end."

"He had time to think about it." Jake kissed Micah's cheekbone, then his temple. "Never a good thing when Austin has time to think."

"At least we didn't have to worry about where he was or what he was doing."

"No," Jake said, and he sighed, rolling over onto his back. "That stage'll come next."

"And how long will the good mood last?"

Jake looked over at the clock on the bedside table. "I'm surprised we've made it this long, to be honest."

"Okay," Micah said. There were still things to worry about, god knew, but his endorphins were high enough to let him relax, at least for the moment. He rolled a bit, edge up against Jake and said, "We're gonna snuggle for a bit. Maybe snooze. Then we'll get up and deal with it all. Okay?"

"Yeah." Jake's arm wrapped around Micah and pulled him in a little tighter. "More than okay."

It was all Micah could have asked for, and a hell of a lot more than he'd had any reason to expect.

Chapter Eleven

JAKE MANAGE TO ENJOY THE peace for quite a while. Longer than he'd have thought possible, really. But at some point he realized that the songs blasting through the wall weren't sexy anymore. They seemed to be old school ska, mostly, and if Austin thought "Mirror in the Bathroom" was sexy there was even more wrong with his brain than previously suspected. Or it could have been a random track off a playlist. Which meant there was no more proof Austin was out there. Was okay.

Jake stayed quiet for another moment, then said, "Fuck." He gently disengaged himself from Micah, who gazed up at him with resignation. "Austin. I need to check on him. I don't want to—I want to stay with you, absolutely. But I can't. I'm sorry."

"I don't mind. I understand."

"You *should* mind, though. Do you think this is all you deserve? Are you doing penance or something? You fucked up in the past, so now you have to put up with someone else's fucked up present?"

"No," Micah said. He sat up and caught Jake's face between both of his hands. "No. I'm not doing penance. I'm not settling for less than I deserve. I *like you*, Jake. A lot. You're hot, and funny, and the sex was good with the potential to be fucking great if we ever have a few less distractions. Things don't have to be perfect—I'm not a princess or something. I'm fine."

"I want more for you."

"Or you want more for yourself," Micah suggested. "And it's totally understandable if you do. I mean, *you* haven't fucked up at all, right? But you're still putting up with all this crap. Stop worrying about whether this is fair for me, and start wondering if it's fair for *you*."

Jake pulled away. The guilt was instinctive, but unwelcome. "What are you suggesting?" he asked. He kept his voice level, but he didn't think Micah could miss the tension that was suddenly in his body. "You think I should walk away from him? Stop worrying about him?"

"No!" Micah straightened. "I just meant—isn't it okay to at least admit that this isn't fair? I'm not saying you should change it. But you're going way above and beyond the call of brotherly duty. I think it's *great* that you're doing it—I mean that. But it's not fair that you have to. That's all."

Jake shrugged. He wanted to accept the words, but...

Micah's face changed. Relaxed, comfortable Micah faded away, replaced with something much more guarded. "Shit," he said. "I invite myself over, throw myself at your dick, and now I'm trying to tell you how to handle your brother? What am I thinking?"

Micah slid over to the side of the bed and started poking through the clothing strewn on the floor.

"No, you don't have to go," Jake said. God, he didn't want Micah to go. Not like this. Not at all. Probably ever. But what was he going to do, chain Micah to the damn bed while Jake when off to deal with Austin?

"I have to go face the music at the half-way house," Micah said. "I blew through curfew last night—I've texted them a couple times to say I was okay, but they're still going to be pissed. The longer I stay away, the pissed-er they're going to be."

"You want me to—I don't know…."

"Write me a note? *Dear Counselors—Micah was late because he was getting fucked.*" He slid into his underwear and grabbed his T-shirt. "I don't think that would be too useful."

"I was thinking more about last night—that's what you're going to be in trouble for, right? Not for being out in the middle of the day."

"It'll be a cumulative thing, I expect."

"So now you're going to be in trouble because of me."

"Nope." Jeans on, looking for socks. "No trouble I can't handle, and because of decisions I made. No guilt needed."

Easy for him to say, harder for Jake to believe.

"Everything's good," Micah said. A lie, but such an obvious one that it didn't feel like an attempt to deceive, just to reassure. "Thanks for this, and for last night—for looking out for me. You had other stuff to worry about, but you still thought about me. That was—great. Thanks."

Micah took a deep breath as if to brace himself for the living room gauntlet, then started for the bedroom door.

"Micah," Jake started, but when Micah turned back to him, Jake couldn't think of what exactly he wanted to say.

"It's cool," Micah said. "I'll see you Monday?"

Jake frowned. Monday. That was it? They'd shared this together, and then, just—Monday? He wanted more than that—so much more. But what could he offer in return? He finally nodded. "Yeah. Monday. Okay."

And that was that. Micah smiled, nodded, and headed out the door. The moment was over.

Jake felt like the world had tilted on its axis far too many times in the last—god, the last eighteen hours? Was that all it had been? Everything with Austin *and* with Micah, and all of it happening way too fast. He needed to regroup, probably. Maybe he should learn to meditate or something.

He pulled his jeans on as he heard the music stop in the living room. Austin talking to Micah. God, please let Austin behave himself at least somewhat. Micah didn't need to be subjected to Austin's completely inappropriate humor, not now, not ever.

But that was stupid. Austin and Micah were friends; Austin probably knew Micah better than Jake did, and would be completely able to judge how far teasing could go.

Jake felt as if he didn't know Micah at all. He'd thought they'd been on the same track, but then Micah had gotten sort of cold before he'd left, sort of—well, Jake wasn't really sure what Micah had gotten. But the relaxed, casual affection he'd shown while they were in bed together had definitely disappeared.

"Hey," Austin's voice said from the other side of the half-closed bedroom door. "You decent? If I open the door am I going to see anything that will scar me for life?"

Jake took the two steps to the door and pulled it open. "What do you want, Austin?"

Austin gave Jake an appraising look. "Micah just left and he seemed kinda down. You're still here and you seem kinda grumpy. I'm just wondering if there's something I should be doing about either situation."

"You could go back in time and *not* play fucking stupid music at full volume for the last forty-five minutes—how's that sound?"

"This is about the music?" Austin didn't look convinced. "If it is—the full volume was your idea, and Barry White isn't fucking stupid. He's a national treasure."

"And the Teletubbies?"

"Also national treasures. Although possibly not our nation."

Jake didn't have the energy for this. "No," he said. "There's nothing you should be doing."

But Austin didn't leave.

Jake sighed and surrendered. "Micah had to go deal with shit at the half-way house. Crap he wouldn't have had to deal with if I hadn't called him last night."

"And you wouldn't have had to call him if it weren't for me," Austin said.

"And if that Moby asshole hadn't called *you,* none of this would have happened."

"If I hadn't already spent a lot of money with Moby, he wouldn't have bothered calling me," Austin said. "One way or another, this all comes back to me. Sorry if that sounds self-centered, but tell me it's not true."

Yeah, this was the self-pity stage of Austin's post-binge routine, coming in just as expected. Jake shoved his brother back a step, making enough space so he could get by and head for the kitchen. "I wouldn't have met Micah anyway if it wasn't for you, so—whatever. It all balances out, right?" He found a clean mug and poured himself a cup of coffee, then turned to see Austin staring at him.

"It all balances out?" Austin sputtered. "Are you fucking serious? I mean—okay, unless that forty-five minutes with Micah was the best, most insanely earth-shattering sex that anybody has ever had since the beginning of fucking time, then, *no*, it doesn't balance out! Hell, even if it was that kind of super-sex, it still wouldn't balance out. I've been making you miserable for years, fucking up over and over and over again, and you think it balances out because I accidentally introduced you to a guy with nice eyes?"

"Now you sound like Micah."

"What? How? Was he—" Austin looked suddenly paranoid. Yup, paranoia was a fun part of the routine as well. Of course, in this case it was somewhat justified. "Was Micah saying we're unbalanced? Like—what was he getting at? Because you've known the guy for two weeks, Jake! He doesn't know shit about you, or about you and me!"

"He wasn't saying that," Jake replied. He suddenly felt every minute of sleep he'd missed the night before, weighing down on him like a heavy blanket. "I think he was just—acknowledging it." And there it was, so simple. "He was just *seeing* it, you know? He wasn't saying anything should change, he was just letting me know he sees that it's hard for me." And was there really anything else Jake could ask for? Just that simple bit of understanding was all he really needed, and when Micah had offered it, Jake had gotten defensive and jumped all over him. Shit. Micah'd had the nerve to speak the truth, and Jake hadn't wanted to hear it because once he did it would be too damn hard to go on living the way he did.

"You picked out a meeting for today, yet?" he asked Austin. "You let me know when and where, and I'll drop you off, pick you up again after." There, that was his duty done. "The rest of the time, though? I'm—I'm fucking pissed at you, man. Not for the music. Just for—yeah, for fucking up, again. For dragging me—for dragging *us*—back into this shit. You're my brother, and I'll stand by you, wherever you are. But goddamn it, Austin, you're going to the same awful places, again and again, and I'm tired of it. It's not—it's not fair. You know? So tell me about the meeting. But the rest of the day? Stay in the apartment, but stay out of my way. Give me some time to be get less pissed off."

Austin looked genuinely startled, and that probably wasn't good. Had Jake never called him on his shit before? Sure, he had. Had he said something different this time? Maybe just the part about himself. Instead of focusing on Austin, he'd focused on himself. Maybe he should have done that a long time ago.

He took his coffee back to his bedroom and shut the door, then found his phone. Micah answered on the second ring. "Hey," Jake said. He felt foolish, but made himself continue. "I bet you haven't even made it to the station yet, huh?"

"Uh, no," Micah agreed. "Still walking."

"Yeah, okay. I just wanted to say—I don't know, I wasn't sure we were okay. Like, when you left—" Jesus, what was he, a man or a child? "Whatever we're doing, I'm glad we're doing it. I don't want to put pressure on you to give more than you can, or more than you want to, and I know you know there's things I can't give you. I can't even drive you home, not when I'm babysitting Austin, not unless we had him in the back seat for the whole damn drive. But I guess I wanted you to know that I *want* to do all that stuff. In a different world? I'd be giving you the full court press, you know? I don't even know what's romantic anymore, but whatever it is, I'd want to be doing it. Taking you out to dinner or cooking for you or buying you gifts or—I don't know. I'm kind of at a loss, I admit. But it's not because I don't think you're worth it. It's not because I wouldn't *want* to treat you right, if I could."

Micah didn't answer, keeping Jake waiting for so long he was about to pull the phone away from his ear to see if the call had been disconnected. But finally he said, "Yeah, okay. I—me too. I've never really done this. What I think we're doing. Like, I've hooked up with people, but never—we're talking about more than a hook-up, right? We're talking about—"

"Jesus, we are a sorry pair. We don't even know the *words* for what we want." Jake sank down on his bed, and despite his words, he wasn't feeling too damn sorry. "More than a hook-up," he agreed. "I don't know, are people still—do they 'date', or is that just in high school? Can we be, like, boyfriends? Is that a thing?"

"I think it's a thing," Micah said. He sounded better. More relaxed than he'd been when he left the apartment. "We can make it a thing."

"Okay. Cool, then. I'm in."

"Okay. So—what does it mean?"

"I'm gonna buy you a present," Jake said. "Not a fancy present. Not expensive. Not something you need to reciprocate at all. But I saw something you need, and I was going to buy it for you and then I didn't because I thought it would be weird, but now I'm gonna do it and it won't be weird at all. It'll be fucking sweet."

"Yeah? A present? When do I get it?"

And there was the complication of Jake's life. "No idea. Monday, if I don't see you before then. But it'd be great to see you before then." They could go away for the rest of the weekend, rent a cabin in the mountains or something, stay in bed all day except for brief trips to the kitchen and out to the porch to look at the forest. Sure, there was nothing getting in the way of that.

"I'm not sure how much shit I'm going to be in at the half-way house," Micah said, and it was a good reminder that it wasn't just Jake operating under limitations. "It sounds stupid, but it's possible I might be grounded."

"Grounded?"

"I think they call it something else. 'Restricted privileges' or something. But—yeah. It's kind of a weird setup."

"But you think it's important to your recovery so you're going to go along with it."

"I don't want to get cocky. I mean, last night was—it was close. And you were there, and that worked out fine—they're for sure going to drug test me, and it's nice to know I'll be clean—but I can't rely on you for that, you know? You've got enough on your plate, and if we're going to be—boyfriends?—then I don't really want it set up so you have to babysit me when I'm feeling weak, you know? That's not what I want from you. So, yeah. I think the half-way house is important to my recovery, so I'm going to go along with their stupid punishments."

"Do restricted privileges include phone calls?"

"They can have my phone when they pry it from my cold, dead hands."

"So you can call me when you know what's what. If you're allowed out, we can try to set something up. Probably here, or somewhere we can take Austin. Sorry."

"It's fine. I get it." Micah sounded like he really did get it. "We'll figure something out."

"Yeah?"

"Yeah. I'm glad you called."

"I'm glad I called, too."

And he was. After they hung up, he flopped back on his bed and let his mind wander. Back over the last couple weeks since he'd met Micah, and then forward. Forward to—he wasn't sure what. But something good, or at least potentially good. Something hopeful. It had been a long time since he'd felt that way, and he knew exactly who to give credit for the change.

~*~*~*~

"PRUNERS?" MICAH LOOKED DOWN AT THE box in his hand, then back up at Jake's expression. They were in the pickup on Monday morning, Austin staring moodily out the window in the back seat.

"Secateurs," Jake said. "They're—well, yeah, they're pruners, but they have a French name, so—classy! And these are really good ones. They're the same kind I have, and see the little holster? It's so you can always have them handy, and then as you're working if you see something that needs to be pruned, you're all set."

"Wow." Micah hadn't really known what to expect from Jake's promised gift, but this certainly hadn't been on the list of possibilities. "And am I actually allowed to use them? I'm getting promoted off grass duty?"

"You can't go crazy. But if you see something that's clearly broken and needs a trim? You can do it."

And that little vote of confidence actually meant at least as much to Micah as the gift itself. "Thanks," he said. He wanted to say more, to *do* more—there had been an awkward moment when he'd first climbed into the truck when it had really seemed like he and Jake were going to *shake hands* in greeting—but Austin's glaring presence was a bit of a downer. So he just pulled the pruners out of their packaging and played with them a little, admiring the smooth mechanism. Then he turned around and told Austin, "I talked to that woman, like I said I would. The social worker? She's the one who pulled strings to get me into the rehab place fast, and she said she can meet with you, if you want, and maybe do the same for you. Maybe."

"Maybe," Austin echoed. "Like I have to fucking *audition* for it? I have to convince them I deserve the privilege of going to their expensive jail?"

"I think to see if you have an attitude that's going to make it worth her while to go out on a limb for you," Micah replied. "So

I'm guessing there's not going to be much point wasting her time, based on that."

"You're going to lecture me on my attitude? Seriously?"

"No." Micah turned around and looked down at the pruners in his hand. A gift. A vote of confidence. Focus on the positive. "I'm not going to lecture you."

"Neither am I," Jake said from the driver's seat, the frustration clear in his voice. "But I'm not going to put up with your crap, either. If you've changed your mind about wanting to go to rehab, you need to come up with another damn plan."

"I can just keep doing what I was doing before," Austin said. "I changed my phone number, so Moby can't call me anymore. That's the only thing that went wrong with the plan last time."

"What if he tracks you down in person?" Micah asked. He had no idea how likely it was that Moby would be that persistent, but it was certainly possible. "Or gets your number from someone else?"

"This really isn't any of your business, man. Fucking my brother doesn't mean you're family, you know."

"Don't be a shithead, Austin," Jake growled. "You don't want to hear the questions from him? You can hear them from me. What happens if Moby tracks you down in person or gets your number from someone else?"

"You know, as a little addition to telling Micah to mind his own business, how about I tell *you* to mind your own business, too? You're my brother, not my jailer. You know you don't have any *actual* authority over me, right? I go along with your rules because *I* decide to, not because you decide."

It was no way to start a Monday morning. Micah *had* been grounded over the weekend but he and Jake had talked on the phone enough for Micah to have warning that Austin was being an asshole, so it wasn't a total surprise. And Jake had seemed reasonably philosophical about it all, with lots of talk about brain chemistry and pleasure centers and all the rest of the terminology. And of course Micah had firsthand experience. Coming back to reality after taking a vacation in the clouds was hell, and being polite and cheerful when you were using every drop of your willpower just to keep yourself from sprinting out the door and straight to the closest supplier? Practically impossible.

But knowing that in theory was a hell of a lot different than tolerating it in person, and Jake was pretty clearly on his last nerve. "You want to go see a movie or something, tonight?" Micah asked, swivelling around to look at Austin. "After we go to a meeting?"

Austin turned slowly away from the window to look at Micah. "Are you asking *me*? Did you get a bit confused there, stud?"

"Slow down—we're not going to sit in the back row and make out, no matter how hard you beg me. I just thought you could use the distraction. Might be good to get out of the apartment?" And Jake could probably use some time to himself, but Micah didn't need to mention that right then. "I've got to be home by nine, but if we hit an early show I could make it."

"Is this going to turn into me going to the movies by myself so you and Jake can have the place to yourselves?" Austin's voice was a pathetic mix of suspicion and self-pity, and the recognition made Micah's skin crawl. He'd been that needy, too. And he couldn't forget that he might be that bad again; just because things were going well for him right then didn't mean they'd stay that way.

So he tried to sound patient. "No. There's no trick, man. It's not like going to a movie with me is some big treat, is it? I mean, I'm flattered, but—"

"Maybe," Austin interrupted. "I'll see what I feel like after work."

It was a stupid situation. Micah felt like he was begging for the honor of hanging out with a sulky brat when really he would much, much rather be spending his free time with the brat's brother. But then Jake reached across the gap between their seats and found Micah's hand for a quick squeeze, and Micah looked at him and saw the appreciation on his face, and it was all worthwhile. Helping Austin meant helping Jake.

So Micah and Austin went to a meeting that afternoon and then ate popcorn and hotdogs at an action movie with lots of explosions, and Jake picked them up afterward and drove Micah home, Austin returning to his brooding in the back seat.

When they pulled up just down the street from the half-way house, Jake turned the engine off and pulled the keys out of the ignition. "I'll be back in a minute," he told his brother. He met Micah half way around the hood of the truck and found his hand, fingers entwining in a way that felt completely new and completely natural all at the same time. "Thank you," he said quietly, and they turned and walked to the sidewalk together.

It should have been scary. Micah shouldn't have been ready for this, whatever *this* was. The plan had been a quick fuck, hadn't it? The idea was to look after himself, focus all his energy on his own recovery, live day-by-day, work the steps—all that good stuff. Getting involved with Jake? It was still a terrible idea, wasn't it?

But the warmth and strength of Jake's hand felt absolutely life-giving. The secateurs in their tiny holster, jammed into Micah's pocket so he wouldn't look armed, felt like a sword he could use to defend himself from any and all danger. And when they stopped walking at the foot of the walkway leading to the house, when they leaned together and their lips met? Surely there was no need for chemical assistance when a simple touch could make Micah feel as if he was floating.

"What did you do tonight?" Micah asked when they drew a tiny bit away from each other.

"Laundry," Jake said. "Not too glamorous, I know. I should have gone sky-diving or something. But just having a tiny bit of time to myself was all I needed. Thank you."

"The movie wasn't bad," Micah said. "Maybe next time me and Austin can do the laundry and you can go out and do something fun."

The light shining down from the porch of the halfway house showed Jake's sly expression as he said, "Maybe we could stay *in* and do something fun."

Impossible not to kiss him, impossible to think there was anything wrong or unwise or anything not perfect and beautiful about the moment. But then Micah's phone sounded its pre-curfew alarm, programmed in the night before at the insistence of the halfway house counsellors, and they made themselves pull apart.

"We're working south tomorrow," Jake murmured, making the prosaic words sound like the sweetest seduction. "We'll pick you up here. Seven-thirty?"

"Wow. I can sleep in."

"I wish I could wake up next to you."

"Not here, you don't. Single bed. You wouldn't have a very restful night."

"It wouldn't be the size of the bed keeping me awake if I was with you."

Micah laughed and gently pushed Jake away. "Someday," he promised. "Soon. But not tonight. And never here."

"Yeah," Jake agreed, and stepped back reluctantly. "Okay. I'll see you tomorrow."

He turned and walked back to the truck, and Micah watched him as he went. The curfew could wait a minute or two, and Micah wanted as much of Jake as he could get, even at a distance.

When Jake reached the truck, he turned around and didn't seem too surprised to see Micah still standing there. He raised a hand to wave, then glanced toward the truck and froze. After a moment he started moving again, fast and jerky. He yanked the driver's side door open, stuck his head inside, and Micah's stomach churned as he realized what had happened. He watched in a sick daze as Jake pulled himself back outside, looked around wildly, and then bellowed, "Austin!"

Five minutes? Had it even been that long? No, less than that.

Micah jogged out into the street and looked both directions, but saw nobody. "Austin!" he yelled, as if his own voice would make a difference.

But there was no answer.

Jake jogged back toward him, his face already drawn and tense. He was holding his phone, staring down at it as if willing Austin to pick up his call, but clearly Austin wasn't cooperating. "He's gone."

"The Link station," Micah suggested, wildly hoping the idea made sense. "You drive, I'll walk. You can beat him there if he just left, and if he's being slow I'll run into him."

"What if he's going somewhere else?" Jake asked, but it was clear he already knew the answer to the question. If Austin was going somewhere else, Austin was gone, and wouldn't be back until he decided to be. "Shit." Jake looked toward the halfway house, then back to Micah. "You should go in, do your curfew thing. I mean—" He scrubbed at his face as if he was trying to wake up. "I can't chain him down. If we find him, what do we do with him? If he wants to go shoot poison into his fucking veins, maybe I just have to let that happen."

"But if he's just being a self-pitying asshole, looking for attention or something, we could get him back." Micah stepped forward. "I'll jog. It'll be good exercise. So I'll hardly be late for curfew at all. You drive, I'll run, and if we don't see him on the way you'll drive me back here and I'll deal with the counsellors."

"I shouldn't be making this your problem," Jake said, but he was moving toward the truck, so Micah didn't think they needed to keep arguing.

He took off at a slow jog, scanning the sidewalks and the driveways and alleys as he went. It wasn't a bad neighborhood, but it wasn't great, either. And anyone who'd been using for any period of time generally developed a sixth sense about finding junk—not quite a smell, but a sort of instinctive pull toward a likely source. On this street, Micah's instinct drew him straight ahead, toward the Link station.

Jake's truck was parked in front of the station, caution lights flashing, when Micah arrived. But it was only Jake standing there, looking miserable. No sign of Austin. "He's not inside?" Micah asked.

Jake shook his head. "There was a train pulling out just when I got here. He might have been on it. I thought about chasing after it and trying to catch him at the next stop, but what's the point? I can't—"

He broke off, but Micah could still hear the words he might have said. *I can't make him do anything, I can't stop him from being a junkie, I can't stand this anymore.* "I know," Micah said. "I'm sorry."

Jake looked at him quickly. "Just sorry like being sympathetic, right? You're not actually blaming yourself for anything? Because you've been great with him. Great *for* him." He took a deep breath as if trying to release some adrenaline from his system, then shook his head. "I didn't want to admit it and he's been better about keeping it on the DL, but I'm pretty sure he's been using, off and on, for quite a while. Looking back, putting little details together... there were times when I'd pick him up after his meeting and it would seem like the other people leaving the meetings didn't know him at all. And you know Austin—it's pretty impossible for him to be in a room with a bunch of people for more than five minutes and not make friends with one of them. I think maybe he was sneaking out and scoring. Then he'd come back and shoot up in his room, in my goddamn apartment. With me sleeping in the room next door like a fucking chump, thinking he was trying."

"Have you mentioned that to him?" Micah asked.

"Not yet. It just sort of crystalized when I went back to the truck tonight. You know? I looked into the back seat and it was like part of me was surprised, but another part? That part totally expected it. With you going to meetings with him he couldn't sneak off from them anymore. So he took off now."

"But there's nothing sneaky about this. He has to know you know, now."

Jake looked about ten years older than he had just a few minutes earlier. "Yeah. No more games." He looked down at his phone, poked angrily at the screen, then looked over at Micah. "You try. Maybe he'll pick up for you."

"I wouldn't count on it," Micah said, but he tried anyway. What else could he do? "There's no point in me calling Moby again. He won't tell me shit, I don't expect, and it might make things worse. If Austin hasn't already connected with him, Moby would know to be on the lookout. I can try a few other people. Make some calls. If Austin's heading back to the old neighborhood, maybe they'll see him."

"You can do all that from the halfway house," Jake said. He jerked his head toward the truck. "Get in and I'll drop you off."

"This feels wrong." Micah moved toward the truck anyway, his body obedient even as his brain rebelled. "I should be with you, helping you. Shouldn't I?"

"Helping me what? I think I'll just be sitting around, going crazy, and I don't really need any help with that."

"I could help you *not* go crazy, maybe."

They were in the truck now, and Jake reached over and caught Micah's hand. "You already are. And I'll call you. If anything happens, or if he contacts me, or—whatever. I'll call. But I don't want you getting into trouble because of me."

"Because of Austin," Micah corrected.

"Because of anything. I don't want you getting into trouble, period. Okay?"

"I wish I could do something to help."

"I wish I could, too. But—you know this, I guess. There's not much to be done from the outside. If Austin wants this? If he wants to keep destroying himself? There's not really anything we can do."

"I wasn't thinking about helping Austin. I was thinking about helping you."

"Thank you," Jake said. Simple words, but said with a depth of feeling that touched Micah deep inside. Jake should have lots of people who wanted to help him. He should have lots of friends, a family—a life. Instead, he had two junkies and far too much responsibility.

But Micah wasn't going to be a junkie anymore. And he'd do what he could to share the responsibility. He'd share as much as Jake would let him, and they'd both just have to hope it was enough.

Chapter Twelve

JAKE SLEPT ON THE COUCH that night, dozing off and then jerking awake every time there was the slightest sound, any suggestion of anything that might be the buzzing of his cell phone or the grinding of Austin's key in the lock. But every time it was a false alarm, and by the time the sun was starting to rise he gave up.

Another text to Austin, the last of at least a dozen he'd sent since the night before, and then he found some breakfast and packed a lunch. He had to go to work, had to make money so he'd be able to pay for the rent of the apartment Austin might come home to, or for the rehab he might someday be ready to try.

Filling the second travel mug with coffee and fixing it to Micah's tastes helped him relax a little. Jake didn't have to go through this alone. It wasn't fair to expect too much from Micah, of course—a friendship and one fuck wasn't a wedding ring, wasn't a promise of lifelong support and comfort. And Micah had his own shit to deal with. But Micah didn't need to do anything that was actually related to Austin in order to help Jake out. It was just nice to have something positive to look forward to, and getting to see Micah definitely fit that criteria.

Jake kept half his attention on the sidewalks as he drove; not an effective search technique, but about the only one he could think of. The whole thing was hopeless, and yet, when he pulled up in front of the halfway house and Micah bounced down the steps toward him, he could feel a bit of energy returning. A bit of optimism.

And the energy kept flowing as Micah climbed into the front seat and started talking. "I sent Austin's picture to about ten people in the old neighborhood, and Tristan's boyfriend is going to help, too. I don't know him so well, but I guess he's turning into some sort of community organizer or something. He's got a sort of spy network set up. It's a bit creepy, but it could be useful for this, right?"

"But what do we do if we find him?"

"I have no idea." Micah's smile was jaunty, but there was something in his eyes that made Jake feel like the optimism was at least partly an act. A brave face and an attempt to do something, even if the *something* wasn't completely productive. Maybe that was the best that could be managed, under the circumstances.

So Jake nodded and made his own smile as genuine as he could. "One step at a time," he agreed. "First we find him, *then* we—beat the shit out of him? Is there any way we could make that seem like a valid therapeutic technique? Because it would be really, really satisfying to punch the little bastard in the gut. I could make it only one hit, but a hard one."

Micah didn't answer, just reached for his coffee and took a sip. It felt strange to make small talk after that, but there was no point in babbling about Austin anymore, not when there was such a total shortage of new information. So they drove quietly. When Micah shifted his mug to his right hand, Jake took his own off the wheel, and just like that they were holding hands, taking turns letting their thumbs wander and explore their limited range. It wasn't sexy, just—nice. Comforting. Jake didn't really want to let go when they made it to the job site, but his self-discipline took over and he tried to look focused and energetic as he hopped out and started directing work.

It was a long day, especially with both Jake and Micah taking breaks every fifteen or so minutes to check their phones for possible updates, but they got a lot done, and Jake should have felt satisfied when he dragged himself back into the pickup after their last job. Instead he was restless and jittery, and that wasn't helped when Micah looked over at him and said, "I'm thinking about skipping my meeting today. I don't think they're actually all that helpful for me—they're more like a way to fill time and give me structure, not anything that actually helps, like, in and of themselves. I think I'd rather go talk to some people in the neighborhood and ask around about Austin. And there's one friend—he used to be my friend, at least—I have to make amends to him, for sure. So if I did that, I'd still kind of be working the program, even without the meeting. I don't know—what do you think?"

"I have no idea." Not useful, maybe, but honest. "Do you have a sponsor yet? You're supposed to get a sponsor, right? Maybe you could ask him what he thinks?"

"Don't have one yet. I keep hopping around to different meetings, trying to find one I like, and they usually want your sponsor to go to the same meetings you do. But—I don't really think I'm going to find a meeting I like. I just—they're not good, you know? For me. A few of them were really focused on the Higher Power part, so I know I don't want to go to them, but even the others? It's kind of like asking someone to choose their favourite kind of dirt to eat. It all sucks, so—"

"A nice rich loam with lots of organic material and just a bit of clay," Jake said quickly. It wasn't really true—he didn't have a favourite kind of dirt to eat—but maybe it was funny? Or else completely inappropriate to say something so random when someone else was trying to make a serious point.

But Micah didn't look upset. "Okay," he said wryly, "I'll keep that in mind. But I'm guessing it's still a sort of 'least awful' option, right? If you were told you had to eat dirt, you'd just sit down and start chewing on your loam; you wouldn't waste time for weeks and weeks hunting for that one dirt that's actually really tasty."

"So you're going to need to bite the bullet on the meetings," Jake said. "Just pick one that's close to home or whatever. And then you'll get a sponsor. But for now—I have no idea, Micah. What do you think?"

"I think my friends are the reason I got clean in the first place. Letting them down, losing them—that's what made me know I had to change. So seeing them? I kind of feel like—okay, I don't know if you're religious—I guess not too much or you would have mentioned it by now, but if you're kind of a quiet believer or whatever, I hope you don't think this is sacrilegious, but—I think my friends are my Higher Power. You know? Like, when I went through all the steps and the counsellors said I could think of whatever I wanted to when they said Higher Power, I thought about my friends. So going to see them—it's kinda like skipping right over the meeting and talking directly to the source."

"Is all that just an elaborate justification, or do you really think it works?"

Jake glanced over when there was no immediate answer. Had he pushed too hard? But Micah was beaming at him. "Thank you for asking that," he said. "Seriously. I need people to ask me stuff like that sometimes. But I think I'm okay, right now. I think that really works."

"Okay, then. Go see your Higher Power."

"And I thought maybe you'd want to come with me." Jake took his eyes off the road again, wishing he wasn't driving so he could look at Micah all the time, and saw him make a face. "I don't want to make it out like a big deal. You're not—I mean, I know we're new, and I'm not looking for some sort of big 'meet the family' experience. But they can maybe help us find Austin, and you'd like them, probably, and, I don't know. I want to see them, and I want to see you, so having all of you together would be really convenient for me. That's all."

"Okay," Jake said. It was easy, really. "Sure. Do you want to go home and get cleaned up, or should we go straight over?"

"It's already past five, and I need to be home by eight—they knocked an hour off because I was late last night. My friends won't care if we're a bit dirty, so if it's okay with you, we should go straight over."

They drove quietly for a while. It was such a strange mix of feelings. Excitement over what was happening with Micah, dread over Austin. Nervousness about meeting Micah's friends, and at the same time a sort of surreal floating feeling, as if any social niceties could never matter when Austin was out there destroying himself and Jake could do nothing about it.

Was he just supposed to go on with his life as if nothing was happening? Sure, Micah's friends weren't completely unconnected to the situation—they might be able to help. But was he going to be shaking hands and making small talk? Was he up to that?

"They put up with me being a total junkie for more than a year." Micah's voice was strangely relaxed, considering what he was saying. "I stole stuff from Tristan's apartment, and he just—he just stopped having stuff worth stealing, so I could still stick around. I'd stolen the TV, and when Tristan got a new one Shane bolted it to the wall with some sort of industrial-strength, totally improvised thing—there was scrap metal welded to it so it'd be too heavy to carry! But they still let me hang around."

Jake wasn't sure what to say to that, so he stayed quiet, and Micah laughed softly. "Yeah. Kinda weird. And obviously I'm—I was—I don't know, maybe I still am—an asshole. But what I mean, is that they're pretty accepting people. They aren't going to give you a hard time about anything. They don't like cops, or most social workers, or, like, big-business types, but you? They'll be fine with you."

"I'm unsuccessful enough to be acceptable?"

"You're real enough," Micah corrected. "It's not about money."

Jake wasn't exactly sure what it meant to be *real*, not unless he flashed back to the damn *Velveteen Rabbit*, and he didn't want to revisit that childhood trauma right then. So he stayed quiet and followed Micah's directions, then found a parking spot not far from the building Micah was eying as if it was some sort of temple.

"I haven't been inside for a while," Micah confessed as they climbed out of the truck and started along the sidewalk. "I had breakfast with Tristan. He said I should come by. But maybe I should have called first." He stopped walking. "I still could. And if it's not a good time we could drive around and look for Austin ourselves."

Jake wasn't sure how to help. He felt a brief stab of irritation—did he really need to be dragged into someone else's drama when he had so much of his own to deal with?—and was instantly ashamed of himself. There wasn't really anything to be done to help with Austin, but there *was* something to do to help with this situation. "Whatever you think is best," he said, which was maybe a bit lame but earned him a grateful smile anyway.

"I'm going to call," Micah decided, and turned away from the building as he pulled his phone out. Then he stopped moving and Jake followed his gaze to see a tall, dark-haired guy walking toward them, a terrier-type dog straining on its leash, clearly heading toward Micah.

"Oh," Micah half-whispered, and then the dog was there and Micah fell to his knees to greet the animal. The owner stood silently, frowning down at the reunion, and there was something in his glower that made Jake want to look around for possible weapons. The guy was big, with ink on his neck and hair cut so short it felt like a statement. And he really didn't seem happy to see Micah.

Then the man's expression softened a little and Jake allowed himself to relax at least somewhat, loosening his focus enough that he could hear what Micah was saying to the little dog.

"I'm so sorry, Dodger. So sorry. I fucked up, buddy. I'm really glad you didn't get hurt—I didn't know you were going to be there, but that's no excuse. I'm so sorry. I'm an asshole."

The dog didn't seem to agree with the last sentiment, at least, as he was still wriggling with excitement and happily licking any part of Micah he could reach.

Then Micah looked up at the inked guy. "I'm an asshole," he repeated. "I know I fucked up. I didn't think about him being in the apartment, didn't think they'd hurt him—I don't know. I just didn't think, and it put Dodger in danger, and if there was anything I could do to change it, I'd change it. But I know there isn't. So, just—I'm sorry. I'm clean, too. A hundred and seven days, but ninety of those were in rehab so some people don't think they should count. Still, even if it's only seventeen, it's the *first* seventeen, and it's going to keep going. I promise."

The guy didn't seem hostile anymore, but still wasn't exactly warm. "You've made promises before," he said, his voice low.

Micah just nodded. "I know. There's no reason for you to trust me now. I get that."

The guy didn't respond right away, just turned and looked at Jake, then back down at Micah. The question was clear, and Micah gently disentangled himself from the dog and stood up. "Shane, this is Jake. Jake, Shane." A nervous look at Jake, and then Micah said to Shane, "Do you know a guy named Austin deSantis? Kinda looks like Jake—same coloring, at least, but Austin's thinner."

Shane frowned at Jake, then at Micah. "He's a junkie? Buys from Moby?"

"Maybe," Micah said reluctantly.

But Jake didn't want to beat around the bush, not as a way to make Austin look less pathetic. "Almost certainly. Definitely a junkie. Definitely used to buy from Moby. But we're not sure just where he is right now."

Shane didn't look impressed with Jake's honesty. "You supposed to be hanging around with guys like that?" he asked Micah. "Is that part of your recovery, or whatever?"

"I ran into him at an NA meeting," Micah said, and he could have left it at that, but apparently he really was committed to the honesty thing, because he continued. "But, no, I shouldn't really be hanging out with him if he's still using. I just—well, we need to find him to make sure he's okay. I'll figure out the rest of it later."

Shane didn't seem to approve of that strategy, and Jake couldn't blame him. But the big man finally shrugged and said, "Me and Moby aren't really talking anymore—he's under some kind of pressure, I think, acting crazy and pushing way too hard." He squinted at Micah, apparently taking in the fading bruise on his face, and added, "Maybe you already know about that?"

"Not the details," Micah said. "But, yeah, I got the general impression."

Shane's attention shifted back to Jake. "Is Austin your brother? You're dragging Micah back into this shit to help your brother? Who probably doesn't even want your help?"

They were fair questions, but before Jake could answer them Micah jumped in. "He's not *dragging* me anywhere. I'm trying to help out a friend."

"I'm following Micah's lead," Jake added. "He says he can handle it."

Shane snorted. "Yeah, 'cause Micah's a great judge of what he can handle."

Shit. That was true, of course. Why was it so easy to forget Micah's past struggles, even when he made no secret of them? Maybe because he seemed so calm now, so in control. But it had been only a few days earlier that they'd stood together in the kitchen, looking down at the baggie in Micah's hand, and Micah had been *shaking*.

"I guess he's a better judge than I would be," Jake said. Micah looked at him with what seemed a lot like gratitude, although Jake wasn't sure it was deserved.

"I'm sorry for before," Micah said. "I mean that. But for now—I want to focus on helping Austin, if I can. We came over to ask Simon if he could help us find him. And I called a bunch of people last night, everyone I could think of who wouldn't be pissed at me. But if you could keep an eye out for him too, that'd be great."

"You've been back five minutes and you're asking for favors already," Shane said.

Micah paused only a moment before nodding. "Yeah. I am."

Shane looked skeptical. "I'm honestly not sure you deserve another chance."

"I don't think it's about what I deserve, necessarily. It's just—I don't know. It's a gift I'm hoping you'll give me, even though I *don't* deserve it."

Jake felt as if he was eavesdropping on a conversation that should have been private, but it was too late to walk away, so he stood quietly as Shane shook his head as if trying to clear his thoughts. "You're good with words," he said grudgingly. "Let's see if you're good with actions, too."

"Thank you," Micah said, and then Shane smiled and Jake wondered how he ever could have thought the man was threatening or scary. With the new expression, he looked like a loveable, if oversized, teddy bear.

"Go upstairs," Shane said. "Tristan will want to see you."

Micah nodded and gave the little dog a goodbye ear scratch. Then he led the way through the broken security door and into a hallway that smelled of things Jake didn't want to analyze too closely. He was meeting Micah's friends, and it felt like meeting his family. It reminded Jake that Micah had already met the only real friend or family Jake had left. One person, currently missing.

Micah the Junkie had more social connections than Jake the Responsible. It didn't seem right, exactly, but Jake wasn't in any position to argue about it.

"You good?" Micah asked when they reached the doorway they'd been heading for. Jake smiled in response and Micah gave a double knock, then pushed the door open. "Hello?" he called. "Anyone home?"

There was an indistinct rumble that sounded like it might be a greeting coming from inside, and Micah took a deep, nervous breath. "We're on," he said, and Jake followed him through the door.

~*~*~*~

IT WAS STRANGE TO BE BACK INSIDE Tristan's apartment. Luckily there wasn't a full crowd that evening, just Tristan on the couch, Simon in the little kitchen, and Trey standing by the window as he so often did, as if he was their sentinel, keeping an eye on the world outside.

"You just missed Shane," Tristan said, standing up.

"They were talking on the sidewalk," Trey reported. Micah had no idea why Trey hadn't already shared that information, but Trey's motives were generally a little hard to figure out.

"It went okay?" Tristan asked. He opened his arms and Micah stepped into the hug, trying to tell himself it was no big deal. He and Tristan had already made peace; the hug was to be expected. But Micah *hadn't* expected it. Hoped for it, sure, but he hadn't been daring enough to go all the way to expectations.

He couldn't let himself get caught up in that, though. It would wreck the casual atmosphere Tristan clearly wanted to maintain, and that wasn't fair to anyone. Especially the group's newest arrival. Micah half-turned and smiled at Jake, then said, "This is Tristan. That's Trey, and Simon. Guys, this is Jake."

There was a mumble of greetings, and Simon said, "Have you eaten? I'm making pancakes."

"Pancakes?" Micah said, and Tristan grinned.

"He's learning to cook, and he's a perfectionist. So he picks one thing and makes it over and over until it's absolutely right." He raised his voice a little and said, "We're almost there on the pancakes, right? You think you're about ready to move on?"

"Don't jinx me," Simon scolded. "I can't unleash my true creativity under this sort of pressure. The pancakes will be as the pancakes will be."

"I love pancakes," Micah said quickly, and looked at Jake, who nodded in response.

It was surreal, really. They sat down and Micah explained about Austin and heard the same warning about Moby that Shane had already given them, and then they just—ate pancakes. Simon told them about the animal shelter where he'd been living, the same one Shane used to stay at, and how it was having trouble with the landlord. They talked about mutual friends, favourite movies, upcoming video game releases. They chatted, just like old times. Like Micah hadn't fucked up, or, just as strange, like Micah was the same guy, now, as he'd been when he'd been so perpetually high he could barely follow a conversation.

Nobody was drinking, though, and that had to mean something. Nobody had pulled out a joint or a pipe, either, like they might have before.

They were pretending it was the same, but it wasn't. It never could be again. And as much of a burden as Micah had been on his friends back when he'd been using, wasn't he just another kind of burden now? None of them were addicts, but they were acting like they were, not having a few social drinks with friends, because Micah was there and they had to take care of him.

He wasn't sorry when Jake looked at his watch and said, "We should head out, if you're going to be home by eight."

"They've got you on a short leash," Trey commented, but nobody else said anything even a little bit negative. Because they had to be careful around Micah, had to be sure they were supportive and gentle.

"You'll let us know if you hear anything about Austin?" Micah prompted as he headed for the door. At least something good should come out of the visit.

Simon nodded. "I'll put the word out. I've got a good idea of where to start."

Tristan smiled with pride in his boyfriend's skills, and Micah tried to memorize the expression. Tristan was happy. That was all Micah really needed. He'd been forgiven, and Tristan was happy. Micah should walk away, satisfied with that. And he should stay away, because he didn't want to be a burden on people he cared about.

He and Jake were outside the building, walking toward the sidewalk, before Jake said, "That wasn't what you expected?"

Micah was startled. Had he been that transparent? Or maybe Jake was just paying attention. "I guess it was. Just—I don't know, I guess it was easier with just Tristan the other day. We had breakfast. It wasn't weird that no one was drinking or smoking up or anything. But tonight? It was weird."

He stopped walking suddenly and frowned at Jake. "You don't have any alcohol at your place, not even beer. Right? Is that because of Austin?"

"I guess," Jake agreed carefully. "I was never a big drinker, but, yeah, I stopped having anything at home when Austin moved in. It's not a big deal."

"It's one more thing you've had to give up."

Jake shrugged. "You think your friends feel like they *have* to give stuff up? I mean, there are addicts who are okay around other people drinking or using. There are addicts who are only addicted to one thing, and seem to be okay with moderate use of something else. Like, you could be a heroin addict but not an alcoholic. But, yeah, you're supposed to be careful about it all, especially when you're fresh out of rehab. You think it's a problem for your friends?"

Micah should keep his mouth shut; Jake didn't need to listen to his whining. But he ignored that common sense and said,

"I think it *should* be a problem for them. I mean, I'm the one who can't handle it, so why should *they* have to give up something they enjoy?"

"Because life isn't perfect?" Jake suggested. He reached out and found Micah's hand. "Because if they have to pick between having alcohol and drugs but no you, or you but no alcohol and drugs, they pick the second. Honestly, Micah, anyone who'd pick the first? Anyone who'd pick substances over a good friend should be worrying about their own addiction issues, not yours."

"It sounds so easy when you say it like that."

"I've seen too much to ever pretend it's easy. But that doesn't mean it isn't true."

Micah wanted to be comforted. He wanted to believe what Jake was saying, and at least right then, with their hands held tight, he mostly did. Mostly. "You ever wish Austin had picked a different meeting to go to the day he ran into me? You ever think your life would be a lot simpler with just one of us to deal with?"

"Simpler?" Jake shrugged, but didn't let go of Micah's hand. "Yeah, it'd be simpler. But I don't think that's really what I'm going for. When I'm on my deathbed, looking back on everything, I'm not sure 'well, that was simple' is what I want to be thinking."

Then he kissed Micah. Nothing passionate, nothing that felt like the start of something, just a quick bit of reassurance and affection. Exactly what Micah needed.

And when Jake stepped away and tugged gently on his hand, saying, "We need to get going if you're going to make curfew," *that* was exactly what Micah needed, too.

But what did Jake need? Not any of Micah's drama, that was for sure. No, Jake needed to find Austin. Maybe Austin wasn't going to quit using, and maybe Jake would have to change their arrangement to make sure he wasn't being an enabler or whatever. But they had to talk; that much seemed clear. There was no way for Jake to move forward, not when he had no idea where his brother was or whether he was okay.

"Is it a long day tomorrow at work?" Micah asked, letting himself be steered toward the truck. "We could go down and check some places out when we're done. Places Austin might be. If you want."

"Will it be too much for you? Last time it was kind of intense, right? Even if Moby hadn't slipped the shit into your pocket, it was kind of hard, wasn't it?"

"What were you saying about things not having to be easy, not having to be simple?" Micah shrugged. "I got through it last time, and I'll get through it again. I can't just live in a cave, you know. I can't run away from it forever."

"It's not forever. You're still new to all this."

Micah couldn't argue with that, and he knew what the smart thing was. But that didn't mean he could do it. "If I'm not looking for Austin, I'll either be with you, watching you worrying about him, or by myself feeling useless because you're off looking for him and I'm too weak to help. None of that sounds like it'd be easier than just going with you. I mean, I agree that I shouldn't go on my own. But if I go with you? I'll be fine."

Jake looked like he was thinking about arguing, but wasn't quite sure what to say. He was too kind to admit he just didn't trust Micah's willpower.

Micah tried to ignore the lack of faith. It only made sense, really—Jake wasn't stupid. He wasn't naïve. He knew how addicts worked. Still, it stung. Nothing Micah didn't deserve, but knowing that didn't really make him feel any better.

"Tomorrow's a brand new day," he said as they reached the truck. "Tomorrow we'll track Austin down and yell at him 'til he cries and you'll figure out a new plan for him. Hopefully one that involves him answering his damn phone when you call him."

"Sounds good," Jake agreed. "Especially the part where we get to make him cry."

"He won't know what hit him," Micah promised, and Jake smiled in response. They held hands as they drove to the halfway house.

Chapter Thirteen

IT FELT ALMOST LIKE HIGH SCHOOL, Jake decided. Spending time with Micah all day, then leaving him at night—it was the opposite direction of most adult relationships Jake knew about. And he wasn't exactly thrilled to be going to bed alone, not with only the memory of that one afternoon with Micah to keep him warm.

Still, it was what it was. Life wasn't perfect, and that was okay.

He definitely didn't want to give up the pleasant stirring in his gut as he drove to the bus stop where Micah would be waiting for him, that anticipation of happiness that was almost as sweet as the happiness itself. Didn't want to lose the excitement of seeing Micah's face light up as the pickup approached, or the strange bashfulness they both seemed to feel for the first moments of being together again.

This morning, Micah busied himself arranging his growing collection of gear in the footwell until they were out into traffic, and then, at the first stop light, leaned over and gave Jake a quick kiss that landed somewhere around the corner of his mouth. Then he drew back to his own seat and laughed softly. "I feel like a little kid sometimes."

As usual, they were on the same wavelength.

But then Micah continued, "I don't think I've ever kissed anyone when I wasn't jammed, or at least stoned. It's different— you know?"

"Well, not first hand, no. I've never kissed anyone when I *was* high or stoned."

"Drunk?" Micah suggested.

"I guess, yeah. Drinking, at least."

"I've never been a big drinker, but it's probably kind of the same. Like, it's—I don't know, it's easier, kind of. Like it doesn't mean as much. Right now, I worry that you'll pull away or I'll do it wrong or I've made a weird mistake or hallucinated the entire thing and you'll have no idea what I'm even *doing*, or why… but if I was high, I wouldn't have those worries in the first place because my brain isn't such a bastard when I feed it what it likes, and even if the ideas *did* occur to me, I wouldn't really care about them, because when I'm using I don't *get* embarrassed, don't get my feelings hurt, don't get disappointed. Nothing really matters, you know?"

"Jesus, Micah, you should start writing advertising copy for the heroin marketing board. You make it sound pretty damn appealing."

"Short term, sure." Micah shrugged and looked down at his shoes. "But sooner or later, you realize that not having the bad things matter means that the good things don't matter, either. I mean, yeah, I wouldn't care if you pulled away, but I wouldn't really care if you *didn't* pull away, either. I wouldn't hurt if something bad happened, but I wouldn't feel good if something good happened."

Jake took his eyes off the road long enough to see Micah's thoughtful frown. Then Micah mused, "I guess that's kind of what it's about. If I want to kick the habit, I have to believe that there's more good feelings than bad feelings in the world. Otherwise, just mathematically, or logically, it would make sense to keep using, right? If I have emotion-neutralizing medicine, and I believe that most emotion is negative, then I should take the medicine."

It was really too early for a discussion this intense, but Jake wasn't going to back away if Micah wasn't going to. "So getting clean—staying clean—it's an act of faith, really. An expression of optimism."

"Yeah," Micah agreed. He still sounded a bit tentative, but apparently the ideas were crystalizing. "So Austin—assuming he's in the same boat I am—maybe he just needs something to believe in. Something to look forward to?"

"Something more than business courses so he can help his nag of an older brother run a business he doesn't actually care about?"

"Shit, Jake, no!" Micah twisted around in his seat, practically bouncing in agitation. "Having a brother who loves him and tries to include him in stuff and give him a stable life? That's a *positive thing*, for sure. I didn't mean he had to look forward to, like, a trip to Disneyworld! And none of this is your job, either. You don't have to be—you *shouldn't* be—the one who comes up with Austin's good stuff. That has to come from Austin, I think."

"He doesn't seem to be very good at finding it."

"I wasn't either, for a long time. But I really feel like I'm on the way, now. I have no idea what it'll take to make Austin get here, but—I don't know." Micah seemed to deflate a little, and it made Jake's chest ache to see it. "It seemed like an epiphany at the time. But I guess it's not actually all that useful, in terms of helping Austin."

"We're allowed to talk about things other than helping Austin," Jake said. "And I'm interested in how you see things."

"Yeah?" Micah took a deep breath. "So—would you be interested in knowing that you're one of the 'good things' I think about when I'm reminding myself why life is better clean? Being with you—even when I'm totally nervous and being a loser about everything—I want to feel that. No filters, no buffers, no medicine needed."

Jake blinked hard, surprised by the sudden rush of emotion. He kept his eyes on the road, tried to remember that he was driving a good-sized pickup through urban traffic, but let his hand reach out in Micah's direction. He felt a lot calmer when Micah's fingers wrapped around his. "That's nice to hear," he managed. He wanted to say more. Something about how he felt—what? Honored? Was that the right word? It was an honor to be that important to someone like Micah; it was a responsibility he didn't necessarily need, but he'd worry about that later. For just then, he'd focus on the positive. "You're one of the good things for me, too. For sure."

"Okay," Micah said softly. "Thanks."

They drove in silence for a while and were almost to the job site when Micah's phone rang. He dug it out of his pocket, looked down at it, then up at Jake. "Shane," he said in explanation, then answered with "Hey. What's up?"

He listened for longer than Jake really liked, and his voice was strange when he said "How sure are you? Is this—fuck. Has Simon heard anything?"

Another pause, and even without confirmation, Jake pulled over to the side of the road. This wasn't a casual phone call. He didn't know what it was, but he was pretty sure he didn't want to be driving when he found out.

"See if you can confirm it, okay? And—" Micah looked almost furtively over at Jake, then said, "If there's cops or anything, can you give them my number? If they need to get in touch with someone?"

Jake felt like he was starting to float away. Cops. Needing to contact someone. Not Austin himself making contact, because—because Austin wasn't in a state to do it? Was that what Micah meant?

Micah ended the call and then tapped away at his phone for a minute. He finished, stared at it like he was willing a response, then turned to Jake. Another one of his deep breaths and then he said, "Nothing's confirmed. Austin might not have been there. But there was a fire last night. A pretty bad one, at one of the squats where Moby's guys do a lot of dealing. People were—Shane isn't sure. He said there were ambulances. No one's said Austin was there, so he probably wasn't—I just texted him, told him he needs to get in touch, *now*. But even if he doesn't text back, he wasn't texting back *before* the fire, either, right? So it won't mean anything. Nothing's confirmed."

The floating sensation was coming back again, and it was tempting to just go with it. A non-chemical version of Micah's heroin vacations, a visit to a place where there was no need to be afraid or frustrated or angry. But Austin might need his help, so Jake had to keep his mind on the job. "Where?" he rasped, surprised by the tightness in his voice. "We need to go there."

"Okay," Micah said carefully. "Near Tristan's. Get closer and I'll get better directions." He paused for a moment, then said, "Should I call Alex? Tell him we'll be late to work?"

It was too mundane, too practical, but Jake nodded anyway and fought to remember the plans for the day. "Yeah. Thanks. Tell him the plaza first, then the Johnstons, then the long stretch of houses out on the hill." He forced himself to drive at a normal speed and not race through traffic. "Tell him I'll pay him overtime to get it finished, if we don't show up to help."

That was what Jake wanted to be worrying about. Employee relations, labor laws, pleasing the customers. Not—no. He wouldn't let his mind go there.

He waited until Micah'd made the call to Alex, then waited a little longer, for something, anything, to pull his thoughts away from their grim fantasies. "Talk to me," he said, and it came out sounding more desperate than he'd intended.

But after a moment's surprise, Micah seemed to understand. "I was looking on the internet last night, seeing all the famous gardens in the world. They seemed—I don't know, they were beautiful, but they seemed kind of artificial, too. Like a poodle with one of those crazy haircuts. The formal gardens for sure, but even the more natural looking ones—they're still not really natural, right? Not when they're all tidy like they are. Nature isn't tidy, I don't think."

Jesus. Jake had been expecting something a little less intellectually involved. But maybe this was good. Maybe talking about the place of gardens in the world of nature was an appropriate distraction. So he tried to do his part, contributing at least a few bricks to Micah's tower of ideas, until Micah's phone rang and they both jumped in their seats, startled and then apprehensive.

Micah looked down at the display, then back to Jake. "Private number," he said, then answered the call.

He listened a bit, and Jake strained to hear but couldn't make out any words over the sounds of traffic. Micah frowned, and said "Yeah. Micah Porter. I'm a friend of Austin's, but I'm in a car with his brother."

A pause, and then, "No, no other family. Nobody close, at least. Look, is Austin okay? Was he in the fire? Jake's going a bit crazy here—we need some information."

Another pause while Micah listened. "Yeah, okay. We're on our way. Do we ask for someone at the front desk, or what?"

Front desk. Hospital? Police station? Jake's mind hopped from one horrible situation to another and wouldn't settle long enough for him to actually start thinking of solutions to any of the possible problems.

Micah ended the call and Jake wanted to tell him to stay quiet. If Micah just kept his mouth shut, if he didn't say the words out loud—

"Harborview Medical," Micah said. "We're supposed to ask for Lynn Askew when we get there."

"She's a doctor?"

"I don't know," Micah admitted. "Shit, I should have asked. I don't—she wouldn't tell me how he is, wouldn't even tell me what happened. But she didn't say 'no' when I asked about the fire."

Jake couldn't keep the images from flooding into his mind. His laughing baby brother, burned, scarred, in pain. Afraid. Calling for Jake, but getting no answer.

Micah stretched a hand out toward his, but Jake jerked away. He didn't deserve to be comforted, and he couldn't let himself be weak. He needed to find Austin and protect him. He needed to make everything better. He needed to get to the goddamn hospital.

"What exit?" he demanded, and Micah started messing with his phone, looking for directions.

Jake sped up. He needed to get to the hospital, get to Austin, make things right again. He needed to save his brother. That was all there was to it.

Chapter Fourteen

THE ROOM WAS TOO QUIET, too comfortable, too pleasant, and Micah knew that was bad. He and Jake should have been rushed to Austin's side or sent to some crowded waiting room or scooped up by the police for questioning. Instead they'd been shown into this tastefully decorated room with its view out over the water and its comfortable chairs and told that Ms. Askew would be with them in a moment. It wasn't what should be happening.

He wished Jake would talk to him, or at least look at him. This was affecting Jake more than Micah, obviously, and Micah wasn't selfish enough to be hoping for comfort. But he was pretty sure he'd feel better if he could at least offer some, if he could get the feeling that Jake wanted him there, or even noticed his presence. But Jake was standing by the window, his hand pressed against the glass as if it was a barrier keeping him from longed-for freedom, and he wasn't saying a damn word.

There was a gentle knock on the door and then it opened to admit a middle-aged woman in a light blue pant suit. As soon as

Micah saw her face, he knew. She looked too careful, too calm, as if there was no rush because—because.

He turned toward Jake, who was staring at the woman with dread. He opened his mouth as if to speak, then closed it again.

She stepped a little closer and Micah resisted the urge to throw himself between the two of them. "Jake deSantis?" she asked, her gaze skimming over Micah and settling on Jake, who managed a jerky nod. "Will you come and sit down?" She stepped toward the arm chairs, but Jake didn't move, and neither did Micah. The woman nodded slowly. "I'm sorry," she said.

Jake jerked as if he'd already heard too much and didn't want any more, but he didn't leave, and after a moment the woman said, "Austin was in a building that caught fire. The fire produced a lot of smoke, and—" She grimaced. "The investigation isn't complete, but the current theory is that he, and several others, maybe had been under the influence of a narcotic. Already unconscious, or barely conscious, when the smoke reached them."

"Just smoke?" Jake whispered. "Not fire. He didn't—he didn't burn?"

"Smoke inhalation," the woman agreed. "No—I'm sorry, I know the details aren't always welcome, but I think it may be helpful for you to know that there were no signs of struggle. He ran out of oxygen while already asleep. He wouldn't have known what was happening."

Jake turned back toward the window, clearly trying to control himself. Micah wanted to tell him there was no need. It was okay to show emotion, okay to be upset, to be devastated. But the words didn't come.

After a few deep breaths Jake said, "I need you to say it. I need to hear the words."

That didn't seem like a great idea to Micah, but the woman didn't seem alarmed by it. She just stepped a little closer and said, "I'm sorry, Mr. deSantis. We've made a positive identification through police records and photo ID. Your brother Austin passed away last night."

Micah hadn't known he was crying until the first tear trickled down his neck. Austin. That laughing, sparkling, maddening force of nature—gone. All the joy he found in the simplest things was lost along with him, and the world was a darker, colder place.

And Jake. Still standing by the window, completely still except for his right hand, slowly opening and closing as if he was trying to grip something, something he could no longer touch or see.

"You can use this room as long as you like—" the woman began, but Jake had started moving at her first word and was practically running by the time she broke off, out the door and down the hall, charging ahead as if he had somewhere to be, something to do.

Micah jogged after him uncertainly. Did Jake need company, or some time alone? If he *did* want company—did he want Micah? A junkie, a loser, someone who didn't know what to say or how to comfort him. Shit. Jake deserved better, but there was no one else offering so Micah kept going.

But going where? He lost sight of Jake after the first corner, tried to retrace the steps they'd taken on the way in and found himself hopelessly lost. Shit, he couldn't even do this right. Jake was hurting, he was alone, and, shit, what if he was waiting for Micah somewhere, what if he was *needing* Micah, and Micah wasn't there?

He found a stairwell and started down it, dialing Jake's number on his phone as he moved. He'd head for the parking garage, try to catch up to Jake there, if the phone call didn't give him better directions.

But Jake didn't answer the call, and when Micah made it to the garage, the truck was gone. Jake was gone.

Another unanswered phone call, a desperate text—*Where r u? Can I help? What can I do?* And then—nothing. There was nothing left for Micah to do. Was there?

No, of course there wasn't. There was nothing for *anyone* to do, because Austin was gone. Dead. It was final, beyond fixing. Whatever he could have done, could have tried, would no longer be any use. The worst had happened. Rock bottom had been reached, but there was no way for Austin to climb back out. Jesus. Austin.

Micah sank down onto the concrete barrier separating the parking area from the ramp to the exit. Austin was dead. Jake was gone. Everything was empty. He looked at his phone and fought the urge to throw it down the ramp. If it couldn't reach Austin or Jake, what the hell good was it?

It could call others, he reminded himself. Jake was alone, but Micah? He didn't deserve it, but he had friends. He had family.

Family who'd been living for years with the fear that they would someday get the same phone call Jake had got, be taken to the same kind of room and faced with the same impossible, implacable reality. He'd been the cause of all that worry. He couldn't do anything for Jake, but that didn't mean he couldn't do anything at all.

The number wasn't in his contacts—it had been in his old phone, but that was long gone, traded away for a few hours of artificial bliss. But they hadn't changed their number since he'd lived with them, so he knew it by heart and after a deep breath he punched it into the phone, then waited through the buzzing ring tones.

He almost hung up when he heard the familiar voice. He didn't say anything in reply to her "hello" and she wouldn't know the number, but still, after an awkward pause, his mother said, "Micah? Is that you?"

"Yeah," he managed. "It's me. I'm okay. I mean, I'm not in trouble or anything. I'm not calling to get help. I just—I just wanted to check in, if that's okay."

"Of course it's okay!" She sounded like she was maybe going to cry, or maybe already crying, and he could feel the tears starting in his own eyes again. "Where are you, baby? In Seattle, or closer?"

"No, Seattle. I'm—I wanted to—I'm okay, but I'm at the hospital. A friend just—the thing is, Mom, I wanted to just say I'm sorry."

"What are you talking about?" she demanded, and he could hear the panic in her voice. "Micah who's with you? What's going on?"

Shit, he couldn't even do this right. "No, Mom, not sorry for—I'm not going to do anything stupid. I'm okay. I meant sorry for before. For all the sh—the stuff I did. For hurting you and Dad. I just—I know I said sorry lots of times before, but I always fu—messed up again afterward, so it wasn't like I was *acting* sorry, you know? I was just saying it. I get that. But this time, I really—I'm sorry, Mom, for real."

"What happened to your friend, Micah? Why are you at the hospital? Are you *in* the hospital?"

"No. Sorry, I shouldn't have mentioned that. That's not—"

"Micah?" A deeper voice, authoritative and strong. "What's going on, son? Why is your mother upset?"

"Nothing's going on," Micah said. A lie, of course, but there was no point trying to explain anything to them. They didn't need to know. "I just called to check in, but I said some things wrong. Sorry."

"Do you need us to come up there? Or should I call the counsellors at the community living center?"

"No. But thank you. For paying for all that, and for offering to come up. I—" He wished he hadn't called. They'd been living their lives, going about their day, and with one stupid call he'd reminded them of their family nightmare. God, he was useless. "How are things down there? You golfing?"

"A couple times a week," his father agreed cautiously. "Would you like to come for a visit? If your counsellor says it's a good idea, we could send you a ticket."

"Uh—soon, maybe. But not right now. I've got stuff going on here. But thanks."

"You're sure you're okay? We can be there in three hours, if you need us."

"No, I'm fine. Seriously. You're talking to the guys at the halfway house, right? They're telling you I'm passing all the drug tests and everything?"

"They say you've had a few curfew violations."

"Could we maybe focus on the positive? The part where I'm clean? That's good, right?"

"It's good." But of course that wasn't enough. "Why have you missed curfew?"

"I've got to go, Dad. I'll call again soon, okay? You can yell at me about curfew then." And he ended the call. Was he a spoiled asshole brat, refusing to discuss something with the man who was paying for his room and board and counselling? Almost certainly. But no one should expect anything better from him. No one smart.

Austin was gone. Austin, who'd understood all this, had known what it was like to be a fuck-up. A fuck-up who still enjoyed his life, who didn't want it to be over, who'd just made a stupid mistake and now didn't have a chance to ever make things better. Austin, Micah's friend.

He typed another text to Jake. *I'll do whatever you need me to. Please call me.*

But there was no response, and he trudged out of the garage and down to the bus stop, alone.

THE BUILDING WASN'T HARD TO FIND. Jake knew the general neighborhood and after that it was just a question of driving around until he found charred wood and yellow police tape.

But once he'd found it, Jake was at a loss. Why had he wanted to see this? What had he thought it was going to tell him?

Maybe it had all been a big mistake. He hadn't actually seen Austin—whoever it was they *thought* was Austin. A bunch of junkies probably weren't too casual about keeping their phones and IDs tidy, right?

Austin was still out there somewhere. Scared. Shit, maybe scared straight. Maybe this mess would be his rock bottom and he'd start clawing his way back up to humanity.

Jake couldn't let himself think about this too much; he couldn't let himself remember that the police had Austin's fingerprints, that there'd be a photograph on the ID with Austin's name, that there were likely other junkies who'd survived and who could have identified him. He couldn't think about any of that. His brother was still alive, and he was scared, somewhere.

He was probably at the apartment. That was how they'd played this game before—Austin would leave, get into some sort of trouble, and come running back so his brother could rescue him.

Yeah, Austin was at the apartment. He was asleep. Jake would drive home and go upstairs and peek in to be sure he was okay, and then he'd call Micah and explain about the misunderstanding. It would all be fine. It would be okay. Austin wasn't—no. He wasn't. He couldn't be.

But Jake didn't put the truck into gear and turn it toward the apartment. As long as he stayed there, as long as he didn't go home, Austin was asleep in his own bed. If Jake went to the apartment and looked into his brother's bedroom, and the bed was empty—

He jammed the truck door open with far too much energy and stumbled out onto the sidewalk. He could smell the smoke, the destruction, and he couldn't let himself think of that toxic mess filling Austin's lungs.

He noticed a couple men in firefighting uniforms poking around at the edges of the building, another man in a dress shirt standing behind them. Investigating, he supposed. Tidying up. Collecting evidence for their use while erasing it from public display. A few sheets of plywood and a good rain and this would be just one more abandoned building, one more shell that used to hold something living and vital. One more corpse.

Jake turned away. He didn't know why he'd come or what he'd hoped to see, but he couldn't face the idea of getting back in the truck, because once he was behind the wheel he'd have no other excuse to keep him from driving home and finding—whatever he was going to find.

"Jake," a quiet voice said from somewhere beside him, and he turned to see Micah's friend Simon watching him with a careful, assessing gaze. "I'm sorry for your loss."

Jake couldn't bring himself to argue. He shouldn't say it out loud, not until he'd actually seen Austin alive. So he just nodded jerkily and turned away.

But Simon didn't take the hint. Fucking ghoul, hanging out at a damn fire scene where somebody—not Austin, somebody else—had just died. The asshole stepped closer, still cautious, and said, "Micah called us. He's looking for you. He's worried."

Micah. Micah and Austin, laughing together, working together—recovering together. Except only Micah had actually done that last part.

And Jake felt a sudden rage overcome him. Micah had been strong enough, but Austin hadn't. Or maybe Micah hadn't really been strong, just lucky. And maybe that luck was going to run out, sometime soon, and Micah would go back to the same shit that had just ki—that had almost killed Austin. And Jake was supposed to just sit there and watch it happen? Supposed to be a helpless witness to someone else he cared about self-destructing?

No, it was asking too much. "Tell Micah he's fired," Jake growled. "Tell him he was only around to keep Austin in line, and since he couldn't do that, he's done."

Simon didn't answer right away. Finally he said, "Is there something I can do, then? Would you like me to call someone, or can I drive you somewhere?"

No, kindness was not good. People who'd lost someone needed kindness, and Jake hadn't lost a damn thing. Everything was fine with him. "No. Just tell Micah to fuck off, and I'll mail him his paycheck."

"Maybe that's not a decision you should be making right now."

"Oh, spare me your condescending bullshit." Yeah, it felt good to be angry. Much better than being sad. "Go running back to your pretty-boy boyfriend and hide in that fucking cocoon of an apartment and mind your own business. Okay? Don't come out here and tell me what I should be deciding, or when."

Simon took a half-step backward. "Fine. Be alone. But I'm not going to be your messenger boy. If you want to fire Micah, or break up with him or—or hurt him, however you've decided to do it? Be enough of a man to do it to his face." Another half-step and then, "Or be even more of a man and don't hurt him at all. This wasn't his fault."

Micah's fault? No, this current pain wasn't Micah's fault. But the future pain when Micah fell of the wagon and went back to poisoning himself? That would absolutely be on Micah, and Jake couldn't be stupid enough to wander into that trap.

"Go fuck yourself," he mumbled, and turned back to the truck. He wasn't in any condition to be in public. He needed to hide. He needed to go home.

So he climbed behind the wheel and he drove through traffic and he fought to keep himself from thinking. When he got home he saw the door to Austin's room, hanging open just as it had been left, and he carefully, slowly took off his shoes and his jacket and set his keys on the table by the front door.

When that was done he made himself do it. Not that big of an apartment: only eight steps to the bedroom door. He made himself take them. And then he took four more steps and collapsed. He rolled into a ball on his brother's empty bed and he cried for everything he had lost.

Chapter Fifteen

MICAH TEXTED JAKE FIVE MORE times, called him twice, and then took the bus over to the apartment and hit the buzzer for ten minutes straight. No answer, no acknowledgement. Austin was gone, and now Jake? Jake seemed to be gone, too.

Calling Tristan didn't help much. There was a bit more news—confirmation that two other junkies had died in the fire, and a couple had been taken to the hospital but were likely going to come through. Micah didn't even ask for their names. It was easier to just think of them as numbers.

About four in the afternoon, in his room at the halfway house, Micah called Alex on his cell for an update. "I don't know what to do," he confessed. "I mean—if he won't talk to me, what should I be doing? Should I just take a bus to where you guys are and help out with that?" Not that Jake was currently too likely to be worrying about his business, but it wouldn't be right to let it fall down around him.

Alex was never quick to speak, but the pause seemed even longer than usual before he said, "Jake called me a couple hours ago. He said—he said you don't work for him anymore." His voice was gentle, but the words hit Micah like a blow.

"He said—what? Why?"

"He didn't give me a reason. He told me to see if I can find anyone else to help out, and said he'll pay Eduardo and me overtime. He—Micah, he didn't say anything about Austin *dying*. He said you and Austin wouldn't be at work anymore. That's all."

Jesus. That was—what the hell was it? Jake was a private guy, sure, but—that private? "Maybe he just didn't want to say the words," Micah tried. Strange that it had been so easy for Jake to say the words that made Micah unemployed, but that was a worry for another time. "Do you know if he's planning to be working tomorrow? Or—" or what? What was left to ask? "Did he sound okay? I mean, obviously he's not *okay*, but did he sound…?"

"I don't know. I'm sorry, Micah. I don't know anything more."

And that was all there was. Micah felt as if he'd been cut adrift. Losing Austin had been hard enough, but had he lost Jake as well?

It shouldn't matter, he told himself as he ended the call with Alex and went back to pacing. None of this should be about him, or even about him-and-Jake. This was about Jake, and what was best for him.

And maybe that meant Micah needed to stay away. A painful reminder, an annoying distraction, a useless acquaintance presuming he was more important than he really was. Some combination of those factors. It didn't really matter what the exact reason was, not when the result was the same. Jake didn't want Micah around, and Micah needed to respect that.

That's what he told himself all that night, and the next morning, too, when he woke up as early as usual and was forced to accept that he had nowhere to go. No job to do, no Austin to joke around with, no Jake to talk to and flirt with and daydream about. Well, the daydreaming he could still do, except he was pretty sure it wasn't a good idea to encourage fantasies that were seeming less and less likely to come true.

Free time was not good for him, though. Already his brain was whispering traitorous suggestions—didn't he deserve a reward after being so good for so long? Wasn't it totally understandable if he had a lapse in a situation like this, with a dead friend and no job and no boyfriend? Who could blame him?

He thought about calling Tristan, or Shane; they'd hang out with him, he knew, but they'd know why he'd called on them. They'd know he was still struggling, still weak, still someone to treat like a fragile invalid instead of a friend.

He threw himself out of bed and pulled on the first clothes he saw, the same ones he'd been wearing the day before. Just twenty-four hours earlier, he'd been doing the same thing, getting dressed in the same jeans and T-shirt, but he'd been buzzing with energy and anticipation, looking forward to another day with Jake.

Now? He tried to put some energy in his step as he headed down the stairs to the kitchen. Andrew was on duty, sitting at the table with a mug of coffee and a paperback just as he'd been the day before, and Micah was tempted to maintain the illusion that nothing had changed. He could pack his lunch, walk out the door, and Andrew would be no wiser.

But it would be a lie.

Goddamn it, this was too hard. Lying would be so easy, and telling the truth was so fucking hard. Micah didn't want to do this anymore. He didn't want to have to fight every damn day, didn't want to look forward to the rest of his life being a goddamn struggle just to—to what? To survive? To trudge along, alone? That was what he was clinging to when the alternative was floating away in peaceful bliss? Was he fucking stupid?

"You okay?" Andrew asked, and Micah realized he'd been standing still for too long, lost in his internal battle.

"Yeah. Sorry. I—" It felt like a test. Like a momentous decision. Micah knew what he should do. He should sit down, tell Andrew the whole thing, and then try to figure out a schedule for the day, meetings and exercise and a balanced fucking diet with plenty of greens and lean goddamn protein. He knew what he shouldn't do. He shouldn't hold it all in, try to figure it out on his own. He shouldn't try to be a hero; he should accept that everyone needs help sometimes and there's no shame in leaning on someone, especially someone who was actually being paid to provide support.

Yeah, it was a big choice. One path led back to addiction, and the other to the drudgery of being a recovering addict. Where was the joy? What was there to look forward to, with Jake pulling himself out of Micah's life? What point was there to any of it?

"I'm going to make my lunch," Micah said, and Andrew nodded, still watching him a little too closely.

The decision wasn't made; it was just postponed. That was the most Micah felt he could manage under the circumstances.

~*~*~*~

JAKE STARED AT THE PHOTOGRAPH. He'd wanted to see the body, wanted to not recognize it and prove that the hospital was wrong, the police were wrong, everyone was wrong. He'd wanted to pass this heartbreak along to some other family and make them mourn their lost son instead of he his lost brother. The hospital had suggested he see a photograph instead, and now he was glad of it. The picture was bad enough, Austin looking so pale, so... so damn dead.

He pushed himself to his feet and the woman, the same one from the day before, stood up with him. She hadn't wanted to show him the picture when he was alone, had tried to convince him to call someone, maybe his friend from the day before, to come and be with him. But Jake still couldn't stand to think about Micah, and he damn well didn't want to ask him to come along to something like this.

"I'm sorry for your loss," the woman said. She was too serene and Jake had to bite back the urge to yell at her, to demand—what? Demand that she let him keep living in denial? "This is obviously a difficult time, but we've found that grieving is a process, for most people, and there are steps that seem to make things easier as you go. The next step in this case is generally to set up some sort of memorial service, for family and friends to—"

"I don't want a damn funeral," Jake snarled. "He doesn't have any family, and his friends—his friends can go to hell! They're the ones who killed him."

She nodded slowly. "It's your choice, of course. But I'd urge you to give it some thought. It's generally valuable to have the chance to celebrate a life as well as to—"

"*Celebrate a life*? Are you kidding me? He's twenty years old and he's been shooting heroin since before he could drive. What the fuck do you want me to *celebrate* about that?"

"It's not about what *I* want," she said, and for the first time he could sense her cool, professional façade slipping a little. She wasn't angry, but she was maybe a little flustered, and seeing it made him savagely glad. This shouldn't be easy for her—it shouldn't be easy for anyone. But she had herself back under control when she said, "This is about you, and what will make it easiest for you to recover from your loss."

"A funeral won't make it easier," he said. "What are the other options?"

"A simple burial with no ceremony is certainly possible. Or cremation—"

He turned away quickly, his eyes finding the window, instinctively searching for escape. Austin hadn't been burned in the fire, but now she wanted to cremate him? Wanted to finish the job?

But what was the alternative? Stuffing him in a box in the ground and letting the worms eat him.

There was no right answer. Jake didn't want any of it; he just wanted his brother back. The soft, laughing baby he'd been, the mischievous little boy, the bold, challenging young man—all of that either burned or rotted, and there wasn't a damn thing Jake could do about any of it.

"Do what you want," he said, heading for the door. "Send me a bill. But no fucking funeral."

"We really can't make that decision for you," she said, but he didn't even slow down. He'd done this for his parents already, and it had been hard, but they'd been responsible adults with their wishes clearly indicated. They'd already bought their damn burial plots, and they'd had friends who'd had ideas for the funeral. It hadn't all been up to Jake.

This time, though? It was just him.

And Micah, if you wanted. Micah would help.

But it was better not to think about Micah. Better not to wonder if things would have been different if Jake hadn't let himself get distracted. Austin had left when Jake and Micah were making out on the street like a couple of horny teenagers; if Jake's head had been where it should have been, Austin wouldn't have gotten away and none of this would have happened. Jake wouldn't let himself take comfort, or, worse, pleasure, when Austin would never know either of those emotions again.

He found his way to the stairwell and kept moving. Austin was dead, and that meant Jake was alone. That was all he deserved.

~*~*~*~

MICAH FOUND FOUR DIFFERENT MEETINGS that day and spent a couple hours at the gym as well. Weights, cardio, anything to tire him out. He went home and showered and then lay on his bed, trying not to think about any of it. Trying not to be lonely, or worried, or sad. Just—numb. It would be so much easier if he could just be numb.

And of course he knew just the recipe to make that happen, but he tried to put the temptation out of his mind.

Not easy to do, of course, and when his phone rang he jerked it out of his pocket so quickly he fumbled and almost dropped it. An unfamiliar number, not Jake's, but that didn't mean too much.

"Hello?" Micah knew his voice sounded desperate, but he didn't care.

"Micah." A male voice, familiar, but Micah couldn't place it right away.

"Yeah?"

"It was a terrible thing, Micah. Really, just a senseless tragedy. How are you holding up?"

The recognition hit hard. "Moby? You're—Jesus Christ, you asshole, you're pretending to be *sorry* about this? Pretending to be upset when it was your fucking den he was in, your shit in his veins that kept him from getting out of the fire? How the fuck did you get my number?"

"Austin gave it to me. Sweet, young Austin—he gave me a lot of things, Micah. Did he ever tell you about that? Tell you how he could be almost as sweet as you?"

Micah's stomach tightened painfully. "You're a fucking pig, you know that?"

"Oh, Micah, don't be so dramatic. I'm a businessman. And sometimes a philanthropist. I truly do care about my community. My customers are family to me, and my family has been hurt."

"Yeah, sure. Look, I've got nothing to say to you. Don't call me ag—"

"We're having a memorial. Word on the street is that the brother wants a private burial. No ceremony. That what you've heard?"

Micah couldn't bring himself to admit he hadn't heard a damn thing. It seemed too early for Jake to have made that kind of decision, but it wasn't like Micah had any experience with the time frames on these things. "It's none of your business, Moby. Leave it alone."

"Austin wasn't the only one who died. This is a loss for a lot of people, and when people are grieving, they should be together. They should take comfort in each other."

Damn it, those words felt true, even coming from Moby's slimy mouth. People *should* be together. Jake might want to bury himself in a hole, but that didn't mean Micah had to do the same. "What kind of memorial? In a church or something?"

"We're still finalizing the venue. But we're planning it for tomorrow night. I'll have someone call you to let you know where we'll be."

Micah could hear the triumph hidden in Moby's voice, and he knew it wasn't misplaced. The memorial was an excuse; that was all. The important part was that Micah would be back with his old crowd, and everyone would be emotional, undisciplined. Maybe it would start with a toast to the fallen, just alcohol, and then they'd move on to some of the pills Micah used to take when there was nothing better available. Maybe that would be as far as it would go on the first night, but once he got started again, he knew it wouldn't be long before he was right back where he'd been. Floating above the world, no worries, no fears. No fucking loneliness.

Yeah, Moby's invitation was a trap. But Micah was pretty sure he was ready to be caught.

Chapter Sixteen

JAKE HAD ERASED MICAH'S MESSAGES from his phone, both texts and voice mails. He hadn't wanted to see them, hear them, think about them.

But lying there on Austin's bed that afternoon, he started to wonder whether Austin had done the same thing with the messages he'd received. Had he erased them, deleting all record that he had people who cared about him, and were worried about him? Was Jake doing the same stupid shit Austin had done?

No. Because Austin was a fucking junkie, his brain fried with chemicals, his judgement totally impaired. He'd been running away from people who were trying to help him, and Jake—well, okay, maybe Micah was *trying* to help, but that didn't mean he *could* help.

Still, Jake hadn't handled it well. He pulled out his phone and typed: *Sorry I didn't get back to you. I'm fine.*

He hit send. It wasn't a great message, but it was something.

A few moments later his phone buzzed and he lifted it to read: *You're for sure fine? You're handling this okay?*

I'm fine, he replied.

Then, from Micah, *Okay, then. If you're fine—go fuck yourself, you selfish asshole.*

Jake stared at the screen. He wanted to deny, explain, ask for forgiveness, but he managed to keep his hands still. This was a clean break. This was what he'd wanted. It was too bad that Micah was angry—*too bad he has such a damn good reason to be angry*—but maybe that was easier. Jake could be the asshole, here. He had to be the asshole; it was the only way to keep himself safe. And to not betray Austin's memory. And—something else, he was pretty sure. There'd been more reasons why it was a terrible idea for him to spend any more time with Micah.

And it was good that the break was clean, because Jake couldn't let his weakness take him into the path of danger. Just the short text conversation—Micah's gentle concern, and then his justifiable anger—had been enough to remind Jake of what he was losing. It was good that he didn't have the chance to go back on his decision, because he wasn't really sure he'd have the strength to stand up to the temptation of running back to Micah.

~*~*~*~

MICAH WAS JITTERY AND NERVOUS. He was almost dancing with anticipation, the same way he used to be when he knew he was about to spend time with Jake.

He'd left the halfway house just after dinner, which meant he only had a couple hours before his still-extra-early curfew, but he wasn't worried about that. The way he was going, a missed curfew was going to be the absolute least of his violations.

A bus and then a bit of walking and he was at the park where Moby had told him to be. In the old neighborhood, but not somewhere Micah had ever spent much time. Now, in the twilight, the scuffed-up grass and ragged trees seemed almost pleasant. He thought about trying to spend more time there, once he started hanging out in the area again, but then he remembered he wouldn't give a shit where he was, once he was using.

He almost turned around. There was a crowd gathering, but none of them had seen him yet, and he could still escape. He could smarten the fuck up and go back to the support of the half-way house. Go back to—to what else? What else was waiting for him other than that half-way existence, stuck between a bleak past and a bleak future? He couldn't impose himself on his friends, his family didn't trust him, Jake didn't want him—fuck it. If staying straight meant feeling this miserable, this self-pitying, this frustrated and angry, then he'd rather be using.

He took a few more steps and a familiar body disengaged itself from the gathered mass. "Micah," Moby said, fond and welcoming. Damn, it was nice that *someone* wanted Micah around, even if it was someone as sleazy as Moby. "It's good to see you. You're looking—" Moby swept his possessive gaze up and down Micah's body. "Robust? You've been working out, have you?"

Micah shrugged. He didn't really want to have this conversation. He didn't want to have *any* conversation. But he couldn't quite bring himself to ask for junk; it would be so much easier if he could blame Moby for this instead of blaming himself. So he waited, and when Moby oozed closer and wrapped an arm around his shoulders, he didn't pull away.

"It's good that you're here. At a time like this, we need to stand together. We need to mourn our lost, but we also need to make it clear we aren't getting pushed around."

What? There was something more in that little speech, something that seemed to be—it seemed to be about an actual issue, not just a way to persuade Micah to accept the narcotics he so desperately wanted.

He could smell the smoke on Moby's clothes, could practically sense the little packets glowing in the man's pockets, and most of him wanted to just focus on that and let the rest go. But there was still enough curiosity living somewhere deep in his brain to make him ask, "What are you talking about? Who's getting pushed around?"

Moby's arm lifted as the man spun around to look Micah in the face. "*We* are! The people who've lived in this neighborhood for years. The ones who aren't quite clean enough, not quite *rich* enough for the new arrivals."

And now that he was started, Micah kind of wanted to keep the conversation going. Anything to delay the inevitable decision, even if he'd already made it. "Who's pushing us around? The cops? They always have, man."

"The fucking *cops* didn't burn down my flop," Moby retorted. Then he frowned. "I'm not saying they give a shit—we all know better than to expect any protection from those bastards. But they're not the ones trying to tidy this place up, trying to make it nice and pretty so they can turn a goddamn profit on their real estate investments."

Micah was talking to his pusher about fucking *real estate investments*? Was that what was happening? He fought back through the words, trying to make sense of them. "Someone burned the flop down? I figured someone just dropped a cigarette in the wrong place."

"And then ran down the stairs yelling, 'Your shithole's on fire, motherfuckers'?"

Well, it wasn't completely out of the question, really—it wasn't like Moby's clientele were known for their extreme mental stability.

But then Moby shook his head and added, "I had people working there—people who weren't fucked up. They could have put out a mattress fire. They said they smelled gasoline right before the assholes started yelling and by the time they got upstairs the fire was out of control."

"Why'd the assholes yell? They're arsonists who don't want to hurt anyone? Is that a thing?"

"They didn't give a shit if they hurt anyone. But they wanted me to know. They wanted *everyone* to know. It's not safe to be in this neighborhood anymore, not unless you're one of the beautiful people. The *rich* beautiful people."

It sounded like paranoia, but Moby, for all his many faults, generally had a fairly tight grip on reality. So Micah asked, "There's been other stuff? Not just this one thing?"

A grim nod. "Nothing else this big, obviously. But, yeah, we've been getting harassed way more often—mostly just someone calling the cops, even at times when nobody was bothering anyone and there was no damn reason to get the shitheads involved. But more obvious stuff, too. Joey Turner—you know Joey? Little Joey, works for me as a runner? He got roughed up the other day, two goons stepping out of a car, grabbing him, slapping him around and then telling him to tell his boss to find a new neighborhood. That kind of shit. We can't stand for it."

Micah nodded slowly. Gentrification. The proletariat being displaced by the bourgeoisie. The endless economic cycle, the Haves stepping all over the Have-Nots in their quest to Have More. It was nothing new, but that didn't make it right.

Moby's rebellious fire seemed to have eased, though, and he was back to his appraising looks at Micah. Moby pulled a silver flask out of his jacket pocket and then, with a little showman's flourish, produced a round green pill in his other palm. Alcohol and oxy, just as Micah had predicted. Yeah, he knew this dance, just like he knew the steps of fucking economic oppression Moby'd been outlining.

The pill, washed down with whatever was in the flask? That was the easy way. But that option wasn't going anywhere. There would always be ways to turn his brain off. Right then, he figured, he needed to keep it turned on. There was work to be done, and he could be part of doing it.

He stepped backward, away from Moby's genuine surprise and manufactured hurt, and said, "I have to do something. I'll—I don't know, maybe I'll be back."

Maybe he would.

But he felt surprisingly strong as he strode out of the park, and when he dialed his phone and heard the familiar voice answer, it wasn't even all that hard to say, "It's Micah. I need your help."

And he got the only answer he could ever expect in return. "Where are you?" Tristan asked. "What do you need me to do?"

~*~*~*~

JAKE WENT BACK TO WORK THE next day. He avoided Alex and Eduardo's concern, tried not to think about the gaping holes where Austin and Micah should have been, and bought a bottle of Jack Daniels on the way home.

He drank it in Austin's room, sitting cross-legged on the bed, then sprawling on the floor, staring at the ceiling, trying to figure out where it had all gone wrong. There were just too many options, though.

He got the urge to tidy when he was already far too drunk to be effective, but continued anyway. He jammed Austin's clothes into clear plastic garbage bags to go—he didn't care where. Just way. He and Austin were close enough to the same size that the clothes would have integrated seamlessly into Jake's own wardrobe; he actually found a couple of his own shirts mixed in with Austin's, but bagged them up anyway. Not many books, but some mementos, stupid ribbons from grade school sports days and a model of the *Enterprise* the boys had fought over when they were kids, and then, in an old cookie tin, a lighter, a spoon, a syringe, all the little tools that made a junkie's life easier: Austin's kit.

Or maybe his spare, since Austin had probably had a kit with him when he'd been wherever he'd gone. Unless the little shithead had been so reckless that he was sharing needles? Goddamnit, Austin—but the irritation melted away as soon as Jake remembered that there was no Austin to be mad at, anymore. Whatever stupidity he'd committed in his last days, there was no point worrying about it. He'd died of smoke inhalation, not AIDS or Hep C.

Jake lurched to his feet, leaving the bottle behind but holding onto the metal box. He stumbled to the front hall closet and burrowed through the shoes and boots until he found the old tool box his not-that-handy father had kept around the house for emergencies. Not too well equipped, but it had what Jake needed.

He flipped the lid open, poked through the contents for the hammer, then pulled his hand back and refastened the lid, hammer still inside. He set Austin's kit on the tile floor, lifted the tool box in both hands and brought it down hard, smashing the end of it into the kit like a pile driver. The box collapsed, but Jake kept smashing, his new tool so much better than the hammer would have been. He could hear the tools flying around inside and their noise added to the satisfaction. Destruction wasn't quiet and it wasn't tidy and that was just fine with him.

He smashed until the cookie tin was completely flat, with bits of it skittered off to distant corners of the now-chipped tile hallway, and only then noticed the red splashes accenting his art work. He flexed his hands and felt the pull on his right palm—he must have sliced it on some rough corner of metal. He turned it over and stared at the crimson mess, and had to resist the urge to stretch the edges of the wound open to make it bleed more.

Austin was gone. Jake was alone. And he *wanted* to bleed.

But his practical side took over pretty quickly and he stumbled his way into the kitchen to clean up and find bandages. On his way, he saw his phone on the table. No texts, no messages. Because he'd covered all his business before he went home for the day, and outside of business there was no one left to call him. He'd taken care of that.

Yeah, he wanted to bleed. But it sure sucked to have to bleed alone.

Chapter Seventeen

"Do we really give a shit if Moby gets pushed out of the neighborhood?" It was Trey who asked the question, but everyone else in Tristan's living room seemed just as interested in hearing an answer. "He's a fucking dealer, and—sorry, man, but most of the people he's dealing to aren't great neighbors. Wouldn't things be better if he moved on?"

"We care if people get hurt during the pushing," Micah said firmly. The night before, after leaving Moby's memorial, he'd met up with Tristan and they'd talked, mostly about ways to help Micah stay clean. Micah had known Tristan would be eager to be part of the solution, but he'd been surprised how painless it had been to accept the help. Asking had been hard, but after that? He remembered telling Jake that Micah's friends were his higher power, and he realized that this was what he'd been missing. He'd named them accurately, but he hadn't surrendered his pride to them. Micah trying to recover without his friends made as much sense as a religious addict trying to recover without his god. And asking his friends for help? It should come as naturally to him as praying would come to someone else. He had to work on that. He *planned* to work on that.

But in the meantime? He'd slept well and woken up with a new sense of purpose, and he'd gone over to Tristan's to recruit allies to the cause. "We care because it won't just be Moby who gets pushed out, either. If rich people are moving in and want to fancy up this neighborhood, you think they're going to want any of us around? You think they're going to want the people who get help for themselves and their pets at the shelter? Fuck, you think they're going to want the Nguyens at their little grocery store when they could have a nice, new Whole Foods or some shit like that? How long's it going to be until the landlords start jacking rents up so regular people can't afford to live here anymore?" He looked over at Tristan and got a supportive nod in return.

But Trey wasn't as easily swayed. "Do we even know any of this is true? It's not like Moby's the most reliable source of information. I'm not saying he wouldn't *know* stuff, but why the hell would he bother telling you the truth about anything? You know what he wants from you, Micah, and this ain't it. Junkies don't fight the power, they just try to get away from it."

"Tristan asked me to look into it," Simon said, and everyone waited for his verdict. He'd been new to the group when Micah had last been part of things, but clearly he'd earned a place of respect sometime since. "It seems authentic. There have been a number of significant real estate transactions in the past couple of years, and there are permits in place for a variety of renovations, demolitions, and new constructions." He looked at Micah as he added, "The building that burned down the other evening was under review; a demolition permit had been requested but there was a concern about possible heritage elements to the architecture. That is obviously no longer a concern and demolition will now be mandatory rather than forbidden."

"Someone's got to catch that, though, right?" Noah. Innocent and optimistic, still believing the system worked.

Shane sounded almost protective as he explained, "If there's enough money, it doesn't matter if they catch it."

"Then the heritage designation wouldn't have been a problem either!" Noah sounded triumphant.

"Not a long-term problem," Simon agreed. "Merely an annoyance. But now the annoyance is removed."

"And they don't care that people died?" Noah asked.

"Junkies." Simon's voice was cold, but he pressed his lips together in a grimace before he added, "They wouldn't consider that a significant loss, I'm afraid."

"So what are we supposed to do?" Trey demanded. "I see why we should care—I bet none of us are on their list of desirables either, right? But they're killing people? They're rich and powerful, and we're—" He looked around the room, then snorted, clearly not feeling the need to make it any more clear what they were. He turned to Micah. "You seriously think we can fight back against something like that?"

"Do I think we can fight?" Micah nodded. "Yeah. I think we can fight. Do I think we can win? I have no idea. But—I know I'm in a different situation than you guys. I know you're starting to build your lives and make things better for yourselves and you've got stuff to lose. I don't. So I'm not expecting any of you to risk anything you've earned. But I—" It was scary to be this honest, but kind of liberating as well. He was pretty sure his counsellors back at the rehab facility would have been really proud of him when he said, "I need to believe in something. I can't—I *won't*—walk around as if things don't matter. If I'm going to live in a little cocoon, not letting myself feel anything or care about anything, I might as well go back on the shit. So, I think this is what I'm going to care about." *Since Jake, the asshole, took himself out of running for that role.* "But that doesn't mean anyone else should care about it. I just wanted to talk to you all about it and see what you thought."

"What does 'caring about it' mean?" Shane asked. He had one hand on Noah's shoulder as if ready to pull his boyfriend back out of any sort of danger. Yeah. Shane on his own would charge into any fight headfirst. Shane with Noah? A different animal. "What exactly are you planning to do?"

"I don't really know." Micah looked around the room at the familiar faces. They seemed interested, at least, and even Trey wasn't arguing too much, so they were more or less on his side. But how far they'd be willing to go on that side? And how far he had any right to encourage them to go? He had less certainty about that.

"Start with fact-finding," Simon said. He made the suggestion sound as obvious as the idea of coming inside out of the rain. "I can help you with that. We need to know what's happening, how fast it's happening, and who's already opposing it. We can't imagine we're the first people to have conversations like this, so we need to network with the others and coordinate our efforts."

"The media," Tristan said, clearly building on Simon's plan. "There are people whose whole job is to find stories like this and publicize them. We could find some of the more respectable people from the neighborhood—people with little kids, working for minimum wage who can't afford to live anywhere else and wouldn't be able to afford higher rent. Make it about them."

"And we need to contact the government," Noah said. It was nice to see him being confident in his own ideas even when the others didn't agree with him. "Maybe it won't work, but we need to at least say that we *tried*. If someone from the mayor's office tries to say they had no idea this was going on, we need to be able to say that's not true, we told you about it on this date and reminded you about it this time and that time. We should at least not make it *easy* for them to ignore us."

"Politicians," Becky agreed. "The ones not in office are always trying to make the ones *in* office look bad, right? So we can give them some ammunition, if we have to. Tell them how we're being ignored—if we are."

"People are going to be scared," Trey put in. "Three people have already died, whether it was on purpose or not. If these developers or whoever are burning buildings down? That's something people are going to worry about. It might scare them out of speaking up."

Shane stood up, just as Micah had known he would, and gave Trey a hard stare. "So we give them reasons to feel safe and protected." He didn't actually flex his muscles, but he didn't really need to, not when he was built like he was.

"We can't out-thug these guys," Tristan protested. "I mean, it won't hurt to have a show of strength, for sure, but I think the real security is going to come from numbers. No one's going to want to stand up alone, but if we can get the whole community involved? They can't burn out the whole neighborhood, not without getting way more attention than they could handle. We need a meeting. We need to make this big."

"Information first," Simon said. "But then—yes. A meeting." He looked over at Micah. "We won't get too much sympathy for the junkies who died, not in the abstract. But if we can personalize them? If we can show that they were from good families and just went wrong, but that their families still miss them?" He paused, clearly waiting for Micah to volunteer something, but when he got no reaction he said, "Your friend. Jake. He should be part of this. A small businessman, working hard for his American Dream, trying to take care of his brother? And all his dreams torn apart with—"

"Okay," Tristan said quickly. "Good general idea, but let's not belabor the point."

"I'm not really in touch with Jake anymore," Micah said, in case anyone in the room hadn't figured that out. "But I can give you his number if you want. You can see if he's interested."

"He'd be valuable," Tristan said softly. "That makes sense to me. But if you're not okay with it—"

"I'm fine. We broke up, that's all. He didn't beat me up or anything. And I see what you're saying. If someone didn't know Austin, they wouldn't really understand why they should care. People think junkies are suicidal anyway, right, or at least don't value their own lives? So hearing Jake talk would help make people care. Sure."

"We should wait until we have something planned, and some more facts. Then I'll contact him," Simon said.

The group went on with their planning, enthusiasm growing with each new idea. Micah let himself sit back a little and watch. This was his new thing to care about, his new reason to not give up and start using again. It wasn't as—pure? As optimistic, maybe, as his feelings for Jake had been. But this was more under Micah's control. Working for social justice wasn't something that could just stop returning his phone calls. There would be victories and defeats, he was sure, but a belief in the possibility of a better world? That wasn't something anyone could take from him. It was his.

No, it wouldn't keep him warm at night or make his stomach flip with just a smile. But it wouldn't abandon him when he needed it most, either, so—he'd take it. It wasn't like he had another choice.

~*~*~*~

JAKE FOUND HIMSELF SETTLING INTO a new routine. Wake up early; make only enough coffee for himself while determinedly not thinking about anyone else he might ever have made coffee for; then drive to work, alone, blaring talk radio as loud as he could stand it to cover the absences in the truck; work hard, no conversation not related to the job, and stay on site as long as there was work to be done; then go home, drink too much, and fall asleep, often in Austin's bed.

He made it past the one-week anniversary of the fire with a little extra alcohol, enough that he had to add hovering-over-the-toilet-waiting-to-puke to his morning routine. At least he had enough sense not to drink the night after that, but his abstinence left him with no way to shut off his brain, no way to ignore his loneliness.

No way to pretend he didn't want to call Micah. It could be an apology—Micah deserved at least that, if not a hell of a lot more. Jake *had* been a selfish asshole. But Micah was an understanding guy, and if Jake asked for forgiveness, Micah would give it to him. He was pretty sure of that.

But then what? Forgiving Jake wasn't the same as wanting to go back to—well, no. There was no going back to the way things were. No more messing around while Austin blasted them with stupid songs, no more listening quietly while Austin and Micah joked in the truck on the way to work in the morning. It was all gone, and there was no point pretending it wasn't.

But there was also no point in pretending Jake was just missing one person when really he was missing two.

He made it through the rest of the week with only a few drinks a night—enough to take the edge off, but not enough to make him pathetic. On Saturday he worked, trying to stay caught up on the work his diminished crew wasn't getting done and trying to keep himself too busy to realize how lonely he was.

His phone rang mid-afternoon, as he was pulling a few stray weeds out of a well-mulched flower bed, and he glanced down to see an unfamiliar number. Probably a customer—nobody else really called him anymore.

But when he answered, he heard, "It's Simon Yeung, Jake. We met through Micah?"

And Jake knew it, deep in his core. This was the call, the one he'd been trying to avoid, the *pain* he'd been trying to avoid. Simon was calling to tell him Micah was dead, too. The drugs had caught him, just like they inevitably caught everybody, destroyed everything they came into contact with. Micah. God, no. Not Micah, too.

Simon apparently got tired of waiting for an acknowledgement and said, "I have some information about the fire that caused your brother's death. I think it's something you should hear."

Jake couldn't switch direction that quickly, not when he was so sure, so completely weighed down with the inevitability of his grief. "Micah?" he managed.

"Micah? He's—well, yes, he's involved in all this. But you don't have to see him if that would be awkward for you. You don't have to do anything, of course. But I think you'll want to at least hear what we have to say."

Jake was already on his knees, luckily, but he still felt weak, almost dizzy with relief. Micah was okay. He was involved in—something, something to do with the fire? But he was okay. "Can we go back to the start?" he managed. "Sorry, I was distracted. You're calling because why?"

"Because we have reason to believe the fire that caused your brother's death wasn't an accident. We see it as part of a larger pattern of intimidation, and we're trying to do something about it."

"Intimidation? What, like a war between drug lords or something?"

"I wish it was that simple. Do you have time to meet me in person? I'm afraid I don't have a car, but I can take transit to you, if you give me a location. I have some documents you should see."

"I can come to you." Maybe it was stupid, like picking at a scab, but if Jake was honest he'd have to admit that there really wasn't any healing going on anyway. There was no scab to pick, just the same bleeding wound. And maybe—no. He couldn't let himself start thinking about Micah. It had been a false alarm this time, but that didn't mean the problem was solved; it didn't mean Micah was safe. So Jake would meet with Simon and hear what he had to say about Austin's death. But that was all. That was all he was brave enough to consider.

Chapter Eighteen

IT WAS HAPPENING WAY TOO FAST. Micah had known Simon was going to call Jake, and he'd known they'd be talking about a meeting. He'd felt strangely uncomfortable about the whole idea, so he'd left Tristan's apartment while Simon was making the call, going to pick up more snacks at the local grocery store. He'd come back, the string handles of Tristan's cloth grocery bags biting into his palms, and heard that Jake was on his way over and would arrive any minute. Yeah, that was way too fast.

Maybe he should just run away. Tristan wouldn't judge him, and the others? Well, they might, a little, but he could handle that. They'd been getting steadily more comfortable around him, less careful, and part of being less careful was that they might poke at him a little if they found a weakness. Nothing cruel, more—investigatory. Evaluative. It was like he was a new member of the group, almost, and they were trying to figure him out. It wouldn't be so bad if they figured out he was weird about an ex.

But, no. Fuck it. Fuck Jake—why should Micah make things easy on him? Well, okay, maybe because he'd just lost his brother, but that was something separate. Micah wouldn't bug him about *that*, but he wouldn't spare him from an awkward encounter, either.

So he stood in the little kitchen and poured pretzels into bowls, mixed up some of the ranch dip that everyone loved so much, and tried to think calming thoughts. This wasn't about Jake, it was about the neighborhood. About Austin. About every person in the world who was just fighting to find a place to stand, and who kept getting kicked back down by the powers that needed to keep them off balance. It was Steinbeck, Springsteen, Bernie Sanders, Malcolm X and Noam Chomsky, all the theory Micah had absorbed over the years, and it was playing out right there in Tristan's living room.

Well, that didn't really count as calming thoughts, but at least it was channeling his nerves in a more productive direction.

He took a trip to the living room, dropped off the pretzel bowls, and went back to the kitchen for the dip. He was working on carrying four dishes when the buzzer sounded and he almost dropped the whole bundle to the floor. "Noam would not be impressed," he muttered to himself. "And Tom Joad never got butterfingers because he was worried about seeing some guy he fucked *one time*."

"I don't think Tom Joad fucked guys at all," Tristan offered from far closer than he should have been. "I guess he was in prison for quite a while, so—maybe. But I think you'd be going beyond the text to make that argument."

"I bet Noam has," Micah retorted, trying to get into the spirit of their banter. "Intellectual curiosity, right? Him and Foucault, after the debate? Burning off a little tension?"

"Oh, yeah," Tristan agreed. "They banged, no doubt."

"Foucault topped. All about the power dynamics, right?"

"All about the power, for sure. But I can see him as a power bottom. Subverting and challenging norms, or whatever."

It was probably a good thing that the knock on the door came then, because Micah was about to get pretty involved in the debate about the various sexual positions and roles two of his heroes might have explored with each other. And while it was an excellent distraction, it wasn't where his brain needed to be right then.

"Stay cool," Tristan said as Simon headed for the apartment door. "This is about something bigger than you guys, right?"

"Right," Micah said, but he didn't like the way his own voice sounded and hurried to drop off the bowls of dip, then make it back to the kitchen before Jake made it down the narrow hallway into the main room.

The kitchen was more of a nook, unfortunately, not a separate room, so Micah couldn't really hide too well. He pulled the fridge door open and jammed his head most of the way into the cool interior; hopefully anyone looking at him would think he was really searching for some lost condiment, not hiding. Hell, hopefully at least one person who might be looking at him would be noticing his fine ass all perked up in the air as he bent over and would be regretting the stupidity of letting something like that walk out his door.

Micah took a deep breath of cool air and pulled his head out of the fridge. He glanced toward the living room and found that no one was even looking in his direction.

Jesus, of course they weren't. The cool from the fridge did nothing to lessen the heat of shame that flushed Micah's cheeks. Jake was there to learn more about the fire that had killed his baby brother, not to ogle some old trick. It was time to grow the fuck up and get back on track.

He grabbed a few bottles of beer from the fridge—the gang had started drinking around him not long after he'd come back into the group—and a can of Coke for himself, then wandered into the living room, trying to look casual, interested only in the important issues being discussed. Oh, was Jake there? Tight half-smile, which was more than the fucker deserved, and the offer of a beer. Jake took the bottle with barely a look in Micah's direction. That was fine. That was good. They were there to talk about more important stuff. Micah found homes for the other two bottles and sank onto the floor near Tristan's feet. It was always comforting to be close to Tristan.

He listened quietly to Simon's recitation of the facts they'd uncovered, and wasn't surprised by any of Jake's questions. Had they spoken to the police? Yes, and Noah gave a rundown on that—investigation ongoing, but no one seemed too optimistic. Had they confirmed all the theories? Well, that was time for

Simon's lists and notes and contacts—the guy was pretty damn good at networking and keeping things organized. Did they have names? Tristan was the one who gently broke the news that most of the real estate had been bought by shell corporations or numbered companies or other quasi-anonymous bodies. Individual names could be found, if Simon worked hard enough, but there was no real reason to believe that the multiple owners of any of the corporations involved had first hand knowledge of what was going on. It was more likely that this was a team of overzealous employees doing whatever they needed to in order to ensure the returns their overlords demanded.

"So what's the point of any of this?" Jake demanded, and as his eyes swept the room they met Micah's for the first time. A short, painful thrill of recognition, and then Jake's eyes kept moving, searching for something more. "What are we supposed to actually *do* about it?"

"About Austin?" Tristan asked gently. "Maybe nothing. I don't—we're not the police. I can't say if anyone's ever going to be arrested for that, if anyone will ever stand trial for what they did to him. We want that to happen, but—I honestly don't know if it ever will."

"But we can keep them from getting what they want," Micah said. He hadn't planned to speak, but now that he'd started, it was easy to continue. It was even easy to look at Jake as he did it and to see not an ex-lover but an ex-brother, someone who'd lost his only remaining family and was struggling to find his way past it. "That's what we're hoping to do. We can't do anything for Austin, but we can try to expose these assholes for what they are, and try to protect the rest of the neighborhood from them. We might not be able to *prove* anything, but if we can at least make them realize we're watching? If we can make them realize that *other people* are watching, and that whatever they do here is going to be noticed? Then at least they won't get what they wanted from all this. There's nothing we can do to bring Austin back, and probably nothing we can do to get justice for his death. But we can at least try to make sure that his killers don't *benefit* from his death. You know? Because—because *fuck them*. That's what it comes down to, in the end."

"Fuck them," Trey echoed. It was a sentiment he was always ready to espouse. But quiet, serious Noah was nodding too, and his "fuck them" came at the same time as Shane's. Micah was vaguely aware of the others joining in, but they weren't who he was focused on. They'd all been part of this from the start, they were all believers, and—well, they weren't Jake. Who was looking at Micah as if trying to read his soul, as if trying to cut past all the bullshit and fear and anger that was holding them apart, trying to see the real Micah he'd known before it all went to hell.

And when Jake nodded, Micah felt as though his whole body was agreeing right along with him. "Fuck them," Jake said, not taking his gaze from Micah's.

Then he rose abruptly to his feet. "Bathroom. I'll be right back."

Micah wanted to stop him, or chase after him, but he'd done that before and it hadn't been too damn effective. So he just sat there, telling his body, his brain, his damn heart to calm down. Whatever had just happened had been about Jake and Austin, or Jake and justice, or Jake and peer pressure. It hadn't been about Jake and Micah because there *was* no Jake and Micah.

And Micah damn well needed to remember that.

~*~*~*~

JESUS CHRIST, MICAH WAS BURNED into Jake's soul. It was melodramatic, he knew, but the passion when he'd spoken, the simple truths and honesty that somehow didn't turn into pessimism and doubt? It was magic; it had to be. Micah was some sort of wizard, enchanting Jake into—

Well, no, okay, *that* was melodramatic. Micah wasn't a wizard, he was just a guy who believed in something. He was brave enough to care, strong enough to keep fighting even when it would be so much easier to just give up. He was an inspiration, maybe, but not magic.

That was what Jake tried to tell himself as he sat there in the apartment, listening to the others making all their plans. They were *all* brave enough to care, and from what little he'd heard about their pasts, it wasn't because they were naïve or because things had always been easy for them so they didn't understand what they were up against.

"It's going to be tricky for a while," Shane was saying, his voice slow and rumbling. "If it seems like we're picking up steam but haven't actually got a big crowd yet? That's when it'll be most dangerous. The people behind this will want to shut us up any way they can." His eyes scanned the room as if looking for disagreement. Apparently seeing none, he continued. "So once we go public with this—as soon as the posters go up, as soon as the public meeting is announced—no one goes anywhere alone. Two at least, three would be better. Always have a cell phone, and if things start to feel even a little bit off, you give me or Trey a call and find somewhere with lots of people to hang out until we can get to you."

Noah looked like he was about to say something but managed to keep quiet. Jake could sympathize. It wasn't easy to see someone you loved putting himself in danger. At least Shane had a good reason for the risks he was offering to take; he wasn't shooting poison into his veins for *fun*.

The planning continued, and Jake let himself relax and watch it all happen. Sure, he spent a bit more time sneaking looks at Micah than he should have, but he didn't get caught at it, and managed to absorb quite a bit of good information from the others. When Micah went to the kitchen to refill snack bowls, Jake wanted to follow him, but resisted the temptation. There was nothing to say, really, was there?

As the meeting wrapped up, Simon ran through a list of tasks assigned to everyone. When he got to Jake, he raised a querying eyebrow. "I think it would be great if you could speak at the public meeting. We want to humanize the lives lost, and you're our best way to make that happen. Do you feel as if you'll be able to do that?"

No! To stand in front of people and confess to his failure? To admit he hadn't been able to keep his baby brother safe? To try to explain to strangers how full of life Austin had been, how much potential he'd had if he'd only been able to get past this one stupid issue? It was impossible. But Jake nodded anyway. "I'm not good at public speaking. But I could say something, I guess."

"And you have more standing to push with the authorities, as well," Simon continued. "I'd be happy to go with you, if you like, but I think you should contact the police and ask them for an update on the investigation. They won't give you any big secrets, but they'll tell you more than they'll tell us. And it's good for them to know that people are watching and expecting answers. It's too easy to sweep these sorts of deaths under the rug when there's no family pushing for resolution."

Jake nodded. He didn't want to do any of this, but he owed it to Austin. And he owed it to Micah as well.

The meeting broke up shortly after and Jake followed Trey and one of the girls, Becky, out of the building. They were at the sidewalk when Trey spun quickly toward him; Becky didn't seem surprised by the move. "You fucked up with Micah," Trey said. Not a question, just a statement of fact. "They say no dating for a long time after rehab, and they say it because of just this sort of shit."

Jake blinked. It wasn't like he was unaware of the rule. "We took a chance," he said.

But Trey shook his head. "*Micah* took the fucking chance. You just let him." He glanced at Becky, maybe looking for permission to continue, and apparently got it. "He almost went back, you know. Almost used again. He's not talking about it and neither is Tristan, but we all know it happened. And it needs to *not happen again.* So if you're going to be part of this? You need to stay the fuck away from him."

"I haven't—"

"You were staring at him like he was the second coming of Jesus," Becky said. Apparently Jake hadn't been quite as subtle as he'd thought. "The fucking googly eyes of regret. And that's not cool. He's not your toy, to pick up and play with when you feel like it and then drop it when you get bored."

"My brother died," Jake said. He was willing to get yelled at for a lot of stuff, but not for this. "I didn't *get bored.* I got—" *Scared.* That was the truth, but he didn't think he was going to share it with these two.

And as they were gearing up for whatever their next accusation was going to be, the door to the building swung open and they all turned to see Micah striding toward them. He was in bare feet, clearly hurrying, and Jake supposed he must have been looking out the apartment window and seen what was happening.

"Leave him alone," Micah said firmly to Trey and Becky. "Whatever you're doing, I appreciate the thought, but I don't need a fucking intervention—not with this. I made my own choices and none of it's his responsibility."

"You *do* need an intervention," Trey insisted. "Or at least protection. We invited this guy into the group because he'll be useful, but that doesn't mean you have to put up with—"

"There's nothing to put up with. He didn't do anything wrong." He frowned at Jake. "*Today*. You didn't do anything wrong *today*."

"And I'm sorry for what I did before. Or at least—for *how* I did it. That was shitty, and I'm sorry."

Trey's snort and Becky's scowl made it clear how unimpressed they were with this, but Micah nodded and he was the one who mattered. "Yeah, it was shitty," he agreed. "But it was a tough time for you. I get that."

"Okay, then," Trey said, stepping between them with his wide shoulders. "That's all settled." He gave Jake a cold stare and said, "So you can go now."

Jake thought about arguing, but didn't really have anything to say. Micah seemed to have mostly forgiven him, and that was all he wanted, really. Wasn't it?

Chapter Nineteen

MICAH LAY IN BED THAT NIGHT, listening to the sounds of his housemates getting ready for sleep, and let himself dream. Just a little. Trey and Becky might think they had to protect him, but they really didn't. He wasn't stupid enough to start thinking he was anyone he wasn't, or that he was heading for some sort of healthy, happy romance. That wasn't for him; he'd learned his lesson.

But he could have *something*, couldn't he? Even just being in the same room as Jake, once the nerves had faded, had been worth daydreaming about. His strong hands, the way he leaned forward when he was listening to someone, his green eyes intent and focused—all familiar, but still special.

Micah's phone rang and when he looked down at the screen he was somehow not at all surprised to see the name on the display. He lifted the phone and said, "I was just thinking about you."

"Thinking about ways to kill me?" Jake asked.

"No. I told you, I get it. I mean—yeah, I was pissed off. Not that you dumped me, or even that you fired me, just—you really scared me. You should have called me back."

"Yeah. And I shouldn't have fired you, either. That wasn't fair."

"Well, if you'd dumped me, I think I would have quit anyway, really. It would have been pretty awkward working together after that." And Micah waited, apparently *not* smart enough to keep himself from hoping. He waited for Jake to say he shouldn't have dumped him, either. But the words didn't come.

Instead, Jake said, "Would it still be awkward? I totally understand if you don't want to work with me anymore. I know I screwed that up. But you were doing a great job. If you wanted to come back, that'd be great."

Micah fought to hang on to his self-control. He wasn't stupid. He wasn't stupid. "What changed? You didn't want to work with me and now you do? Why? What's different?"

There was no immediate answer, which was just as well because it gave Micah a chance to refine his thoughts. "I mean, why'd you dump me in the first place? You fired me because you dumped me, so—why'd you dump me?"

Of course, as soon as he asked the question he wanted to retract it. Did he really want to hear Jake spell it out? Couldn't he just leave well enough alone?

And apparently Jake was about as unenthusiastic as Micah, because it took him a long time to answer. Just as Micah was about to say it didn't matter, though, Jake said, "Mostly it was stupid. I was—you know. I wasn't thinking too well. The only part that really still makes sense is—" He paused, and Micah wished they were in the same room for this conversation. He wanted to be able to see Jake's face to know whether he was searching for the words that would best explain, or the words that would hurt least. "I guess the only part that still makes sense is I just don't think I'm strong enough to do it again. I mean, I've been through this before. I've loved a junkie, and—I just don't think I can do that again."

Micah nodded, then realized it wasn't going to transmit too well through the phone line. "Yeah," he said. "I—yeah. I get it."

"You do? You don't think I'm being unfair or something? Like, I'm blaming you for Austin's mistakes?"

"I've got enough mistakes of my own. I don't need to borrow any of Austin's." Micah felt suddenly tired, as if he could set the phone down and sink into his pillow and sleep for—forever, maybe.

"But you're getting past yours. You're *doing it*. You're working the program even if you don't like it, you're staying strong—"

"Jesus, Jake, what are you arguing for? I'm letting you off the hook—it's not you, it's me. I'm the problem, you're fine, you're making a good decision. Why are you arguing with me about it?"

"Because you're not a fucking problem, Micah! This *is* my fault. I'm the one who's not strong enough, not you."

"I almost used," Micah said. "And I only told Tristan about it, nobody else. I mean, the rest of the guys figured it out, I think, or maybe Tristan even told them; I don't know. But I didn't tell anyone at my meetings, I didn't tell the counsellors here—hell, I haven't even told them I'm fired yet. I just keep going over to Tristan's during the day, working on planning or whatever, and they assume I'm going to a real job. So in terms of me working the program? I wouldn't give me too much credit for that, Jake, not when I'm going to meetings every day but not actually telling them what's going on."

Another uncomfortable gap in the conversation before Jake said, "You told Tristan? You said you didn't want to open up to them. You felt like they couldn't be natural around you if they knew you were struggling. What happened to all that?"

"I grew up, I guess. I decided—I decided my pride wasn't the most important thing. I needed help, so I asked for it."

"That sounds like working the program to me."

It was stupid to feel proud, stupid to still want Jake's approval after everything. But apparently Micah wasn't quite as smart as he'd been wanting to pretend. Still, he couldn't be completely reckless. "I can't work for you, Jake. Thank you for offering, but, no. It's not a good idea."

"Why not?" Jake asked cautiously.

"Because—because *I'm* not strong enough for that. I think I can more or less handle it with you working on the neighborhood project. I can make that work. But going back to the way things were, except *not* going back? Like, still seeing you every day, but not—not any more than that? Just working? No. I don't think I could do that. I don't think I could see you, talk to you, be with you all the time and not—" *Not be in love with you.* But Micah wasn't going to use those words, not like this.

"I really fucked this up, didn't I?"

"No. I think—I think it was fucked up from the start." Micah tried to make himself believe the words. He was smart. He *had to be smart.* "It wasn't a good idea. In a different world, with different histories, I bet we'd be a scorching couple. But in this one? We don't really make sense."

Jake didn't answer right away, then said, "I know a few other guys who might be hiring. I can give them a call if you—"

"No," Micah said, a little too loudly. "No. I don't need you to look after me, Jake. That's not your job. I can—more or less, I can accept it that you don't want to be with me because you think I'm a pathetic junkie who's on his way to a relapse. But don't you dare start patronizing me. Don't try to give me your fucking charity."

"I didn't mean it like that." Jake sounded miserable, which was pretty satisfying.

"Okay," Micah said. "But that's how I'm going to take it, so don't go there." He took a deep breath. "I'm glad I got to know you, Jake. I really am. I'm glad I got to know Austin, because even though it hurt to lose him, it was still worth it. All of this was worth it. You know? So you don't owe me anything."

Another pause, this one long enough that it seemed like Jake might have hung up. "Thank you," Jake finally said. "I— yeah. Okay. It was worth it." A breath, and then, "I've got to go, Micah. Thanks for picking up the phone. I'm sorry I didn't do the same for you."

And then he really was gone, and Micah was left alone. Again. But he felt better. Not happy, not by any means, but peaceful. He felt like he'd had the right thoughts and said the right things, and there was a certain satisfaction to be taken from that. It wasn't much comfort, but it was enough, at least for right then.

ANOTHER WEEK. JAKE STILL FELT Austin's death like the wound of a sharp knife, but it was no longer *all* he felt. He'd been through the process of grief before, and was reasonably sure this was natural. Things were—proceeding. He was adapting, learning to think of Austin less, to sometimes remember the joy instead of just the pain. And as he worked through it all, he felt at least some of his sorrow being drained away to be replaced by anger.

And that was good. Anger gave him energy and focus and direction. It gave him something to think about besides Austin, besides Micah.

So by the next Sunday afternoon, standing in the basement of the Unitarian church and waiting for people to start arriving for the community meeting, he was feeling pretty good. It helped that

Micah was standing right next to him; maybe he didn't want to work with Jake anymore, but he was at least being supportive. And that was enough, until Jake saw how many chairs had been set out and how many people were filing in.

"I was thinking it would be, like, someone's living room," he whispered to Micah.

"Strength in numbers," Micah replied. "And once we started talking it up, a lot of people were interested. Shane and Simon both have really good networks set up—they got the word out, and people trust them."

Well, Jake would have been happier if they'd been trusted a little less. "This is too many people. My speech is—it's not really a speech. I just thought I'd talk. But not to this many people—it won't work."

"Sure it will. Why not? It's still just talking. And it's not like we're counting on you to get the information across—that's Simon's job. You're just here to remind everyone that real people have already been hurt by this mess. Simon's the brain, you're the heart. It's okay if the heart is a bit—well, a bit emotional. No one will mind."

This was the guy Jake had dumped and fired and shut out of his life. This smart, kind, generous man. Jake had treated him like shit, and Micah had called him on it and then moved on. Damn it. Jake was an idiot.

"What if I say the wrong thing?" he asked.

Micah frowned. "I don't think there is a wrong thing. You're just talking about Austin. Be honest. You'll be fine."

Yeah, because Jake was so great at being honest. But Micah seemed to believe in him, so he had to at least try to live up to that.

His nerves settled somewhat as the meeting started and Simon presented the information they'd gathered so far. He told the crowd about the people they'd contacted and pointed out the three local reporters who'd been persuaded to come and at least listen to what was said. He ran over the plans, such as they were, and stressed that it had to be a community effort—if there was any chance of winning against something like this, everyone would have to stand together.

And then it was Jake's turn. Simon had been smooth and calm and collected, talking like a politician or a lawyer or something, and Jake had to stand there with his calloused hands and battered heart and try to make people—try to make them feel something.

"Just be honest," Micah said, and gave him an encouraging smile.

Jake stood up. His legs were shaky, but they followed orders and carried him to the front of the room where there was a little platform he had to step up to. Then he turned, looked at the audience, and froze completely. There was simply no way he could force a sound out of his throat.

A painful few moments, then a loud, barking cough behind him, followed by another. Every eye in the place, including Jake's, turned to see Micah, half-standing, holding a hand up in apology to the crowd, gasping and hacking and choking. What the hell? He hadn't even been eating anything. Tristan looked over from his spot beside Micah and almost grinned. Then he put a hand on Micah's back and patted soothingly, his expression a caricature of friendly concern.

Micah was faking it. Giving Jake a chance to collect himself, drawing attention away for just a few moments, hopefully enough time for Jake to get his brain on straight. He took two deep breaths, Micah's coughs faded, and Jake turned back around to face the audience. He didn't want to imagine any of these people naked, but he found one face, an older woman sitting toward the back, and she smiled gently at him and he began to speak.

He wasn't great. He knew that. But he did what he could. He talked about Austin as a little kid, curious and energetic and constantly in trouble, but so charming and happy that the trouble never seemed to stick. He wondered out loud whether that had been part of the problem later, whether permissive parents and a doting older brother had somehow made Austin think he was magic and nothing bad could ever happen to him.

But something bad *had* happened. Simon had already covered the facts, so Jake let himself speak for a moment about his imaginings. How he hoped Austin had been asleep and just stayed that way, but how sometimes he worried that maybe he'd woken up and tried to get away, but the smoke had been too thick and he'd been scared, and maybe he'd yelled for his brother to come get him, come help him, but Jake hadn't come.

The nice older lady lifted her hand to her cheeks and that was when Jake realized he was crying a little himself. In front of all these people. He brushed impatiently at his eyes, shook his head and said, "It was hard to accept all this when I thought it was just because Austin had been stupid and unlucky. But hearing that it was Austin being stupid and unlucky *and* someone else being greedy and reckless, or even deliberately cruel? That's not something I can accept, not without trying to do something about it."

He glanced back at Micah, and there were tears on his face, too, but he wasn't wiping them away. He wasn't ashamed of them, because he was strong enough to accept his own feelings.

"I'm going to fight," Jake said. "I'm committing myself to figuring out who's behind all this and making them pay. I hope the police will take care of most of that for me, if I push them hard enough. I want these bastards in jail for a very long time. But I've talked to the police a couple times already, and—" He shrugged. "I'm not sure they're going to be able to do much. At best they might catch the guys who lit the fire, but even that's a long shot, and it's way less likely that they'll be able to do anything about the guys *behind* the arsonists, the guys who are looking to profit from all this. So if the only way for them to pay is to be sure they don't get what they want out of this neighborhood, then okay. That's what I want to do."

"Easy for you to say," a man called out from somewhere in the middle of the crowd. "There's nobody left in your family. Nobody else to worry about. Some of us have kids, and you want us to go to war with thugs who've already killed three people?"

Simon was stepping forward, but the comment had been directed at Jake, and he wanted to be as honest as he could with all this. So he said, "I can't tell you what chances to take. I can't tell you what you should do. I think it makes sense to believe there will be strength in numbers, and the more people involved, the less risk there is to any individual. I think it makes sense to believe that these people aren't stupid, and they know they won't get a lot of attention for burning out some junkies, not compared to if they went after a family man or a child. But at some point..." He looked over his shoulder again and saw Micah sitting there, leaning forward, listening as if he truly believed Jake had words worth hearing. Jake turned back to the man in the audience. "At some point I think we need to let go of what makes sense, and do what we think is right. I think we have to be strong enough to take chances, even if they scare us. Because if we don't?" He stopped. This wasn't something he needed to say to a guy with three kids. But it was something he needed to say for himself. For Micah. "Life is scary. Caring about people is scary. I can't tell you what you should do, or what chances you should take. But I know that

245

for myself? I want to face my fears and make my decisions based on what I think is right. Not on what I'm afraid of." He frowned. "But—that's just for me. I don't have kids, so I don't have to make that hard decision. I can't tell you what to do." No, he couldn't tell that man what to do, but he could damn well tell *himself* what to do. He didn't have kids to worry about, just himself. And for himself? He didn't want to be afraid anymore. "I'm going to fight," he told the crowd, and then he turned and walked back over to where Micah was sitting.

THE FORMAL PART OF THE MEETING wrapped up quickly after Jake stepped away from the podium. It seemed like everyone had a lot to talk about, though, and the crowd broke up into little clusters, some more agitated than others. The minister came over to talk to Jake, and then one of the reporters, and Micah sat in the background, wondering whether he'd heard what he thought he'd heard and whether it meant what he thought it meant. And, of course, trying to figure out how he felt about any of it.

The alarm on his phone went off before he got anything sorted out in his mind, and he stood up, actually relieved by the chance to escape. He thought about saying goodbye but ended up chickening out and slipping toward the exit without saying anything to anybody.

He was almost there when he heard Jake's voice from not far away. "Micah? Are you leaving? I was hoping—I thought maybe we could talk."

Micah turned around. He might as well get it over with. "I have to go to a meeting. Because I'm an *addict*. I can't skip it. I have to take it seriously."

Jake looked a little taken aback, which was probably fair. Whatever message Micah had been trying to send, he'd made it far too vehemently. But Jake recovered quickly and said, "Yeah, okay. Do you want me to pick you up afterward? Drive you home?"

"No." And *yes, god, yes.* But that wasn't the smart thing to say. "It's not far from the house; I can just walk. Thanks for offering, though. And good talk—good job." He turned then, and made it out of the building without any more interference.

Of course, he immediately regretted his quick exit. He shouldn't miss the meeting, no, but he could have accepted a ride home, couldn't he? He could have been a bit less abrupt, a bit less—panicked? Was that what he'd felt?

He tortured himself with those questions on the bus ride to the church where the meeting was being held—damn it, the same one where he'd first met Austin—but didn't come up with any answers that did him any good.

The meeting was like so many others, but at the end, as he was backing away to avoid the group hug, his gaze caught on the guy who'd led the session, the same man who'd done it that first time and who'd seemed—human. Kind. Micah hadn't been ready to deal with anything like that then, but now? He found himself moving toward the guy, who saw him coming and smiled, then stepped a little off to the side so they could talk in private.

It should have felt sleazy, maybe, but it didn't.

It *did* feel awkward, though. The guy held his hand out and said, "I'm Lawrence."

"Micah. Hi."

"You doing okay, Micah? I've been glad to see you every time you've shown up."

"I'm—yeah, I'm okay. I'm—fuck, I don't know, I think okay is about as good as I can go."

"Okay's just fine. You've only been out of rehab for a month or so, right?"

"Yeah."

"And you've stayed clean?"

"A couple close calls."

"Those are inevitable. The important part is to keep working."

"Yeah, I'm—in my own way, I'm doing that."

Lawrence smiled. "Congratulations." Then he leaned a little closer, another move that should have seemed skeevy but didn't. "Would you like to pray with me, Micah?"

"No." Micah stepped back. "No, not at all."

Lawrence didn't seem that offended. "Just talk, then? About anything in particular?"

"Yeah," Micah said. "I want to talk about fucking." He felt like an asshole as soon as the words were out of his mouth. So juvenile, trying to shock this guy who was just trying to help. And so pathetic, considering how completely unfazed Lawrence looked.

"I'm going to assume you have someone in mind?" Lawrence prompted. "And—possibly you're concerned about the no-relationships-for-a-year guideline?"

Okay, Lawrence was good. "Yeah. Maybe. I mean, I'm not even sure if that's what he meant. I *think* it was, but I'm not sure. I just—okay, it's not the fucking part. I'm good with that. Already did it, and it was fine. But then he dumped me, and it was—it was hard. I mean, there was other hard stuff going on the same time, but—yeah." Strange how he could discuss Marxist theory with an adequate vocabulary but could only discuss his feelings at the preschool level. That was a concern for another time, though.

"You feel as though it was a threat to your recovery? You were tempted to use again?"

"Yeah."

"But you didn't?"

"No. I told you, I've been good."

Lawrence shrugged. "It's not a question of good or bad. But—okay. You were involved with someone, he broke up with you, you felt tempted to use but didn't, and now he wants to get back together with you. Maybe."

"Yeah." Maybe Micah could work out some sort of deal where Lawrence could just do his talking for him.

"And you're wondering if it's a good idea, in terms of your recovery?"

Micah nodded.

Lawrence said, "How the fuck would I know, Micah?"

"What?"

"I'm happy to listen if you want a sounding board to talk it through, but the answer isn't going to come from me. You know that. It's got to come from you."

"But—the rules. The steps, the brown book. I mean—there's a way we're supposed to do this."

"Not starting new relationships isn't part of the twelve steps. And even if it was—how many of those steps are you really following to the letter? Any of them? Or are you just borrowing the general ideas and—how did you say it? Working it in your own way?"

"So—wait. You're saying…?"

"I'm saying you need to make this decision for yourself. If you want to use the rules or the twelve steps or whatever else as an excuse, that's fine with me—I won't rat you out. But I'm sorry, Micah—I also won't try to make a decision for you. Step four involves making a fearless moral inventory of yourself. If you've done that? Then you're in a much better place than me, or any other human being, to decide what will hurt your recovery and what will help it. So, if you want to pray with me, or if you want to bounce ideas off me, I'm here for you. But if you just want me to tell you what to do? Go buy a fortune cookie."

"A fortune cookie? Really?"

"Psychic hotline? Eenie-meenie-miny-moe? I'm not even going to tell you which totally arbitrary decision-making tool to use. Not my place."

"I—wow. This is not exactly what I was expecting."

"I hope you're not too disappointed."

Micah smiled. No, he wasn't disappointed. "I don't have a sponsor yet. I'm not crazy about all the god at this meeting, but otherwise, it seems okay, and it's a good location. I think I might make this my home base. I don't suppose you know anyone willing to do a little truth-telling to an obnoxious addict in the name of sponsorship?"

Lawrence's smile was more than a little smug. "Welcome to the fold, Micah. I think I can help you out with your sponsorship issues. What you do about your ex, though? That is completely up to you."

Chapter Twenty

JAKE DIDN'T CALL MICAH. HE WANTED to, but the brush off had been pretty damn clear, hadn't it? Jake'd had his chance, one time, and he'd blown it, and that was that. So he went home after the meeting, did his laundry, cleaned the apartment, tried to ignore how empty Austin's room looked—then called the landlord and gave notice that he'd be moving out at the end of the month. As soon as he said it, he felt like a weight had lifted. Every square inch of the apartment was imbued with memories of Austin, and a lot of them weren't all that good. Jake needed a fresh start, even if it was a start on his own.

He was already asleep by the time his phone rang, but when he looked down at his call display he forced himself awake and cleared his throat to be sure he didn't sound dozy. Then he answered the call, and heard Micah's quiet, "Shit. I woke you up."

"What? No! I mean—yes." Jake glanced at his alarm clock. "It's almost midnight; I get up early. Yeah, you woke me up. But it's not a problem."

"I can't believe I'm fucking this up already."

Jake struggled to sound more coherent. "I'm not sure what 'this' is, but nothing's fucked up, I don't think. Are you okay?"

"Yeah." Micah's snort might have been amusement, but it sounded more like disgust, aimed at himself. "I'm fine. I was just thinking about stuff, and I got up the guts to say something, and I guess I totally forgot about the time. That's kinda a junkie move, huh?"

"Are you high right now?" Jake demanded. "Have you used?"

"What? No!"

"Then it's not a junkie move. You're fine." And then, feeling as if he was stepping away from the shore onto ice of indeterminate thickness, he said, "What stuff were you thinking about? What was it you wanted to say?"

Too long of a silence before Micah said, "I don't want to mess up your sleep schedule. It's totally fine if this isn't a good time. But—earlier, it seemed like you wanted to talk. Is there any chance you wanted to do that now? Like, do you want to go for a drive?"

"Now?"

"It doesn't have to be now."

But there was something about the way he said it that made Jake think maybe it *did* need to be now, before—something changed? "Won't you get in trouble with your curfew?"

"Yeah. I'm going to move out. I want to get closer to the old neighborhood, and... I don't know. I think I'm done here. I think I'm ready to go."

"It's been just over a month, hasn't it? That's not very long."

A pause, and then Micah said, "Yeah. Sorry, I shouldn't have bugged you. Bad timing. Sorry. Go back to sleep."

And then he hung up, and Jake was left staring at his phone. He was pretty sure he'd screwed up, but he wasn't really sure how. He was supposed to have just gone along with a midnight drive? The drive itself was no problem, but it didn't make sense for Micah to violate curfew. It didn't make sense for Micah to move out of the halfway house, really.

Except—except. Damn it. Those weren't decisions Jake should be making. Well, the drive was partly his decision, sure, but if Micah decided to move out of the halfway house, that was up to Micah. Jake had to trust his judgment about what was best for him. Because if he didn't trust Micah's judgment, how could they really start a relationship? If Jake thought Micah couldn't make his own decisions, then obviously Micah couldn't decide whether or not to go out with somebody.

Which was framing the whole issue in terms of Jake's interests, of course, which probably wasn't a good thing, but there really wasn't a way he could think of that made it his place to decide whether Micah should move out of the halfway house or not.

He should let it go. He should go to sleep, wake up in the morning and figure it out. Instead, he poked at his phone screen and then waited impatiently.

"It's really late," Micah said. "Why are you calling at such a stupid time of day?"

And just like that, Jake relaxed. This was Micah. It was going to be okay. "I was just lying here, awake for some reason, and I was thinking about taking a drive. The last time we talked you were thinking the halfway house was still good for you and you should follow their rules, but I thought I'd maybe just give you a call and see if your thinking on that had changed. Because if you thought it was a good idea, I'd really like to go for a drive about now."

"I'll meet you in front of the house," Micah said, and again he ended the call.

But this time, Jake didn't feel hung up on. He wasn't being dismissed, he was being allowed time to get in his damn truck and go pick up his—his friend. That was all he should count on, he reminded himself.

Still, he pulled on a pair of jeans he'd been told made his ass look good and then a Henley he'd always liked on himself. Didn't hurt to advertise, surely.

He jogged out of the apartment and down to the parking area, ran every yellow light on the way to Micah's, and told himself to calm the fuck down so he didn't ruin it all. Whatever *it* was.

As promised, Micah was waiting in front of the house, and for a moment it felt like old times. Jake driving, Micah waiting, Austin—damn it. No. Not old times. But, still, that didn't mean new times couldn't be good. Jake had to make himself remember that. His whole life couldn't be a memorial to his brother.

Jake pulled to the curb and Micah climbed in so quietly Jake wondered if he was the only one having memories of how things had used to be. Of course, Micah might just be remembering that the last time he'd been in this truck was before Jake had dumped, fired, and ostracized him.

"Thanks for calling," Jake said as Micah did up his seat belt.

"Nope. No way. You called me, buddy. You didn't like it when I made a suggestion, so, fine, this is all *your* game now. Your idea. So—yeah, Jake, thanks for calling."

Well, that was probably fair. And fair or not, it seemed like how it was going to be. "So, where do you want to go? I mean, the 'go for a drive' thing was my idea, so it's about time you chipped in with something, right?"

Hopefully Micah's silence was because he was appreciating Jake's rhetorical skill rather than being pissed off. They were all the way to the end of the street, heading for the highway before Micah said, 'Go to the old neighborhood. We can drive around and scout out apartments."

"At midnight."

"Midnight is one of the times that I'll be in my apartment. So, yeah, we might as well check them out at that time."

Jake turned in the appropriate direction, then said, "Your parents were paying for the halfway house, right? Are they going to pay for the apartment, too?"

"No. I mean, I haven't asked them, but even if they wanted to—no. I didn't spend much of the money you paid me, and I think I've got a line on a new job."

"Yeah?"

"There's a non-profit that wants to pay Simon to organize the resistance in the neighborhood, and he's got money for an assistant. He offered the job to me." Micah shrugged. "The non-profit has to approve me, I guess, so—that might be a problem. If it is, I'll have to figure something else out."

"If you need a reference, I could give you one."

"Thanks."

They drove in silence for a while, the headlights of oncoming cars about all they could see, then turned off the highway and into the neighborhood Micah wanted to call home.

Jake took a deep breath. It was nice to just *be* with Micah, but he needed something more. Driving aimlessly through dark streets was something, but it wasn't enough. There had to be some sense of the future, even if it was bad news. So he said, "I wanted to talk to you today, at the meeting."

"Yeah. Sorry. I—I had to go, but I didn't have to be quite that quick about it."

"But you wanted to get away from me. You didn't want to hear what I had to say."

"Not—I don't know. I kind of—well, fuck it, Jake, I guess I got a bit scared. You'd know about that, right?"

"You seem to have recovered faster than I did."

"Yeah, maybe. I mean, I had a pretty good—well, really, I had a fucking useless talk with my new sponsor, but he kind of reminded me that I didn't need him, you know? I have to know myself, and make my own decisions about what chances I'm able to take."

"And you decided to move out of the halfway house, based on that conversation?"

"Seemed like a chance I could handle."

A part of Jake was screaming at him to shut up and not push it, but he kept going anyway. "And you decided to call me, based on that conversation?"

"I—holy fuck, is that a *fire*?"

Jake's gaze followed Micah's. It was just a dull glow; it could have been a neon sign, set a bit back off the street, but then it flickered strangely, and his foot hit the accelerator.

Micah had his phone out as they drove forward. Someone at the other end picked up just as they pulled to the curb, and Micah said, into the phone, "Holy shit. The vet clinic's on fire!" The flames weren't that high yet, at least where they could be seen. Licking up the outside of the building, halfway down the narrow walkway that led to the back alley, spreading fast. Micah turned to

Jake, panic on his face. "Simon sleeps in there. Call Simon, or Tristan if he doesn't answer! Shit, shit, shit!"

Then, as Jake jumped out of the car, phone in his hand, call made and waiting to connect, Micah got more controlled and started relaying the address and other information to the 9-1-1 operator.

Jake kept his phone pressed to his ear but kept moving, up the steps to the front door of the clinic, where he bashed his fist against the iron door. *Come on, Simon! Answer the phone, or hear the door. Something. Please, Simon. Let me help you!*

Micah appeared beside him, eyes wide, phone still clapped to his ear. "I hung up on 9-1-1 once they said they were sending firetrucks," he yelled. There wasn't much noise from the fire, not yet, so the volume wasn't needed, but was totally understandable. "I'm calling Tristan. Have you got Simon?"

"Fucking voice mail," Jake said, and hit the button to redial.

"Same with Tristan," Micah said, and Jake could see the real fear in his eyes. Micah loved Tristan, worshipped him, and maybe he was with Simon, maybe they were both inside the building. With the smoke, the flames.

"Call Shane," Micah ordered, and scrambled off—toward the fire.

"Damn it!" Jake bellowed, but he made the call, and for once was rewarded with someone actually answering.

"The clinic's on fire," Jake bellowed. Now there actually was enough noise from the fire to make yelling justified. Terrifying how fast it was spreading. "Micah and I are here, but we can't get in. We can't reach Austin—" Fuck. No. "Tristan. We can't reach Tristan or Simon."

Jake's attention was drawn by the shattering of glass and he squinted through the smoke to see Micah sweeping a long metal bar—a temporary parking sign, maybe—around the edges of the window at the front of the building. And then—god, no! Jake sprinted forward, but he was too late. Micah had pulled himself up on the windowsill and tumbled into the smoke-filled interior of the building.

It was a nightmare. It had to be. None of this was real. Jake was still at home in bed where he damn well should be, and this wasn't actually happening.

That was what his brain tried to tell him, but his body knew better and it drove forward, phone dropped on the ground behind him. He hit the windowsill with a grunt, tumbled himself up and over, felt the broken glass on the floor bite into his hands and knees and didn't even slow down. Micah was in there, somewhere, searching for his friend, searching for the only person who'd believed in him and supported him reliably.

"Micah!" Jake bellowed. And then, just in case, "Tristan! Simon!"

The crackling roar of the fire was getting louder and the smoke seemed almost like a blanket, muffling sound, but Jake was still pretty sure he heard a response from somewhere further into the building. Closer to the fire.

And instead of fear, Jake felt a strange sense of calm. If it ended here, it ended here. There was only one person who might mourn him, and that person was already deep into the fire. If Micah didn't come out of this, then there was no reason for Jake to come out, either. So he stepped forward resolutely, the smoke thicker with every step, and he bent down beneath it not to save his own life but to make sure he was still useful by the time he found Micah.

There was an open door on the left, and he stumbled through it, yelling "Micah!" And was rewarded with someone grabbing his arm. He whirled and saw not Micah, but Simon, sooty tears streaking down his angular face.

"Take him!" Simon ordered, and thrust a—a plastic crate into Jake's arms. Jake stood, trying to figure it out, and Simon grabbed Jake's shoulders and shoved him forward. "Door's over there."

Jake stumbled into motion, and as he moved forward he sensed a difference in the wall in front of him, an absence of structure, a gap—a door, as Simon had promised. He pushed his way through the smoke, found the opening, tripped over the stairs that took him outside, and was met with strong hands on his shoulders.

"Put him over there," Micah ordered, and then he was gone, running back into the inferno.

Him. *Him.* Jake lifted the crate to eye level, blinked past the smoke, and saw a furry face with two beady eyes staring back at him. He wasn't sure about the species and didn't really care. He just dropped the crate roughly where he'd been told to and headed back inside to find Micah.

Who was, of course, on his way back out, struggling under the weight of another crate. "There are more!" he yelled, and Jake wondered why the hell either of them cared.

Except.

Smoke. Trusting someone to be there for you and then dying alone. Coughing, gasping, confused, frightened.

Jake pushed his way back into the building and found Tristan struggling with one end of a metal crate. Jake grabbed the other end and was shocked by the weight but adjusted his grip and lifted anyway, and the two of them shuffled their way back out into the alley where the collection of caged animals was growing.

"We need to find Duck," Tristan yelled, as if he thought the words made sense. They were going to look for a duck? "You guys keep working here!"

Then he was gone back into the fire and Jake and Micah trailed after him, searching for more animals to extract.

There were plastic carriers stacked by the door, and it seemed as if the job was to pull the animals out of the wall cages, stuff them in the carriers, and take them outside. Micah seemed to have figured this out quickly, either because of prior knowledge or just because he was smarter than Jake; either way, he was in charge. It was too smoky to be sure which of the wall cages were empty and which might have a small animal cowering in the back corner, so Jake and Micah opened them all and half-climbed inside, searching, half-blind.

It was impossible to track time. Probably only a couple minutes, but it felt longer. At some point Jake became aware of flashing lights cutting through the smoke, and then of water dripping down through the embers. He kept working, though, because there were still more cages to be checked. More creatures to be saved. More lives that shouldn't end in smoke and terror.

"Last one," Micah yelled at him as they staggered back into the building. Jake could feel the burns on his skin from embers that had popped in his direction, could barely breath, had been crying for what felt like his lifetime, but there was one more, and Micah was going in, so Jake followed.

Micah leaned inside the cage, searching for anything furry, and that was when Jake saw Simon, stumbling out of the dense hallway smoke, a limp cat-shaped lump in his arms. Tristan was behind him but he fell and Simon turned, reached back for him with one arm, and was clearly faced with the choice. He needed all his strength to get Tristan out of there. He needed to abandon the cat they'd risked their lives searching for.

But he didn't. "Go!" Micah yelled, and Jake went. Micah knew when he needed help, and this wasn't one of those times. Jake caught the cat before Simon dropped it all the way, waited long enough to be sure Simon had a good grip on Tristan, then turned to see Micah heading out the door ahead of them, a plastic carrier held awkwardly in front of him. Jake stepped aside and waited while Simon dragged Tristan free, then followed them, cat in his arms, out into the smoky-but-breathable air of the alley.

Chapter Twenty-One

MICAH GASPED FOR BREATH. THE AIR in the alley wasn't good—not by a long shot—but it was *air*, which made it a million times better than the toxic sludge inside the clinic.

The firefighters had arrived and a couple of them were shuttling the crates of animals down the alley to fresher air, and a team of paramedics were down by the road, working with Tristan, with Simon—oh. With Duck. Jake had handed the lifeless body of the cat over and was standing there, staring, as the paramedic dutifully fitted an oxygen mask over the animal's face.

Micah weaved toward them. He'd been aware of Jake shadowing him out of the building, refusing to go ahead until Micah was clear, but once he'd been safe, Jake had disappeared. Off to seek help for the stupid cat, who was *not* an Austin surrogate. Micah refused to play that game, refused to let the loss of an animal in any way echo the loss of a vibrant human life—except he couldn't ignore the expression on Jake's face, the despair made more tragic by the trace of hope that still survived.

It's just a cat, Micah wanted to say as he found his place by Jake's side, but he knew it wasn't true. Not for Simon, but not for Jake, either. So he stayed quiet, but he leaned in, and when Jake leaned back he braced himself so he could support the weight.

They all stared at the animal and the paramedics so intently that when Micah saw the first tail-twitch he thought he must have imagined it. But then the cat's front leg jerked and Jake gasped and they all leaned forward, closer to this miracle.

"We need to keep the oxygen going," the paramedic said, and took a firmer grip on the cat as if this was all part of her daily duties.

Micah realized his hand was gripped tightly in Jake's, but didn't even think about pulling away. It all seemed sort of petty, now. Micah's worries about letting Jake down or being distracted from his recovery? Jake's fears of losing someone else to drugs? Neither of them had been afraid of almost dying in a fire that night, but that had turned out to be the biggest danger they'd had to face.

Micah squeezed Jake's hand and turned to find that he already had the man's full attention. "I don't know what you were going to say earlier today," Micah said. "But if any of it was about giving us another chance? I'm in. I want to do that. If you think you can trust me? I'll live up to that." He stopped, realized how far ahead of himself he was getting, and added, "If you don't think you can trust me, then, you know, fuck you, but we can talk about that some other time."

"I trust you," Jake said, and it sounded sincere, not defensive. "I know things could go wrong, but that's just—it's just life, right? Nothing's for sure. If I'm going to really live, I've got to take chances, and there's no one I'd rather take a chance on than you."

And that was enough, for that moment. Micah turned back to look at Duck, who was getting more energetic with every breath he took, and leaned into Jake's solid side and let himself feel safe, at least for the moment. There was someone setting fires, and addiction was always going to be hard to fight through, and Jake had too much pain already for him to be able to easily absorb more. Nothing was perfect. But it was real. And that was good enough for Micah.

~*~*~*~

THE NIGHT DRAGGED ON FAR TOO long. First the fire, then working with the others to load the rescued animals into various vehicles to be transferred to a variety of sites the clinic staff tracked down, then talking to the police and fire investigators, recounting what few impressions Jake could come up with about the source of the fire... it all seemed endless, but by the time the sun had come up the work seemed to be done.

A woman from the café down the street came down with coffee and pastries and expressions of sympathy and support, and that was something. It was hard to be sure how many people were crying because of emotion and how many because of smoke, but quite possibly it was a combination of the two for most of them. Jake didn't care about the clinic itself, really, but he felt a cold fury at the idea that this fire had almost certainly been set by the same people who'd killed his brother. It might not have been intentional that people had died in the first fire, but clearly these bastards hadn't learned from their mistake, hadn't repented or gotten more cautious.

"We got lucky, this time," Micah said, leaning into Jake's shoulder in a gesture that had grown familiar, and more than welcome, over the course of the night. "But these fuckers need to be stopped." He looked over at the police. "Hopefully they see that."

Jake nodded. His anger was the only thing giving him the energy to stay on his feet. Well, his anger and Micah's support. "I think we can leave now, right? We've talked to everybody, the animals are sorted out, Simon's going to Tristan's—are we done?"

"Yeah. You aren't planning to go to work, are you?"

"I'm planning to go to bed. Well, shower first, but then bed." He felt suddenly shy, but reached for Micah's hand anyway. "I'm thinking mostly sleep, but—if you wanted to join me, I'd like that."

"It won't be weird?" Micah asked. He kept his grip on Jake's hand but swivelled so they were standing face to face. "I mean, the last time I was there...."

"It might be weird, but if it is, that's okay. Weird is going to happen. Painful is going to happen. But it'll be easier to deal with both of those things if you're with me."

"Okay, then," Micah agreed, and they turned and headed for the truck, still holding hands.

"Hey!" a voice called after them, and they turned to see Trey jogging down the sidewalk, holding something out in their direction.

He got close enough that Micah could say, "Is that a plant?"

"Yeah," Trey said, as if it was obvious, which it really was, now that he was closer. "It's Simon's—I snuck in to see if there was anything I could pull out of his room before the fire guys taped it all off, and this was on the windowsill. All his clothes and stuff were on the far side of the room and they're burned, but I thought maybe this could be saved."

Jake squinted at it. "It's an African violet. He can buy another at the grocery store for a dollar ninety-nine."

"This one was a gift," Trey said. Apparently the guy was a bit more sentimental than he seemed on the outside. "And you work with plants, right? Do you think you could save it?"

"I work with outdoor plants. I'm not really an expert on this sort of thing." But Jake reached for the plant anyway and Trey surrendered the surprisingly heavy pot with no argument. "It'll depend on the roots, I think. The top's pretty scorched, but if the roots didn't get boiled it might put out new leaves. I can try to nurse it along, if you want."

Trey nodded briskly. "Good. Let me know how it goes." Then he turned and headed back to the crowd.

"I think he likes you," Micah said lightly as they started walking again. "Trey's only bossy and dismissive with—well, with everybody, but I think he was *extra* bossy and dismissive with you. That's a good sign."

"Great," Jake said, and as they climbed into the truck he handed the plant over for safe keeping.

"You're part of the gang, now. There's no escape."

"I don't think I want to."

"We're going to find out who set the fires," Micah said. He sounded—not quite dreamy, but as if he was speaking as much for his own ears as for Jake's. "It's going to take a long time and it'll be a lot of work, but we'll do it. We'll make them pay."

"Yeah," Jake said. He didn't seem to have much hunger for revenge, but he could get behind the idea of protecting the community. His brother didn't need him anymore, but that didn't mean nobody did. "Okay. We'll find out who did it."

Micah slid around in his seat the way he did when he wanted to have a real conversation, but he didn't say anything.

After a few minutes of silence Jake glanced over and saw that Micah's eyes were shut, his mouth open just a little as he breathed in his sleep. It felt like another sign of belonging, one much more significant than Trey's attitude. Micah trusted Jake enough to fall asleep in his presence. Jake was in charge of getting them both home safely, navigating the dangerous world with his precious cargo. For the first time he could remember, the addition of a new responsibility made him feel calmer instead of more anxious. He could do this. It was a privilege to be *allowed* to do this.

When he got to the apartment building he thought about cruising around the block a few times to give Micah a little more rest and himself a little more time to savor their little bubble of safety in the cab of the truck. But then Micah coughed a little, working up some of the gunk he'd inhaled earlier, and he opened his eyes and smiled sleepily at Jake. "We there?"

"Yeah." Jake found his parking spot. "You want me to carry you?"

Micah grinned. "I remember that. When my dad would carry me inside after I fell asleep in the car. I loved it—I felt so warm and safe."

"I'll give it a try," Jake said. "But—"

"You can spoon me in bed instead, how 'bout? Just as good, and hell of a lot less likely that you'll put your back out or drop me down the stairs."

"Deal."

So they staggered up the stairs together, made their way into the apartment, and together they stopped by the door to Austin's room. "It just seems like such a waste," Micah said. "He was so alive. All that, gone...."

"Yeah," Jake agreed. He tightened his grip on Micah. "It was a waste. And that's—I don't want to sound morbid, but that's kind of the message I'm trying to take from all of this, now. For a while there—well, you know. I was afraid of losing someone else, so I sucked back into my shell where I'd be safe. But you know, *that* would have been a waste, too, if I'd kept on trying to do that. I can't honor his life by refusing to live mine. Does that make sense?"

Micah nodded silently. Then he reached his hand out and ghosted his soot-blackened fingers over the bedroom door. "I'll take care of him for you, Austin," he said. "As much as he'll let me. I promise."

Well, that was sweet, and maybe Jake should have left it at that, but instead he said, "That wasn't really the dynamic between me and Austin. I think you know that. He didn't do a whole lot of taking care of me."

"Not yet," Micah agreed calmly. "But he loved you. If he'd had a chance to get his shit together? He would have taken care of you when you needed it. He didn't get that chance, but I've got it. So I'll do it for him." He smiled, then gently shoved Jake toward the bathroom. "So get in that shower. You stink like smoke and you need to clean up before you go to sleep."

"You going to come with me?"

"There's no room."

"We'll make room," Jake promised. And they did.

Interlude 3.1

"I WANT YOU TO MOVE IN HERE," Tristan said. He was chopping tomatoes for a multi-layer nacho dip and he said the words as casually as if he'd been asking Simon to pass him the cheese grater.

"Until I find another place," Simon said carefully. He'd lost all his possessions and been made homeless twice in the last half a year and felt like it might be time to do *everything* carefully.

But apparently Tristan didn't share that sentiment. "No," he said. "I mean, that's okay, if that's what you want. You're totally welcome to stay here for a while. But what *I* want? I want you to move in here, for good. Or we could find somewhere else and move in together. That's what *I* want." He glanced over at Simon and smiled his bright, beautiful smile. "I just thought I should tell you. I'm not going to sulk if I don't get my way, but it seemed stupid to not even say anything. What if you wanted it and I wanted it and we both didn't say anything because we were shy or whatever and then neither one of us got what he wanted even though we wanted the exact same thing?" He selected another tomato. "That would suck."

"Move in," Simon said. Apparently the idea was taking a little while to sink into his brain. "Here."

"Or somewhere else. Whatever. The key thing is I think we should live together. We spend most of our time together anyway, neither one of us has a lot of stuff, Duck likes it here—but I'm sure he'd also like it somewhere else, if you wanted—so, you know—I think we should do it." He scooped the chopped tomatoes into a bowl and selected another one. Simon was pretty sure there were already more chopped tomatoes than they'd eat in a week, but he didn't say anything, and Tristan kept talking. "I'm okay if you don't want to. I mean it. But—yeah. I think it'd be good."

"I could pay rent," Simon said. He was thinking out loud. He didn't have a full time regular job, but he was doing contract work for a variety of businesses in the neighborhood and had enough money coming in to get by. "And utilities. I could do that."

"I wasn't really thinking of it as a financial benefit, but, yeah, you could pay, sure."

"Duck does like it here," Simon mused, and Tristan smiled at him and set down the knife.

That was when the commotion started at the doorway. Wild banging, shouting—familiar voices, bellowing Simon's name.

"Is that Micah?" Tristan demanded, quickly wiping his hands and then heading for the door. "Jesus, you moving in is kind of a moot point if he gets me kicked out before you get around to it."

Simon trailed behind him and stood in the hallway as Tristan opened the door. Micah shoved past him, Jake trailing behind—and Micah was holding something in his hands, stretching it out to Simon like an offering. A thick disc of yellow metal, the size of two or three hockey pucks melted together—

"Is that *gold*?" Tristan demanded, and then quickly shut the door behind Jake.

Simon reached out for the metal and Micah dropped it into his hands. Heavy. Very heavy. Simon turned his attention to Micah and waited for an explanation, but Micah turned to Jake, who said, "Trey rescued your African violet from the fire. He said it meant a lot to you, so I was trying to help it out. The leaves were scorched, but plants can often come back if their roots are strong, so I lifted it out of the pot to see what the damage was like, and there was hardly any soil. Almost all of the space in the pot was taken up with *that*." He shook his head in disbelief. "Did you know it was in there? And *is it* gold?"

Simon gazed down at the chunk of metal and played over the words his aunt had spoken when she'd given it to him. She'd practically *dared* him to smash the plant to bits. If this was gold—and it really, really seemed to be—what did it mean that she'd wanted him to have something valuable, but only after he'd destroyed the gift that was the last link to his family? To her? "I don't know," he muttered. Then he lifted his gaze from the metal and fixed it on Jake. "Was the plant okay? The roots? Will it live, do you think?"

Jake seemed taken aback. "Uh—I don't know. I'm not a houseplant expert, to be honest. The roots looked okay, so I just jammed a bit more potting soil in to fill the hole where this had been and put it back in the same pot. I think it'll be okay."

"She told me to repot it," Simon said, the words coming back to him as he tried to sort through it all. "My aunt. She said plants need space to thrive, and I thought it was a metaphor. I thought she was trying to tell me it was good that I was leaving the family. But really—shit. She was telling me where she'd stashed her *real* gift."

"It's a nice plant," Tristan said. "Even without the gold. I liked the flowers."

Simon stared at him. It *had* been a nice plant. And hopefully it would be again, if its roots were strong. "She gave me a lump of gold hidden in a cheap plant," he said, trying the idea out to see if it felt like something his aunt would do. It absolutely fit.

"It's a few pounds at least," Micah said. "That's worth a lot of money, right?"

"Yes," Simon agreed. But his attention was caught by the expression on Tristan's face as he moved toward Micah.

"It's worth a lot of money," Tristan said, his expression

intense. "And that could be traded for a lot of drugs. But you didn't keep it, Micah. You brought it over here, for Simon."

Micah drew back. Not a lot, but enough to be noticed. "Yeah," he said levelly. "I didn't steal from your boyfriend."

"I didn't mean—" Tristan broke off and frowned. "Shit. I don't know why—I meant that as a compliment. As, like, a celebration. Before you got clean, if you'd found this you would have kept it, right? But you're clean now so you didn't. That's all I meant."

"Not quite all," Micah said. "Because you were surprised. Impressed. You thought maybe I'd still act like a junkie if I got the chance, and you thought it was a big deal that I didn't." A half-step back and he shook his head. "I don't blame you. I'm the one who fucked up. I can't expect everyone to just forget about all that. It's not a big deal. Don't worry—"

Jake moved fast for someone as muscular as he was. And he was light on his feet as he swivelled around and slid between Tristan and Micah. "You did great," Jake said firmly, and then there was a quick kiss. "We believe in you." Another kiss. "And even if we didn't, it'd be okay, because *you* believe in you." Another kiss, slower this time. "Right?"

Micah's hands crept up to grip Jake's hips. "It's not his fault," he whispered. "It's mine."

"There's no fault, Micah. Just people doing their best." Another kiss, this one firm and somehow final. "No fault, just a huge fucking lump of gold." He kept his grip on Micah's hand but turned around to face Simon and Tristan. "It smells like you guys were cooking dinner—sorry if we interrupted. We just—well, it was pretty exciting. But we should—"

"Stay," Simon said quickly. "Tristan and I had just decided to move in together. Here. I'd like it if my first act as an official resident of this building was to invite you both to stay for dinner."

"I don't—" Micah started, but Tristan stepped forward quickly and took his free hand, the one Jake wasn't holding.

"We fuck up," Tristan said. "You do, I do—everybody does. We make mistakes and then we get past them. You and me—we've been through a lot of rough times. I'd really like it if you and Jake could stay tonight to help us celebrate a *good* time. You know? I want you to be part of that."

A wordless communication between Micah and Jake, operating at a pretty high level for so early in their relationship, and then they smiled almost in synchronicity. Jake said, "Congratulations. Living together—that's a big step. And a chunk of gold is always worth celebrating."

"Always," Tristan agreed.

Simon stepped back and let Tristan lead his guests—*their* guests—into the living room. The apartment was a shithole. Simon had a lump of gold in his hands. Tristan had a steady income from his refusing-to-be-a-blackmailer past. If they wanted to move somewhere better, they could.

But this apartment was the home base for all of Tristan's friends. Simon's friends. This apartment was full of love of all kinds. This was Tristan's home. It would be Simon's home. He couldn't ask for more, not when he already had everything he ever needed.

Interlude 3.2

"IT'S NOT A LONG-TERM SOLUTION." Shane wanted to get that out of the way before anyone else felt they had to point it out. This wasn't a great idea, and he'd probably missed a bunch of problems that would make it absolutely unworkable, and he didn't want anyone to feel awkward about having to shut him down. Still, he'd wanted to at least make the suggestion. "We wouldn't be able to take any animals overnight—not unless we could get one of the other clinics to board them for us. But for the vaccinations, and for the social workers to keep meeting people? I think it might be okay?"

"It's brilliant," Dr. Anderson said. She was glowing with excitement. "It could be *better* than the stationary clinic, couldn't it?"

"The old clinic was a good way to get people out of their safe zones and help them learn to follow social rules," Lena mused. She was clearly thinking as a social worker, as focused on the humans as her wife was on the animals. "But there were certainly some people who weren't ready for that, and I think this could be a really useful tool for bridging that gap. Ideally we'd have both—the mobile clinic for the harder to serve clientele, and the fixed clinic for those who are ready for a challenge."

"So setting up a mobile clinic is a good idea for now, at least," Dr. Anderson said, "And then we'll try to keep it going once we rebuild." She beamed at Shane and he could feel the approval wash over his body like the first sip of hard alcohol on a cold day.

"I need to be with you whenever you go out," he said quickly. "You don't have to pay me for all the hours if there's no budget for it, but you can't be going into those places alone, or just with a social worker. It wouldn't be safe."

"I don't like turning you into a security guard," Dr. Anderson said with a frown.

Shane could see Noah's worried nod from his peripheral vision, but he shrugged. "You know I won't be rough with people, right?"

"I'm not worried about you being rough, I'm worried about you getting hurt."

"Better me than you, and also *less likely* me than you. I won't go looking for trouble, and I'm big enough that people don't want to start things with me."

"*Usually* they don't want to," Noah corrected. "But if they do?"

"It won't be any more dangerous than what we're doing now," Shane said. Worrying about his safety was *not* the priority they should be focusing on. "It'll be fine. And we can make it clear to everyone that we're not carrying any of the good drugs in the van."

"Okay," Dr. Anderson agreed, and the rest of the group nodded their acceptance of the idea.

The sensation wasn't completely familiar to Shane, and it took him a while to find a name for it. But sitting there at their usual café, he and Noah on one side of the booth, Lena and Dr. Anderson on the other, talking about things as if they were all equals, all chasing the same goal? Shane was proud of himself.

He was part of this. They were a team. And as a team, they weren't going to let the fire interfere with their important work. They weren't going to let themselves be scared off or discouraged.

Yeah. Whoever had started the fire hadn't known who they were messing with. But sooner or later they were going to find out.

Shane was looking forward to the show.

Interlude 3.3

"SIMON IS *MAGIC*," JAKE WHISPERED. "And my hero. Simon is my magic hero."

Micah rolled his eyes. He loved being able to roll his eyes at Jake, loved having that level of comfort, of confidence in their relationship. It had only been a week since the clinic fire, but already they felt established as a couple, even as they both worked out the conventions of their new relationship.

Now, in the kitchen of Jake's apartment, with Simon only a few steps away in the living room, Micah turned and gave Jake a quick kiss. "Simon is good at paperwork and organizing things. That's not actually magic." He shrugged. "But if you want him to be your hero, that's okay. Whatever it takes to get you to stop killing yourself with bills and invoices every night. I want us to work hard during the day and then *play hard* at night."

"Okay, that part sounds good, but I stand by my 'magic' assessment. He's got it set up so I can just enter numbers in one place on the computer and then all this math gets done for me and it spits out the right total in the right place! That's magic!"

"I'm pretty sure that's a spreadsheet, you doofus."

"Call it what you want. I'm calling it magic."

"Okay," Micah said. If Jake wanted to call it magic, he could. "And have you talked to Alex? Is he going to find the staff for his crew?"

"He says he's got it under control." Jake stole a carrot from the pile Micah was slicing. "And Tristan's sure he wants to work with you and me instead of just sitting around collecting his money for doing nothing?"

"He says so. I think he might have a slightly more spiritual view of what we'll be doing than you have, though. He's been talking a lot about nurturing and communing with nature. I think he'll do the work, but—you know. He might be a little sentimental about some of it."

"He can be as sentimental as he wants to be as long as he keeps loaning me my magic hero."

"Uh huh. Can you set the magic cooking box to five minutes for those potatoes, please?"

"You already poked them?" Jake checked as he hit the buttons on the microwave.

"Yeah," Micah confirmed.

Then he took a moment and tried to collect the details. The cozy domesticity, complete with Jake's inane appreciation of basic office software. The smells of good food cooking, the comfort of having a friend in the living room, giving them valuable help in exchange for a meal that wasn't going to be anything special.

It was a life. It was *Micah's* life. Hard to believe, but it really seemed to be true.

He hadn't done anything to deserve it, but people didn't always get what they deserved, for better or worse. It was unearned, but he'd be damned if it would be unappreciated. So he absorbed the details and stashed them away in his memory. This was reality, and he couldn't imagine any reason to want to escape it.

Coming Soon

Pure Bred, the fourth (and final) book in the *Shelter* series

Excerpt:

TRISTAN'S LIVING ROOM WAS CROWDED. Seemed like it was always crowded these days, even more than it used to be, and Trey didn't like it. It seemed like everything was changing way too fast, leaving him behind. He'd never been quick, but that didn't used to matter, not when he was hanging out with everyone at Tristan's.

Now, though? There was a guy *in a suit* standing by the window where Trey usually stationed himself. The guy had taken off his jacket and loosened his tie when he'd seen how everyone else was dressed, but as far as Trey was concerned the damage had been done. Once a suit, always a suit. And he didn't trust suits.

He also didn't trust assholes who took his spot by the window. So he lurked in the kitchen, glaring at the interloper and scowling at the rest of the crowd, who all seemed totally fascinated by this visitor.

"So I don't think there will be many successful court challenges," the suit was saying. "We're certainly willing to help support you with any legal actions that make sense, but our organization is running on a limited budget, so we can't afford to throw money or time away on long shots. The strategy we'd like to follow in this situation is based more on lobbying and publicity. The two fires give us a strong human-interest angle. They might have been designed to intimidate, but as long as we don't let that happen, I think we can make them work in our favor."

Trey cut his gaze over toward Jake. The guy's brother had *died* in one of the fires the suit was talking about, so it probably didn't sound good to hear them being treated as a positive. But Jake looked stoic enough. Micah was holding his hand pretty tight, though. Micah might be a junkie, but he wasn't stupid.

"So, moving forward," the suit said, "We'll want to be working with some of you quite closely in order to fine tune our message and make sure we're presenting it in the most positive way." He glanced around the room, and Trey didn't think he was imagining it when the suit's eyes seemed to rest on him for a little longer than the others. "Some of you will likely be most effective in the background," he said, and Trey snorted softly. Yeah. The background, that was where he belonged.

"But everyone's contributions will be important," the suit continued. "And in order to help coordinate it all and to ensure that communication is as streamlined as possible, we're going to assign a dedicated staff member—well, an intern—to this project for the next four months. I'd like to introduce you all to Seb Tanner." He raised an arm as if he was going to offer a hug, then gripped the new guy's shoulder instead.

Seb Tanner was a suit. He wasn't *wearing* a suit, but that didn't change what he was. His khakis were pressed, his light blue button-down starched and properly tucked in, his blond hair flipped in a tidy wave across his tanned forehead. Suit on vacation, suit-casual, junior-suit—the precise definition didn't matter, because they all featured the word *suit*. Even his smile was suit-worthy, confident and friendly, as if this guy had never in his life been introduced to someone who wasn't absolutely thrilled to meet him and really, really hoped to be able to get to know him better.

"Thanks, Gary," Tanner said, and smiled at the older man as if Tanner was the one in charge and the main suit had just been allowed to make an introduction. Then he turned to the room. "I want you all to know that I've been reading the file on this for two days straight, and I'm appalled by what I've seen. Gentrification is one thing, but the high-pressure tactics, the intimidation, the disregard for human life or property?" Tanner shook his head. "It's the kind of situation that made me want to get involved in community organizing and public interest work in the first place. I'm really proud to be a part of this movement, and I'm really looking forward to fighting on your behalf."

"For four months." It was Simon, his eyebrow raised as he looked Tanner over. Yeah, if there was anyone in the crowd who'd be able to out-confident someone like Suit, Jr., it would be Simon. "You're passionate about the project, you're going to fight, fight, fight... for four months. And then you'll go back to school, I assume? But this 'project' isn't going to be finished in four months. Is it?"

Tanner kept his gaze locked on Simon's but didn't even look flustered. "I'm here to do what I can within the time frame I have available. I'm hoping to work with locals to set up communications and establish a general structure to use going forward. But, no, I wouldn't expect the project to be finished by the end of the summer. That's why Gary is here, to ensure continuity."

Simon sat back, but didn't look completely satisfied. Trey shifted impatiently. Contacting the Seattle Communities Team had been Simon's brilliant idea, so if he wasn't happy with the way things were going, it wasn't likely that anyone else in the room was any more satisfied. But this meeting was Simon's baby, so if he wasn't going to fight, no one else would, either.

But that didn't mean they wouldn't cast meaningful glances at each other. And it looked like Suit, Jr., was picking up on those looks, and the meaning behind them. "I know you guys started this," he said softly. "I know you've done a lot to get the resistance off the ground. And I know I'm young, and not an expert. But I have access to experts, and I have time. This is my only job, my only priority, for the next four months. I think we can all work together, and I think we can make things happen. I wouldn't be here if I thought I couldn't be useful."

He sounded like he really believed it. Like he'd lived a life where being useful and wanted was the default position for him and he saw no reason why that situation should change.

What a shithead.

~*~*~*~

SEB WASN'T USED TO FACING THIS kind of skepticism. He wasn't used to people looking at him as if he was an outsider who had to *earn* their respect instead of just receiving it because of who he was. Who his father was.

He loved it.

He'd rise to the challenge, he'd show them he was worthwhile, he'd have them eating out of his hand within—well, okay, he shouldn't get carried away. There'd be no hand-eating, although there were a couple of them whose mouths he wouldn't mind getting to know a little better. But, no, that wasn't what he was there for. If he wanted something like that, if he wanted to find a rough, tough guy to put him in his place—and looking out at this crowd, he was pretty sure that was *exactly* what he wanted—he'd find it somewhere else. Don't mix business with pleasure. And damn it, Seb, keep your mind on your job!

He checked that his face was still wearing its expression of interest and admiration for Gary, then let himself scan the audience again. It was a strange crowd, a mix of almost-grown-up street kids with a couple guys nearly as preppy as himself, then some older people—social workers, small business owners, community members—that sort of thing. About twenty people who had apparently become the core of the resistance to the area's gentrification push.

His eye was caught by the guy standing in the little kitchenette. Damn. A perfect mix of physical power and emotional frustration. If Seb was lucky, maybe throw in a little self-loathing homophobia and get a fuck to remember. Oh, yeah. The guy was built like an oversized gymnast—fairly tall, but still somehow giving the impression of compact strength. He'd be totally impersonal, totally in control. No kissing or any of that shit, unless—oh, god, yeah, unless he bent Seb over and *bit him*, like a lion controlling his mate.

Seb felt his cock shift and pulled his mind back to what he was supposed to be thinking about. Yeah, yeah, plans for the next meeting, smaller sub-groups working on different goals, all the stuff he and Gary had talked about on the drive over. The importance of working as a team. Sweaty, angry sex was an effective team-building tool, wasn't it? Maybe he should mention that as a possible topic for his senior thesis. He'd done a term in England the year before and gotten a good start on his research— he could go for a little cross-cultural flair and title it "Nontraditional power exchanges in business relationships—valid reasons to 'fancy a bit of rough'." Hell, yeah. He could probably get that published.

"Right, Sebastian?" Gary said, and Seb smiled enthusiastically, if somewhat vaguely. Gary didn't seem like the type to go off script, so, sure, he was probably right.

The meeting wrapped up then and Gary guided Seb out as soon as they could manage without seeming rude. "They need some time to think it all through, and we'll support them as they do that. But this is an emotional situation for them, and we're pushing them to think strategically, not emotionally."

"They did *ask* for help," Seb said as they walked down the street to Gary's car. "Do we really have to persuade them to take something when they were the ones who asked for it in the first place?" And then, totally unbidden, the image of the ripped guy from the kitchenette making Seb ask for it, making Seb beg—holy shit, he needed to get laid. This was getting stupid.

"People often have a vague general idea of what they're looking for," Gary explained, apparently oblivious to Seb's distraction. "But when we arrive and start making things concrete, they may not be as pleased. Often they just want us to give them money, but our funding doesn't allow for that. We offer expertise, not cash."

Seb nodded. The kitchenette guy had seemed resentful, and this context made his reaction make sense. It also made it a bit more difficult to be turned on by his anger. The guy was just as angry at *Gary* as he was at Seb, and there was absolutely nothing sexy about Gary, not unless you were kinky to an extreme Seb didn't even want to begin contemplating. "So we give them some space and they realize they need us and come running back with their tails between their legs?"

"They aren't dogs, Sebastian. And we need them just as much as they need us—our mission statement involves working *with* communities to address social issues. If we can't carry out our mission, there isn't much reason for us to exist as an organization."

Seb didn't answer that. He didn't like the idea of needing anyone. Wanting? Oh, he was just fine with wanting. But need was a different thing altogether.

"And I don't think space is going to be the answer," Gary continued. "Not for this group. They've got some strong personalities at work, and they're already fairly well connected in terms of community leaders. They're primed and ready to go, and if we give them too much time, they're going to start acting on their own, without our advice and expertise. They'll either have initial success, in which case it will be difficult for us to persuade them we can offer any more help, or they'll have initial failure, which will mean we have a lot of cleaning up to do. I'd rather avoid both scenarios."

"So what's the plan?" Seb asked. Gary didn't have a lot of flair, didn't have that flash of brilliance that attracted Seb to people, but he knew what he was doing. And he was, technically,

Seb's boss this summer, although Seb preferred to think of him as a guide or mentor.

"I want you in there with them. You're young; a lot of them are young. I want you to build on that, get to know them, earn their trust."

"It sounds like I'm going undercover." Seb wasn't objecting to the idea; really, it sounded intriguing.

But stick-in-the-mud Gary shook his head. "Be honest. Get them to trust you by being worthy of their trust. We're on their side in all this."

"Yeah, okay," Seb agreed. He was already thinking back to the guy in the kitchen, the barely hidden anger, the muscles—he could spend some time with him, for sure. And, really, to know Seb was to love him. There shouldn't be any problem with the rest of his assignment. "I'm in," he said. "I'm ready."

Gary didn't look entirely convinced, but that was Gary's problem. Seb smiled to himself and let his mind wander. He'd made a good decision when he took this internship. It was going to be a very interesting summer.

Other Books by Kate Sherwood

(all m/m – for m/f see Cate Cameron at

www.catecameronauthor.com)

Feral – first book in the *Shelter* series – NA contemporary drama

Lap Dog – second book in the *Shelter* series

Sacrati – fantasy/alt history

In Too Deep – NA contemporary drama

Chasing the Dragon – angst and adventure!

Mark of Cain – contemporary drama

The Fall, Riding Tall – two book contemporary drama

The Shift – contemporary fantasy novella – monster hunters!

Room to Grow – contemporary drama novella

The Pawn, The Knight – two book futuristic drama with plenty of

angst

Poor Little Rich Boy – contemporary drama

More than Chemistry – light contemporary novella

Beneath the Surface – contemporary drama

Dark Horse, Out of the Darkness, Of Dark and Bright – three book

contemporary drama with extras

Shying Away – NA drama

Lost Treasure – contemporary drama

About the Author

Kate Sherwood started writing about the same time she got back on a horse after almost twenty years away from riding. She'd like to think she was too young for it to be a midlife crisis, but apparently she was ready for some changes!

Kate grew up near Toronto, Ontario (Canada) and went to school in Montreal, then Vancouver. But for the last decade or so she's been a country girl. Sure, she misses some of the conveniences of the city, but living close to nature makes up for those lacks. She's living in Ontario's "cottage country"–other people save up their time and come to spend their vacations in her neighborhood, but she gets to live there all year round!

Since her first book was published in 2010, she's kept herself busy with novels, novellas, and short stories in almost all the sub-genres of m/m romance. Contemporary, suspense, scifi or fantasy–the settings are just the backdrop for her characters to answer the important questions. How much can they share, and what do they need to keep? Can they bring themselves to trust someone, after being disappointed so many times? Are they brave enough to take a chance on love?

Kate's books balance drama with humor, angst with optimism. They feature strong, damaged men who fight themselves harder than they fight anyone else. And, wherever possible, there are animals: horses, dogs, cats ferrets, squirrels... sometimes it's easier to bond with a non-human, and most of Kate's men need all the help they can get.

After five years of writing, Kate is still learning, still stretching herself, and still enjoying what she does. She's looking forward to sharing a lot more stories in the future.

Find out more about Kate Sherwood and her books at her website: www.katesherwoodbooks.com

Follow Kate Sherwood on Facebook, too.